CAGED

THE CAGED SERIES

AMBER LYNN NATUSCH

CAGED

Design by Clarissa Yeo
Layout by Incandescent Phoenix Books

An Amber Lynn Natusch Book

www.amberlynnnatusch.com

ISBN-13: 978-0-9849464-4-0

First Edition: 2012

ALSO BY AMBER LYNN NATUSCH

The *CAGED* Series

CAGED

HAUNTED

FRAMED

SCARRED

FRACTURED

TARNISHED

STRAYED

CONCEALED

BETRAYED

The *UNBORN* Series

UNBORN

UNSEEN

UNSPOKEN

The *BLUE-EYED BOMB* Series

LIVE WIRE

KILLSWITCH

DEAD ZONE

WARHEAD

The *FORCE OF NATURE* Series

FROM THE ASHES

INTO THE STORM

BEYOND THE SHADOWS

BENEATH THE DUST

The *ZODIAC CURSE:*

HAREM OF SHADOWS Series

EVE OF ETERNAL NIGHT

Contemporary Romance

UNDERTOW

More Including Release Dates

http://amberlynnnatusch.com

www.facebook.com/AmberLynnNatusch

http://www.subscribepage.com/AmberLynnNatusch

For Rhys,
Mommy loves you.

ACKNOWLEDGMENTS

Though this project started as a humble little story that I just couldn't ignore, it is what it is today because of the amazing people who volunteered their time, energy and creative input to help me see this through. Publishing CAGED is not only a success for me, but also for them.

Amanda Zabski (aka, the other ten percent of my creative brain) is single-handedly responsible for getting me out of my own way, helping me craft, mold and shape the story lines, and pushing me when I feel like throwing in the towel. This book never would have gotten where it is without her. Literally.

I would be remiss if I didn't give an enthusiastic nod to my cheerleading duo, Virginia Nicholas and Eryn Bagley. Virginia is always the first person to read the rough draft from cover to cover and give me her general impression, whereas Eryn likes to take the chapters I write as I write them (which are usually horribly out of order) and comment along the way. I love you both, but I think you're becoming Ruby addicts.

Since I write like words are flying out of my head with

little to no regard for grammatical accuracy, I desperately need my friend and editing drill sergeant, Jen Krom.

Jamie Rosen is my graphic designer extraordinaire. He takes what I see in my head and makes it into a haunting cover, which is admittedly no easy task.

My husband Bryan is, and always has been, the yin to my yang. Luckily for me, he loves to research things ad nauseam, and is a total tech-whiz with computers, programs and all things internet related. He prepared everything for publishing so I wouldn't have to. He truly is one of the best.

To those I haven't directly mentioned who have contributed to the success of CAGED in any way, please know that I love and appreciate you. Now, on to the next project...HAUNTED!

PROLOGUE

I saw my first tree that day.

I was twenty-eight years old.

I lifted my face from the fine, white, powdery snow that I lay in to see it. It stood dead ahead of me, tall and strong. It looked nothing like I had imagined; bigger, rougher. I struggled to drag myself over to that strong tree, propping up against it with the hope that its strength would somehow inspire my own. I looked up to see the billowing clouds dance across the sky. Dad had always told me that snow came when the clouds were thick and full.

I was in shock—I could *see*!

My hand floated up to my face involuntarily, stopping before making contact. I observed it, slowly turning it different ways to familiarize myself with it. My eyes then darted quickly away to the rest of my body. They, not my hands, scanned myself. Seeing the state of my leg quickly turned my shock into horror as memories slowly leaked back into my consciousness.

My parents are dead.

I had been told from a young age that those born

without sight tended to compensate with their other senses. I never felt like that was true of me, exactly, but I always had the ability to sense the strong emotions of others as if they were my own. An empath, as it were. When I said that I *felt* someone's pain, I meant it literally.

My parents were yards away, but I couldn't get to them. I felt their terror as death came for them violently. Distracted, I never heard their attackers coming for me. The tearing of my shirt's fabric was my first sign of their presence. I could feel the warmth of their hands as they grabbed and pawed at me, ripping material off along the way. I had no idea how many of them there were.

As the screams of my parents faded, the attackers turned their undivided and unwanted attention on me. I never was one for being the center of attention, and that moment was no exception. I could feel the cold wind on my entire body as I started to black out.

I was so afraid...

When I awoke, I didn't know whose blood was on me, but I knew it wasn't mine.

I didn't know how I got to wherever I was, but I knew I was hurt and unable to walk.

I didn't know what day or time it was, but I knew I was alone, terrified, and missing a chunk of my life that I could not account for.

Despair closed in on me, and I tried to pull myself together long enough to figure out what to do. I needed to splint my leg. I needed to find shelter. I needed to find my parents' bodies. I needed to do a lot of things. The only thing I seemed able to make myself do was curl up in a ball by that big tree and stare at the world around me.

My entire body shook. The bitter cold assaulted my bare skin that had been left desperately exposed to the elements.

I seemed too detached from the situation to care—a paralyzing state of shock taking over.

I never heard the voices as they approached from the distance. They were white noise, indecipherable, until one called out to me. The voice was unfamiliar, yet fell on my ears like an old friend's. I tried to yell, but instead of a thunderous "over here," a mere squeak came out. Much to my surprise, he acknowledged, then ran towards me at a speed I hadn't known a human could possess, but I guess I wasn't really an expert.

A sudden, brief jolt of horror shot through me. *What if these are the people I've been trying to escape?* I went from elation to panic in a nanosecond. I struggled to find a way to stand up, only to be weighed down by the burden my right leg had become. I wanted to escape. The compulsion to run nearly tore me in half.

I can't die this way.

My breathing became more rapid, shallow, and completely ineffective. I felt the darkness coming again. Just as my final grip on consciousness faded, I saw him. I thought he was an angel, sent by God to bring me home, to bring me to my parents. A dream come true, during my worst nightmare.

The contrast was beautiful and frightening.

1

"**S**hit! Just when you think you're running out of places to slice yourself with questionable looking metal scraps, some fresh real estate pops up and introduces itself to the harbinger of tetanus," I muttered to myself, jabbing my finger with the copper I was remaking into a bracelet. *If I can stave off lockjaw for another week, I'll consider myself the luckiest person alive.*

Once it was clear that the bracelet wasn't really interested in being sized, it gave me an excuse to cut out early and head upstairs to plan the events of the evening. The odds weighed heavily in favor of a salad for dinner with an HBO movie chaser, but it was an easy bet since I was the one stacking the deck. After doing a final run-through of the shop to make sure everything was shut down and straightened up, I made my way out the main entrance to an already bustling scene. All of the local restaurants that lined the old, cobblestone New England streets were lit up, creating an inviting ambiance for the people who filled the streets, making their way to the various establishments. I loved to walk around downtown, crowded with brick buildings dating back to the 1700's. Portsmouth, New Hampshire had a lot to offer for a small city, without the drawbacks of being in a much bigger urban scene. No worries about being mugged on the way to your car, no fear of a drive-by shooting while out jogging, no stabbings, no gangs; virtually no violence at all, random or otherwise. Best of all, no murders. That alone sold me on it.

I quickly soaked in the view and turned to lock the door. *Maybe I should actually go out tonight. Maybe loosen up and actually participate in socialization?* As I shoved that crazy talk far into the depths of my subconscious, I worked on unlocking the adjacent door that led up to my personal space, my second-story apartment and third-floor loft studio. I bought the three-story brick building with my inheritance. It was one of three things I owned that had any ties to my parents at all.

Even though I'd moved to Portsmouth nine months earlier, I hadn't really made many friends. In fact, I hadn't really made *any* at all, which made it a tad difficult to have a social life. I never gave too much thought to it, though. Everything was so chaotic after the death of my parents, and having to assimilate into a seeing world only complicated things further. Although most things were easy enough to pick up on with a little study and help from those around me, I constantly encountered unknowns. Driving was beyond intimidating, and it had taken me months to muster the courage to even try it at all. I had kept my dad's car because of how much he loved it, and I wanted to have the opportunity to see the nuances that he always spoke about that made it such a fantastic ride. It was the second of the three items linked to my parents.

When I entered the corridor, I heard a faintly familiar

sound and shot up the stairs to get into my apartment. *Is that my phone?* Nobody ever called me. I knew two people in town, and one of them owned my favorite Chinese restaurant.

I highly doubted that my take-out was calling me.

I barely got to the phone in time, only to hear a pre-recorded message reminding me that my recycling schedule had changed and I needed to put it out Monday instead of Tuesday. *Good to know.* After noting that on my virtually empty calendar, I turned the TV on for some dinner-making background noise. It was the only conversation I seemed to be a part of.

I giggled at some ridiculous show involving the strange mating rituals of drunken co-eds as I pieced together my salad. *Tonight I'm going to live on the edge and add avocado.* I really did need to get out more.

Feeling as though my IQ was dropping in direct propor-tion to the rapidly increasing beer count on the show, I decided to try the local news. I turned to a feature on the most recent bar/restaurant/club in town. I put my knife down, because multitasking had never been my thing, and watched the footage. The place looked promising. It had a fabulous contemporary decor that was very Euro-trendy and an actual live DJ spinning. *Interesting.*

I watched as they flashed clips of people dancing, bartenders fixing whatever drink was en vogue, and a montage of interviews with delighted patrons. *Maybe I really should try going out, it looks like fun...but drunk people always look like they're having a good time.*

I loved to dance, but the bar scene completely intimi-dated me. I'd never had the guts to go more than once. In college it was too difficult because someone had to be with me constantly to guide me through the melee so as to avoid injury from a variety of sources. Apparently drunken people were accidents waiting to happen. The one and only time I went I managed fifteen whole minutes in the bar before some idiot backed into me. He knocked me into a waitress; she fell into a group behind her, which started what could best be described as a procession of human dominoes that ended with a very pissed off bouncer and us getting tossed.

How bad could it be? I can always leave if it blows.

I caved and decided that going out for the first time ever by myself was the plan. I then frantically tried to find appropriate attire. My style was best described as delightfully random. I relished the opportunity to mix vintage with boutique finds and high fashion with Goodwill bargains, topping it all off with the perfect accessory. I was always complimented on the originality of my outfit. I suppose they could have been backhanded compliments; I wasn't very good at reading expressions. I never worried about it, though. I loved the freedom of being able to choose what I wanted to wear.

Before I got too far into the process, I sought inspiration from Gwen Stefani's "What u Waitin 4." I liked to go through life with my own little soundtrack blaring both internally and externally; I thought it was good for the soul. Since nobody on the news feature looked overly dressed up, I settled on some low-rise jeans that were skinny enough to toss on my favorite (and oh-so-expensive) chocolate brown, faded, four-inch stacked heel, knee-high boots with the buckle on the side. *I SOOOOOO love Jimmy Choo.*

As if it were important what top I wore (because my boots were so amazing), I grabbed a long-sleeved, grey and navy mini-striped top that came down low on the hips and covered me when I bent over. My boots were showstoppers, but I didn't want to run the risk of mooning the bar-goers every time I bent down or sat in a chair; I liked to try to keep my bits to myself. The slight transparency of the top demanded that I put a camisole on under it because I wasn't into flashing the girls either.

If my dressing went seamlessly, my hair and makeup were a whole other story. Sometimes you went into battle knowing you were going to get your ass handed to you on a platter. I tried my best to tame my shoulder-length, platinum-blond, curly hair, though I was convinced it was possessed and had a personal vendetta against me. The potential for greatness was there, but I hadn't quite figured out how to extract it. I had been told on numerous occasions that it looked like Sarah Jessica Parker's in *Sex and the City's* early seasons, only bigger. Having never watched it, I had no idea if that was good or bad. I managed to get the frizz out of it using some kind of expensive goo that I was certain just weighed it down slightly. Since it took the edge off, I considered it a wildly successful encounter. As for makeup, my strategy was simple—try not to look like a ghost. I'd learned that being obscenely pale was not generally socially accepted. Society 1, me 0.

I did my best to apply a little stain to the apples of my cheeks and clear gloss to my lips. The intricacies of eye makeup application still eluded me. My fair complexion didn't pull off a lot of color well, so I never tried. I didn't want to upstage my ocean-blue eyes, so I kept my eye shadow neutral and accentuated with highlighter. Eyeliner and mascara were an ER excursion waiting to happen. I tried my best to not get the liner in my eye or on too thick. If I kept mascara to the general region of my lashes, it was a wild success. Luckily for me, my lashes were impossibly long, so I had a big target.

Once the ritual was completed, I gave myself a once-over in the mirror. *Not too shabby.* Beauty was a funny thing to gauge when my blindness had left me without societal cues for nearly my whole life. What I found attractive wasn't necessarily what others did. Sometimes I found myself completely baffled by the movie stars, sports gods, and socialites in the media who were worshiped by the masses. I didn't see it. Sure there were those that you just couldn't argue (Brad Pitt for example), but only one face had ever stopped my breath, and I was very certain I'd never see anything that compared to it for the rest of my existence. Some treasures were only meant to be found once.

10:36pm.

I assumed that was an acceptable time to head out. I didn't want to be too early and look stupid arriving alone.

At the door, I stopped to load my favorite magenta leather handbag with my wallet and keys. I rifled through the clutter on the console table, looking for my platinum band. The ring was the last of the three things I owned with any connection to my parents; I rarely ever took it off. *Maybe I left it in the shop.* Not wanting to stall my going-out momentum, I decided to look for it when I got home. I locked up the apartment and headed downstairs. I broke out into the crowd of people meandering through the streets and locked up behind me. A girl could never be too careful, even in Portsmouth.

The club was only a few blocks away from my place, so I filed into the crowd of people going my direction and kept pace. For entertainment on my trip, I listened in to conversations that were entirely too private to be had in the busy streets. I learned all about how difficult it was to treat chlamydia, especially the third time around, from the group of early twenty-something women directly in front of me.

Perhaps someone should have the "friends don't let friends get STD's" discussion.

Behind me were the drunken ramblings of some middle-aged businessmen discussing whether the size, shape, or texture of a woman's anatomy was her most important quality. It sounded like shape was ahead for a while, but size made an amazing push from behind to come through victorious in the end. *Men really are that predictable.* I crossed the street, not only to escape the increasing anxiety I was feeling while listening to them, but also because I needed to make a left at Market Street.

As I approached the club, I was disheartened to see a line flowing from the entrance down the street. *What is this, Boston? Great.* I sighed audibly and joined the rest of the cattle in the queue. I hoped with any luck it was going to move quickly. I felt so exposed being by myself when everyone around me had friends or significant others with them. *I'm so lame.* If I'd had my cell phone, I could have pretended to be texting while I played games on it. While I was lost in thought, somebody elbowed me from behind to indicate the line was moving and I'd better catch up. I frowned back at the owner of the elbow in question and he smiled wickedly at me. *Creeptaaaaastic.* I made a mental note not to look in that general direction again.

As I started to reflect on why this was the world's worst idea, the bouncer came out and started picking people out of the line to go in. *There's a selection process? I don't remember seeing that shit on the news.* As I turned to duck out of line, a hand caught my elbow and gently spun me around.

"Don't you want to go in?" the bouncer asked.

I half-smiled and nodded.

"Well then, today's your lucky day, Chica."

Indeed it is.

"Thanks" was all I managed to mumble as I walked past him to the entrance. I felt the cold looks tear through the back of me as I passed everyone waiting in line. I glanced back to see Creeptastic arguing with the bouncer and pointing at me. I didn't wait around to see what that was about and put on speed as I went through the door. One flash of my ID and a smile later, I was in. Not wanting to relive my domino disaster of undergrad past, I made my way very quickly to the bar. I found the back corner where it connected to the wall and tucked myself into the last seat. I figured if I surrounded myself with as many stable surfaces as I could, it would greatly decrease the odds of a repeat performance.

I wasn't a big drinker, but the scene there would have driven anyone to it. There was barely enough room to pass between individuals without grossly encroaching on their personal space. Being very attached to mine, I decided that in order to loosen my grip on it, I would require some liquid courage. Thirty minutes, twenty-five dollars, and three G&T's later, I was ready to rock. My dancing shoes were ready to go cut some rug all over that place. Just as I was getting off of my perch at the bar, I got a strangely uncomfortable yet familiar feeling. My breath started to come rapidly and I felt all the blood drain from my face. It was at that moment I felt an unwanted hand on my shoulder. I choked down a scream. *I'm in public. I'm fine. Nobody here is going to hurt me. Breathe.*

I slowly turned to face Captain Touchy-Feely. *SHIT!* The Captain was none other than Creeptastic. *How did he get in here?*

Feeling slightly relieved for the moment, I asked, "How the hell did you get in here?" People skills were not my forte.

He put his hand around the back of my neck and drew

me towards him. "I thought you were going to leave me out there in that line. I had to convince the big guy that you were hard of hearing and didn't realize that I wasn't behind you while you went in," he said.

My pulse was in my throat. He was smiling at me, but the look was predatory and the energy and intent behind it were nothing short of malicious. I tried to keep my shit together while every fiber of my being was yelling "get the fuck out of here." Since no overly untoward gesture had been made, I opted for defusing the situation.

"Guess I am. I never heard you and I wasn't aware that I should have notified you of my entrance approval, dear."

He laughed abruptly and moved closer still, until our toes were in danger of touching and my back was pinned up against the wall.

"Dear, is it? I was hoping our pet names would take on a more...*flavorful* quality."

I struggled to gracefully evade both his position and hold on me. My poker face was alarmingly close to failing, and I needed to get some distance between me and the psycho. As I ducked my head around his hand in a fluid dance-like move to the downbeat of whatever song was playing, I said, "I don't do flavorful, and I certainly wouldn't do you." So much for the defusion game plan.

His eyes flickered something I didn't understand as he violently grabbed me by my shoulders.

"Who said I was giving you a choice?"

I not only saw, but felt, what he intended. *Not again. Please, God, not again. No, no, no, no, not again.* I was paralyzed by my fear. I didn't shout. I didn't run. I stared into the face of a psycho and did nothing. I felt the tears stinging the backs of my eyes and then it happened again. My vision started to narrow and go dark. I was going to pick that time to black out. *Classic. That would give him exactly what he wanted: an easy excuse to carry me out of here unquestioned and go do whatever sick things he was planning on. Focus. Focus! Do not do this. Fight!* But it was no use. There was no fight in me, giving truth to the old adage: those who don't learn from history really are doomed to repeat it.

alm.

That single thought resonated through me as I felt a warm presence envelop me from behind. I slowly regained my vision and saw two strong and heroic hands reach around me, grabbing the offender's wrists to pry his hands off of me.

"She doesn't seem to want to buy what you're selling," my savior said. I couldn't see his face, but something about him was commanding. He compelled my restrainer to do his bidding with an energy so powerful the hair on the back of my neck raised to attention. He emanated power. There was no threat of violence in his aura, though judging by the size and strength of his hands he was no doubt capable of it. Captain Creepy slowly withdrew his hands without taking his eyes off of my hero.

"It seems as though you're interrupting our conversation," Creepy growled.

"I think your conversation is very much over. I think you're going to leave here immediately and never come back. I think if you don't, there will be a price to pay, and you can't afford it. Am I making myself clear?" Hero asked.

Something new flashed through Creepy's face. *He's afraid.* He paused for a moment, flashed me an evil grin, then turned slowly and walked away without a word.

I hadn't realized that I was shaking until one of those amazing arms reached around across my chest and gently drew me back to his wall of strength. It was a friendly gesture with no hint of sexuality. Comforting. It took me a moment to realize that he had been talking to me. He leaned over my shoulder and spoke directly into my ear.

"Are you okay?"

I nodded.

"Did he hurt you?"

I shook my head no. He chuckled and his chest shook against my back.

"Are you capable of speech?"

I stammered, "Yeah, uh yes... yes I am."

Smooth, Ruby. Very smooth.

"Do you want to move yet?" he asked casually, as if he weren't troubled by which way I might answer his question.

I slowly turned to face him, my nose brushing against his slim-fitting, baby-blue button-down shirt. It covered a very lean and muscular chest. My eyes quickly scanned down his Euro-cut jeans to his Diesel sneakers. Nice choice. I didn't so much lift my head to see him as angled my gaze to his face. He was looking down at me curiously and smiling. When my eyes met his, I almost fell over. I said a quick "thank you," turned around, and hauled ass through the bar. I heard a faint "wait" trailing off behind me, but had no interest in retreating to him. It was *him*. I was sweating by the time I got to the door. I glanced back to see that he was following me out. *SHIT*. He was only a few yards behind me.

I tore through the doors and took off running full speed down the street. I got more than a few looks of concern from bar-goers, and I even got a "Run Forrest" comment from an especially original frat boy.

I must have lost him somewhere in my Olympic-level sprint back to the apartment because there was nobody around when I unlocked the main door on the street. I gave a final look as I closed the door behind me and quickly locked it right after.

I leaned against the main door and slid down to the floor. I was exhausted and in shock. Wild and unwanted memories started racing through my mind.

I opened my eyes to see a man. My breathing stopped short and I stared. I wasn't aware of the movement of my arm until I could actually see my hand touching his face in adoration. He was smiling at me. I closed my eyes and explored his face with my hands as I'd done a million times to others throughout my life. My hands could read beauty, expression, and age in a way that my eyes could now only hope to achieve. He caught my hand, shaking from the harsh winter cold, and held it while he yelled for someone else to give me a coat. It was big and he wrapped it all around me. The warmth that lay in the layers of down felt amazing against my nearly frostbitten skin. He picked me up in his arms and told me that I was going to be all right; he'd make sure of it. Suddenly we were moving quickly through the woods; it was all I could do to keep conscious. He asked me questions to try and keep me alert but it was to no avail. The last thing I heard was him yelling at me to hang on.

When I awoke a week later I was yet again alone. Alone in a room of flashing screens, bleeping monitors, and so many tubes. Everything was stark white like the snow I was found in, only far warmer and safer. I looked around the room for any token from my parents to show that they had been waiting for me to wake up, and then it hit me. There would be no more tokens. Those days were gone; taken from me. As reality washed over me, I wanted to cry. Instead, a fierce but soundless wail erupted from me. It eventually morphed into an uncontrollable sob that possessed my whole body, shaking it violently. I continued on like that until an intern came to check on me.

I suddenly remembered how I got to the hospital, that I was rescued from the woods. I asked who it was that brought me in, but there was no record of anyone. I'd been brought to the ER and checked in, but when the nurse came back to get additional information from the man who brought me, he was gone.

I couldn't wrap my mind around what just happened, but it was exceptionally hard to focus on anything other than the racing of my heart at that moment. It had to be the running.

Though I hadn't seen a lifetime of faces, I'd never seen anything that rivaled his, and I never thought I would see it again. When I asked about him at the hospital, nobody had any information to help me find him. No name, number, address, etc. I'd never wanted to contact someone more, and the reasons were many. I still had no recollection of that night beyond the initial attack that led to the death of my parents. The doctors later told me that I had injuries consistent with physical assault and exposure, but not rape. They weren't sure how my leg had been broken and said that I was a medical miracle because of my acquired vision. None of them had seen or spoken to the man who brought me in. The experience left me with a whole lot of nothing aside from confirming the obvious: I was wounded and alone.

I spent a couple of months in a rehabilitation facility, needing extensive physical therapy for my leg. I couldn't walk on my own, and I had nowhere else to go, no family to rely on to help me do the most basic of activities. With a lot of free time on my hands, I spent the greater portion of it daydreaming about those magical eyes and the face that framed them so beautifully. I wanted to know whom they belonged to, where he lived, and why he left.

I was one to believe that things happened for a reason, and that God, the universe, or whatever you wanted to call it, had a greater plan than mere humans could begin to wrap their minds around. I also, however, liked to romanticize the most insignificant things. In combination, the two could lead to delusions of all kinds. Part of me wanted desperately to say that it was no coincidence that we were in the club that night, but luckily my inner realist was there to cut that idea off swiftly at the knees. *He probably didn't recognize me. He just wanted to make sure I was okay. It seems to be his MO.* And with that happy and esteem-boosting bit of reality, I was off the floor and heading up to my apartment. A shower was in order to wash away the memory of the evening. If ever I had needed reinforcement to uphold my policy on not doing the social scene, that evening was it. Bar 2, Ruby -20, and counting.

3

The days passed slowly, sometimes painfully, with a constant inner dialogue that revolved around my mystery man. I woke up thinking about him, went to work thinking about him, and ate lunch thinking about him, until it was obvious that my day would be utterly wasted in an obsessive fog that rendered me useless. My original frustration with knowing nothing about him always returned. Attached to it were unwanted feelings associated with being alone in a hospital room for weeks with nothing to occupy my time but trying to remember what happened and find a way to track him down. My mental calisthenics were utterly fruitless, unless developing an ulcer was considered productive.

On day eleven I actually considered stalking the bars to see if I could hunt him down. That should more than adequately demonstrate the depths of my desperation, considering the score between the bar and me. Later that day I started to come to my senses, realizing that I was about to hit new lows. I didn't want to get so desperate that I eventually found myself lying in a gutter, covered in questionable fluids, before I smartened up. Getting the answers I sought just wasn't worth obsessing over.

At that point that I regained some composure and did what any self-respecting woman would do in the situation; I immediately started lying to myself to make it all more palatable. I found myself rationalizing things, like that wasn't actually him, and that nobody could truly have their own guardian angel. It was all purely coincidence. I was amazed at the complete bullshit I could feed myself, easily swallowing it when it best suited my purpose.

By day fifteen I really had myself believing the shit I was slinging. I thought about it far less often. Unfortunately, when I did, my curious nature would override my common sense, and my mind would wander back to lingering questions I was so eager to ignore. The power of my damaged psyche knew no bounds. None at all.

On day sixteen I found myself thundering furiously around my store (my dad always told me that I sounded like a five-hundred pound man when I walked), trying desperately to find my platinum ring. I was certain I'd placed it in the back studio a couple of weeks earlier while working on a woven metal bracelet. My mind was analogous to a steel sieve: strong but leaky. I abandoned all reason and started searching every nook and cranny in the whole place. *It has to be here. It can't be gone...it's all I have left.* I felt the desperation like a vise around my chest, creating a direct relationship; as one increased, so did the other. If my desperation had worsened, I would have passed out.

I was bent over in the corner of the room, wedged in between the front counter and a display case, burrowing under a cabinet, armed with a flashlight to see if the ring that I knew I didn't take off in that room could have fallen underneath the wooden structure. Though I wasn't shocked when I didn't discover it hiding coyly under there, I certainly was surprised that the tinkling of the entrance bells startled me enough to whack my head with enthusiasm against the cabinet when I shot up to attend to my customer. As I turned, trying nonchalantly to rub down the growing goose egg on my head, I was greeted by a familiar voice.

"I don't think it's safe for you to ever be left unsupervised. You seem to find danger in the most innocuous places, don't you?"

Holy shit! Him again...

I was extremely capable of deluding myself, but even I couldn't do it when I was faced with said delusion in the living flesh, in broad daylight, and in my very own place. It also didn't help that he seemed all too aware of who I was. I tried my best to appear amused at his comment, though I found precious little funny about the situation. I was again rendered incapable of speech, an impediment I would one day have to focus on correcting. As I silently willed myself to speak, he rescued me from myself. Again.

"You must have really hit your head good. I've never seen a woman at such a loss for words," he chided with a wicked grin on his face.

"I...uh...it really hurt!" I stammered. Clearly *that* was what I'd waited all this time to say to him.

He moved across the floor quickly with a utilitarian grace that was mesmerizing, coming to stand before me. He reached up and gently removed my hand from my head. The intensity of his presence made me shiver.

"Let me see. I need to know if we're making another trip to the hospital," he said as he examined my frozen form. I could barely breathe.

"There's no blood, so that makes it a less interesting

story for later, but better for now. Do you feel dizzy? Faint? Nauseated?"

Apparently he was not only a hero but a trained medical professional too. *Is he going for sainthood?* I soon found him asking me an all-too-familiar question.

"Can you speak?" he asked softly, still grinning that grin that made me think he found this whole situation entirely too entertaining for my liking.

"Yes, I can. Sometimes I just choose not to," I said with just enough hostility for him to realize I didn't enjoy being the butt of his joke.

"Sorry. I didn't mean anything by it. I was just concerned that you might have a concussion; you really hit your head pretty hard on the cabinet," he said while consciously wiping the smile from his face. It appeared to take a considerable amount of effort for him to manage the task, but I appreciated both the effort and the outcome.

"What exactly were you doing down there?" he asked innocently.

"I lost something. A ring."

He turned his head somewhat mockingly to look around at the showroom, full of jewelry, most of which were rings.

"Not those. This one is important, personal. I can't lose it. Ever," I said as my voice slowly softened, becoming mournful. He smiled a different smile at me as he told me he'd help. Even after all my months of obsessing about this man, needing to know who he was, his name, and his memories, he paled in importance at that moment.

"I have to find my ring."

4

We spent the next two hours tearing apart my store, then putting it back together. Both tasks were accomplished with nearly exclusive silence, barring the few "excuse me" and "oops, sorry" utterances. I was starting to lose hope when, finally, he popped his head through the door separating the showroom from the back studio, a cheesy grin plastered across his face. He walked towards me extending a cupped hand, in which a well-worn and engraved platinum ring was delicately laid.

I screamed with relief and delight, snatching the ring from him and putting it on. Before I could think clearly, I jumped into his arms and gave him the biggest bear hug I could, legs wrapped tightly around him and all. I stayed there for about fifteen seconds before I realized that my koala impression was not only completely inappropriate, but horribly awkward. With as much grace as I could gather, I climbed down the man-whose-name-I-still-didn't-know. I dropped my gaze to the floor, wanting to crawl into a hole and die.

"Thank you," I whispered.

"You're welcome?" he said, pausing in an effort to draw my name from me.

"Ruby. My name is Ruby."

He chuckled before responding.

"I'd say it's nice to meet you, but I think we're well past that stage by now," he said, reaching his hand towards me. "I'm Sean."

Like a reflex that I couldn't control, "Nice to meet you too" flew out of my mouth, completely disregarding the point he had just made.

His face was as perfect as I'd remembered. He looked like a supermodel, but roughed up somehow. Harder. More rugged. His eyes were a green I wouldn't have thought possible. They were so clear and bright, the color of new grass in the spring with hints of a darker, hunter green shade that shadowed the outer edges. They were by far the most amazing things I'd ever seen, and seeing them again was like the first time; I was awestruck. They were framed by beautiful eyelashes that were far too long and thick to belong to a man; it really wasn't fair. His cheekbones were angular, almost harsh, with a five o'clock shadow that likely showed up only minutes after he shaved. His nose was the perfect balance of symmetry, stateliness and size, being prominently featured, but not too large to look right. His mouth was a shade of reddish-pink that looked like he just got slapped (or brutally kissed), bringing all the blood to the surface of that delicate skin. They were more thin than full and had just the right amount of Cupid's bow. To sum it all up, he was perfection.

I, however, was not.

I came out of my stupor to see him studying me—not in a sexual way, but clinically, as if I was a lab animal doing something interesting in my little cage. He shifted his attention to my store full of jewelry once he noticed me noticing him. I stayed silent while he wandered around taking everything in, again in a very studious fashion. *I'm guessing he's not actually a fan of fine accessories.*

"You made these?" he asked. There seemed to be a sense of appreciation in his tone.

"Yes. I find vintage, broken, or ugly pieces and find ways to rework them. I recently started working with recycled metal, plastics, and other unusual things. It seems to be gaining popularity. I think people like the idea of supporting the 'green' movement."

"They're...*unusual*," he replied, lightly fingering a beaded necklace on display.

"Unusual, eh? Is that a good or bad thing...or do I want to know?" I asked. I smiled uncomfortably, awaiting his response. He seemed to really think about his answer before he spoke, as if it were paramount that he get it just right.

"You have a distinct point of view, unlike anything I've ever seen before. You combine color, metals, and materials in a way that should create a visual disaster, yet it's so beautiful in an original way," he said with a steady tone. *Maybe he really does appreciate jewelry.* My face flushed and warmed with his compliment, and I instantly turned to shy away from him. "You're very talented," he added. It stopped me in my tracks.

I turned in slow motion to face him, needing to see if once again he was pulling my chain. When I met his eyes, it was clear that he'd meant what he said, and all I could pull together in response was a measly "thanks." I knew it was beyond weak, considering the level of compliment I'd just received, but it was something so unexpected and unfamiliar that my brain hadn't finished processing it before my mouth independently replied. I lacked a lot of social graces due to my sheltered childhood, but even more than that, I lacked praise to which I would have needed to respond. My parents were never quick with a compliment, and it left me feeling a little lost when his was so easily given.

I was so excited upon receiving the news that I asked one of the other graduate students in the lab to drive me home right away. It wasn't often that a non-doctoral student was published, and Professor Lewellen had made a special trip to our building to give me the news in person. My research on neurophysiology and its effects on the human immune system was being published in the American Physiological Society's Journal of Neurophysiology.

I had been working on this connection since my undergraduate studies after a random chance discussion I had had with a chiropractor I met while studying in a nearby coffee shop. He had mentioned a link between improper nerve function and the immune system, and he was so passionate about his clinical experience with it that I started to wonder if there was really something to it. I dedicated all my free time to researching the connection, and since I had more of that than I cared to admit to, I accomplished a lot before ever entering my masters-level program. I had compiled a summary of extensive research, clinical application and trials, as well as case study statistics, and presented it to Dr. Lewellen for his review. He said it was amazing research with compelling information, but neglected to mention was that he was going to submit it to journals for review on my behalf.

I felt like a kid on Christmas the whole way home in the car. I could barely sit still or shut up. It was probably good that I couldn't see the expression of my poor classmate, who I'm sure was entirely disgusted with my antics by the time she dropped me off. I forgot to say thank you for the ride as I jumped out of the car and made my way up the driveway, white cane flying from side to side. I ran through the door shouting for my parents, who upon hearing my cries immediately thought something was wrong and crashed upon me in a panic. When I convinced them there wasn't anything wrong, which took quite some time, I gave them the good news. Being academics themselves, I thought they would gush over such an accomplishment, especially for someone at my age and level of scholastic achievement.

What I never would have expected was the silence I was met with. Neither said a word for a good minute or two. When I figured that they were in quiet shock, I reached over to feel my mother's face to read her expression. What I felt was something smacking of indifference and irritation. Did they not hear me? I opened my mouth to ask if they had, but my father quickly asked which journal it was to be published in. When I told him, all he said was "Oh. Not the British Journal of Medicine? That's disappointing." My mother quickly added, "There was no reason to come storming into this house causing that kind of a scene over that." In that moment I was the embodiment of dejection in ways that neither would ever live to understand. It was also at that precise moment I realized that their imperfection of a child might never accomplish enough to make them proud.

When I snapped out of my not-so-fond-memory, I found Sean looking at me with a careful, patient expression on his face. He was slighted neither by my lack of manners nor by my flightiness.

"You sure that head is feeling okay?" he asked politely.

"Sorry, I just thought of something. It's not important." I feigned a smile to try to sell my response.

"Well then, Ruby, I'm off to grade some desperately boring papers. It was great to...meet you. Finally." And with that he turned on his heels and headed out the door with the same abruptness that he had come and gone with before. *So that was it? What I've been obsessing over for months? All that lead-up for "gotta go grade some papers, peace out bitch?" Oh hell no!*

"Why are you here?" I blurted out as quickly as I could before he completely escaped through the door.

"Ah...isn't that the million dollar question?" he said, turning gracefully to face me. "Why am I here? Why are you here? Why are any of us here? Didn't take you for a philosopher, Ruby." He flashed me the toothiest grin before letting go of the door. Unfortunately, it shut off my response to his rhetoric.

I bet he wasn't sorry that he didn't get a chance to hear it.

5

I spent the rest of my evening trying to figure out how I was ever going to get some answers out of Sean, if that even was his real name. I couldn't think clearly enough when he was around to actually formulate a well-thought-out and coherent, not to mention pertinent, question. Just the sight of him got me so frazzled that all higher brain functions shut down, making it nearly impossible to do anything above breathing and staying upright. I may as well have just grunted and banged on things to communicate with him; it probably would have been more effective. I had sworn off men a long time ago, so it wasn't that I wanted him; it was simply his face. It was mesmerizing, like staring at the most beautiful piece of art.

His uncanny ability to disappear as quickly as he showed up made my predicament even harder still. I worried that I was going to have to resort to criminal activity to keep him in one place long enough to get what I wanted from him. I wasn't necessarily opposed to physical violence, but I heavily questioned my ability to knock him out with a solid blow to his head and then immobilize him with rope or one of those crafty zip-tie things. He had at least a hundred pounds on me. My semi-kidnapping fantasy hardly seemed that morally reprehensible given the circumstances. At least then I could have gotten some concrete information from him: full name, phone number, workplace, life story, etc. Cover all the basics.

I chuckled to myself at the mere thought of clubbing and interrogating him. I imagined doing it up *Law & Order: SVU* style, sans partner. I had to admit that in all the weirdness and strange coincidences, which I still didn't believe in, he never emanated anything but a calming and neutral energy. Had he bad intentions or evil plans for me, I would have picked up on it. At least I *hoped* I would. But there was still something that seemed just a little too convenient, and my gut resonated the slightest sound of warning. I tried to focus on that feeling and strengthen it for better interpretation, but I couldn't. No matter how hard I tried, I just couldn't put my finger on it. So I chose to ignore it instead.

Maybe he was my consolation prize: lose your parents, gain a strange hottie. My mind constantly ran over the possibilities until, for the sake of my sanity and my under-eye circles, I conceded that he was just a very strange individual who looked like a Greek god and really enjoyed saving me. I drifted off to sleep, wondering when he might choose to drop in again, and what tragedy he'd snuff out in the process.

6

S aturday proved to be a lucrative day for the shop. I sold ten pieces in six hours, which may not sound like many, but when some of them fetched a price tag of five hundred dollars or more, it made for the beginnings of an excellent shopping spree for me. And a fatter check for Uncle Sam come quarterly payment time.

There were a couple of pieces that I was sad to see go, including my absolute favorite; it too had found a new home. I had made it from an amazing sapphire ring that I found washed up on the beach in Maine. It was extremely old and in horrible condition, but the round-cut gem itself had remained remarkably perfect according to the guy I took my gems into for assessment. After I dismantled it, I remounted the stone in an obnoxiously huge white gold pendant that amounted to nothing more than a really thick disk framing the bezel-mounted stone. The end result was bold, elegant and fashion-forward, not a piece for the average girl. Luckily, the young doctor who purchased it had impeccable fashion sense by my estimation, and I was certain that she'd take care of my baby. It also made me an easy twenty-five hundred dollars. The profit margin on it was huge, given that the stone had been free and I had a great contact for getting gold at a really reasonable price.

I was still glowing about the sales of the day while I closed up the books. It really illustrated how much of a banner day it was at REWORKED because I *hated* the business part of being in business. I was happiest being stuck in the back and left alone to design. Accounting was for the birds, or the nerds, as was often the case.

After locking up, I rushed to my apartment in a frantic state, needing to find a barrage of items quickly so I wouldn't be late. The best part of my day was yet to come, and I had to get my ass moving. Saturday evening was reserved for a sacred activity: dancing. I took classes only a couple of miles from my house at a fantastic studio that offered a comprehensive selection of styles with amazing instructors. I always started with ballet for the evening (as all dancers should have a strong background in the basic principles of ballet). Next was jazz, then tap, and last but not least was hip-hop. It was my most recent addition, but rapidly proving to be my favorite.

I liked to run the two miles to the studio to get warmed up before starting barre work, but, unfortunately, I was at a total loss as to where my running shoes and iPod were. Running without music was not an option. Ever. In fact, I never understood how anyone could do it. I firmly believed in having an ongoing soundtrack to my life, courtesy of my teenage years listening to Ally McBeal. Striding down the streets of Portsmouth to the studio was a perfect time to apply that notion. Thankfully, I located both my shoes and iPod so I could run with both tunes and protected feet.

I arrived at class just in the nick of time, tearing off my outerwear in the lobby until I was down to the required dress of pink tights and black leotard. After I slapped on my thigh-high leg warmers, I positioned myself along the barre with the others. An hour later, I was thoroughly limbered up and ready for the rest of my classes. The four hours of dance made for a long evening, but I didn't mind. It was better than anything else I would have been doing any other night of the week.

Hip hop ended after a wicked combination that our instructor had just learned in New York City was firmly drilled into our brains and bodies. I had the shakes from lack of food and was in dire need of replenishing fluids. If I'd wrung out the sweats I was wearing, I could have filled a Nalgene bottle.

I changed quickly after class and put on my iPod before waving in the general direction of everyone as I walked out onto the street. I secured my messenger bag so that it wouldn't bang around while I ran back home. My legs seemed especially tired that evening, so I started off walking, hoping that they would quickly be inspired to get with the game plan to run home.

The trip through town could be a bit unnerving in the dark. Winding through the main streets of the city was safe, but I could freak myself out sometimes, ducking down alleys and roads that weren't well traveled during the evening. There were always people out when I hit the bar district, but other than that, they were few and far between.

I'd never actually *walked* home before, and after about ten minutes, I started to realize why. Running seemed to numb my awareness of certain things in a way that walking did not. I didn't get as much time to focus on the upcoming dumpster and what could be lurking behind it, or what could be around the dimly lit corner lying in wait. Even worse than the general anxiety I was giving myself was the very definitive feeling that someone was following me. I was picking up on something that was not especially warm and fuzzy, but whenever I turned to see if someone was there, I was alone. Very, very alone.

And I slowly started to panic.

My legs soon realized that running was in our collective best interest, and off we went. As I began to run, I hoped the malevolent energy around me would lessen, but it didn't. With my increasing panic came increasing speed. I hurdled over objects in the street and wove through parked cars like a heat-seeking missile aimed straight for the warmth of home. I didn't look back anymore, knowing that whoever was throwing that energy my way would inconveniently not be seen. Common sense dictated that it would be best to take out my earphones, but the thought of hearing my pursuer disturbed me too much. Beyond that, I needed the adrenaline rush that Rage Against the Machine's "Killing in the Name Of" was giving me, although the title wasn't very reassuring.

I was about two minutes from home when I neared Market Street. There would be people out for sure on a Saturday night, so I thought I'd be in the clear. I rounded the corner to see precious few walking the streets. It was an improvement, but not what I'd hoped for.

As I neared home, I reached around to my bag in a desperate effort to find my keys, all the while chastising myself for not having them already in hand. Personal safety was never my strong suit and I was painfully aware of it at that moment. After two blocks of searching, I managed to pull my keys from the bag, only to immediately fumble them. They flew through the air in slow motion, and I help-lessly watched them crash to the pavement and skid underneath a parked car.

"Shit!" I muttered angrily to myself.

My timing couldn't have been more off. At that particular moment, the street was clear of any life that I could see. Still, I felt that negative energy there, nagging at me. It wasn't getting stronger, but it wasn't getting any weaker either. Having no other options, I threw myself onto my hands and knees, trying to figure out the best way to retrieve my keys from under the high-end Mercedes that was running some wicked defense. When I realized I couldn't reach them any other way, I flopped down on my belly and wiggled under the perfectly engineered undercarriage, midway back towards the far tire.

"Gotcha!"

I had my keys in hand and was ready to inelegantly worm my way back out the way I'd come in. I turned to check my trajectory and immediately felt ice shoot through my spine. In my line of sight was a very large and very manly pair of shoes. As I lay there sweating, trying to concoct a plan, my attention snapped to the two pairs of equally masculine shoes on the other side of the car. *Great...they're multiplying!*

"Hey, Jay? Did you park the car on a girl again?" an unfamiliar voice shouted.

"Nope. This one wasn't there when I pulled up," replied the man I assumed was Jay.

"Have no fear gentlemen, I know this one. I seem to get this view of her *often*."

Sean...

I launched myself from under the car to see him smiling down at me first before his gaze drifted over the top of the car to his friends. I was certain they were finding great amusement in both the situation as well as my general appearance. I was covered in sweat and dirt, and wet from the puddle I'd managed to land directly in under the car.

"Is there a reason you were getting familiar with my exhaust system? You wouldn't happen to be a fan of German engineering, would you?" Sean asked.

"Actually, I am," I replied with a haughty tone. "I dropped my keys...I had to get them. This is *your* car?"

"It is," he said. "One of them, anyway. We were just heading home. Where are you headed looking so..." he asked, gesturing at me strangely. I couldn't tell if he was amused or confused by what I had going on.

"Home," I replied, trying to wipe some of the nastiness off of my shirt.

"You seem stressed. Something wrong?" he asked with obvious curiosity.

"Uh, no. No, everything is fine," I said unconvincingly. I did realize as I was saying it that the energy that had me diving under his car was gone. Completely. "I'm just hungry. I need to go home and eat something."

"Do you need a ride?" he asked while looking me up and down, no doubt assessing the damage my dirt-covered body would do to his car's leather interior.

"Nope. I'm good. Thanks," I blurted as I started off down the street.

"Do you need an escort?" he asked, my back still facing him.

"Not necessary," I said without looking over my shoulder. Mortified didn't begin to cover what I was feeling at the time. I wanted, just for once, to not make a *complete* ass of myself in front of him, but that seemed too much to ask.

He said nothing in response, but I heard the growl of his car's engine as it started up. I continued down the street at a brisk pace; running was out of the question, as my body was way too spent. The threat appeared to be gone anyway.

The Mercedes purred as it pulled up slowly next to me, the window lowered so he could speak.

"Be sure to keep a firm grip on those keys, *Ruby*."

"I'll be sure to do that, *Sean*," I said, forcing a smile.

He smiled back, turning up the stereo as he pulled away. While his speakers pumped The Fray's "I'll Look After You," the words hauntingly echoed through the street—and my mind.

I guess he believed in theme songs too.

7

And so my *relationship* with Sean grew. I found myself not-so-randomly running into him here and there. He found himself popping up gallantly when I needed something, and annoyingly when I wanted desperately to be alone. He was irritating in a charming way, making me want to both strangle him repeatedly and gaze into his amazing green eyes, losing myself in them. I couldn't have been more awkward around him; he was completely unnerving.

I eventually stopped putting much thought into the deeper questions that surrounded him and moved in a different direction. If interrogation wasn't going to be effective, I would try a different tactic altogether. I would try to be his friend. It was a stretch for me, taking me way outside my beautifully crafted comfort zone, but necessary to accomplish what I wanted.

Over the weeks of coincidental run-ins, we learned more about each other. For all the oddities plaguing our situation, I found that he really filled a void that I hadn't known was there. Being around him felt right and I wanted to leave it at that, but it wasn't that simple. Through a stroke of genius I realized that my best strategy would be to exploit our friendship. I would slowly lull him into complacency so I could subtly start to extract answers from him without him being any the wiser. Indulging a curiosity over coffee, an innocent question over lunch; these were things that friends shared.

And share he would.

8

When I was in need of the perfect vintage get-up in Portsmouth, there was really only one place I went. *Better With Age* was a trendy boutique not far from my own shop. It carried not only the hottest vintage finds ever, but also mixed in new stuff from local and undiscovered designers, as well as top-shelf jeans. I could tell a lot about a store by the jeans they sold.

The owner, Veronica Marks, a.k.a. Ronnie, was a petite, good-looking, forty-something single mom, who may have spent a little too much time in her younger years partaking in the overindulgence of the eighties and all that that implied. She was quick-witted, sharp-tongued, and a pit bull when it came to her teenage daughter Peyta. She was a walking contradiction, with her Greenpeace ideals and Kabbalah excerpts plastered all over the shop, and a front counter that housed her Glock 9mm. I idolized her. She was the closest thing I had to a friend before Sean.

I pushed through the entrance to her store and smiled at the expected sound of tinkling bells. A flash of brown hair popped up from behind the counter to greet me. Ronnie appeared to be having another one of her "I just wanted to try something different" episodes; her formerly shoulder-length, red hair was shorn to a pixie cut and dyed chocolate brown. The new hairstyle was stunning with her bone structure, but it took me a minute to fully absorb the change, as it completely altered her looks.

"Ruby Tuesday, what can I do for you today?" she asked, smiling as she made her way towards me. "I just got some amazing new shirts in. They're still in the back. You want me to grab them for you?"

"Sure. I'm game."

A wide smile overtook her face as she turned and went through the beaded curtains leading to the stockroom. I rummaged through the racks until she came out with both arms full of fabulousness. She laid it all down on the counter and started organizing it by size, speaking aloud as she did so.

"Nope...that won't fit. Bad color. Too short...ooooooh, but this one is perfect," she said as she pulled a cream blouse out and held it up to admire the sheer fabric. "Now, you need some different pants to try this on with," she mumbled while looking down at my yoga capris. She had a valid point. "I'm going to pull some jeans for you. And I've got those knee-high riding boots you've been eyeing for weeks still in your size. I'll get them for you."

I took the blouse over to a mirror and held it up against me to see if the color would wash me out more, or play into the creaminess of my skin.

"What's the occasion, anyway? Something special I should know about?" she called out, her voice echoing from the back room.

"No. Not really," I replied casually.

"Baloney! Something is up with you. This is the sixth

time you've been in here this month alone. What's with the sudden interest in your appearance? You've got impeccable style, girl, but let's be honest, you don't exactly rock it out 24/7," she said as she gave me the once-over. Again.

"Hey, sometimes a girl just wants to be comfy!" I retorted.

"That's my point. You seem to be more interested in not being comfy. Present outfit excluded. So who is he?" she asked.

"He who?"

"Whoever it is that's making comfy less of a priority."

"Nobody, Ronnie, really. I just felt like beefing up the wardrobe," I said.

"If that's the story you're sticking to...," she said, trailing off.

"It is. Give me those jeans so I can go try this thing on. Weren't you getting boots for me?" I asked with my most demanding tone.

She smiled.

"Peyta must have moved them. I'll have to go back and rummage around. Worst case scenario, I'll text her to find out where she's stuffed them. Damned teenagers. I really should fire her," she said with a wicked smile.

"Let me know how that goes for you. Seventeen-year-old daughters are notoriously unforgiving," I tossed at her as I walked over to the curtained changing area. I heard her laugh heartily as she disappeared into the back again, in search of the Frye riding boots.

As I changed into the handpicked outfit, The Dave Matthews Band's "Crash Into Me" came over the speakers in the shop. It was clearly a sign. I'd always had this theory that it couldn't be a bad day when that song came on the radio. I smiled to myself in the mirror as I pulled the blouse on and arranged it so it sat perfectly on my frame. A pair of cognac-colored boots were thrust into the dressing room just in time.

"Thanks," I told the disembodied arm.

"You're welcome. I forgot that Peyta wears the same size as you. I think she was hiding them for herself. You'll never believe where I found them," Ronnie replied, chuckling to herself.

As I unzipped the boots to put them on, the jingling bells signaled another customer entering. "Can I help you?" Ronnie asked, sounding a little sweeter than usual.

Hot guy for sure.

"Got any vintage rock shirts? Preferably something from the seventies?"

Oh. My. God.

"Sure. Over there in the corner. I have some in the back too. I'll go pull them for you," she said, sounding all too happy to oblige.

As soon as the coast was clear, I stuck my head out to see Sean standing where Ronnie had directed him, rifling through the tees.

"Do you work on your stalker qualities, or are you just stalker-tastic by nature?" I asked him while his back was facing me.

"Ruby," he said without turning around right away. When he finally did, the remnants of a smile were barely visible on his face. "Nice outfit," he said, giving me elevator-eyes.

"Evasion and flattery will get you nowhere. Do I need a restraining order or what?" I asked, trying desperately to stifle the grin that was tugging on my lips, threatening to expose my true sentiment.

"Maybe," was his only response.

"I found these four in the back. They look like they should fit you," Ronnie said as she shot through the strings of beads.

"It's not for me, but thanks. The size should be fine."

"Is it your boyfriend's birthday?" I asked mockingly.

"Don't worry, Ruby, he's just a friend. You know it's you I really want," he kidded. I turned eighty shades of red.

Ronnie cocked her head to the side as she watched us, clearly amused with something as the right corner of her mouth twitched and turned up. I rolled my eyes at her and bit the proverbial bullet.

"Ronnie, this is Sean. Sean, Ronnie."

They exchanged pleasantries before Ronnie focused her attention back on me.

"Just beefing up the wardrobe my ass," she said with the piercing eyes that only a mother could possess. I said nothing in response.

"I'll take this one," Sean said, breaking the brief silence which I had no intention of filling.

Ronnie turned to him and took the shirt before heading over to the counter to ring up the purchase.

I scoffed to myself and muttered something under my breath.

"What was that?" Sean asked.

I sighed heavily in an attempt to convey my displeasure with repeating myself.

"I said 'so much for that theory'."

"And what theory would that be?" he asked casually.

I sighed again.

"My theory that it can't ever be a bad day when Dave Matthews sings 'Crash Into Me' on the radio."

He smiled boyishly.

"You like that song?" he asked.

"It's one of my faves. Why?"

"You do know what it's about, don't you?" he asked, choking on a laugh.

"Apparently you do, so why don't you enlighten me?" I asked, getting frazzled by his persistence.

"It's about masturbation. He's a Peeping Tom, Ruby," he said just before he roared with laughter.

"You're disgusting. It is not...it's about *love.*"

The more I tried to defend my tune, the harder he laughed. Ronnie finally cleared her throat from behind the counter.

"It's forty-five dollars, please," she said to Sean.

He wiped the tears that were welling in his eyes from the strain of his outburst.

"Sorry," he said as he reached into his pocket and pulled out the necessary cash. "Here you go."

He took the bag that Ronnie extended to him before turning back to me.

"I guess your theory was wrong. You really do look like you're having a bad day."

"You're an ass" was all I could muster in response.

"Never claimed to be anything else," he said as he strode past me, flashing his impossibly green eyes down to mine. "You should buy it. Especially the boots. I have the perfect place for you to wear them," he said plainly. "I'll see you soon, Ruby."

I stared blankly at the door through which he'd just exited, completely speechless. I heard Ronnie come up beside me.

"I'd do more than beef up my wardrobe for that one," she said, her comment laced with innuendo.

"It's not like that, Ronnie," I defended.

"It should be, Ruby. It really, really should be," she said, staring me down. "Now go take that off so I can ring you up. You heard the man, he's got plans."

I begrudgingly dragged myself back to the dressing room. I emerged wearing my comfy clothes, bringing the others up to the counter.

"I don't really know him that well, Ronnie. I'm getting to know him, but sometimes we have the strangest interactions, and he pops up so randomly. The whole thing is just a bit weird."

"Nothing in this world is random, Ruby. Remember that," she said, grabbing my hand as she handed me my bag. "Nothing."

I had never seen her so serious, and was completely baffled as to what I missed that caused such a change in her demeanor. I smiled, trying to soften the mood.

"Thanks for the help. Guess I'll see you soon."

"I guess you will," she replied with the same curling of her mouth's corner.

"Tell Peyta I'm sorry about the boots. I'll give them a good home," I said as I pushed the door open.

"I'd rather tell her about what you did in them."

I pretended not to hear that one.

9

"So I was thinking," Sean said with a mouth half-full of some greasy concoction he purchased at Dunkin Donuts, or "The Dunk" as he liked to refer to it. "You said that you've never been into the city. I think we should go down this weekend and I can show you around...do whatever you want to do."

"I believe what I said was that I've never *seen* the city before. My parents took me once to Boston. So what exactly do you have in mind?" I asked with a tone of caution and incredulity. "I should warn you that my idea of a good time doesn't involve a trip to the Green Monster or Hooters."

I was quite certain that if a person could pierce your body with a stare and subsequently cause internal organs to combust, my pancreas would have been ablaze given the glowing eyes pinned on me.

"Ruby, are you implying that beer, boobs, and baseball are what I consider to be a good time?"

If the shoe fits...

"Is there a polite way to answer 'yes' to such a question?" I asked as I giggled nervously. I thought I was hilarious, but

Sean didn't seem to subscribe to that brand of humor, a lesson I'd learned over the previous few months.

Something else to work on.

He scowled at me, but chose not to continue the conversation in its current direction.

"I was thinking more along the lines of trolling around the city, going to the park, museums, galleries, dinner, dancing, whatever you want to do."

"So let me get this straight. You are going to drive me into the city, do whatever I want to do, go wherever I want to go, eat whatever I want to eat, and dance? I thought you didn't dance? And who, exactly, is going to pay for this excursion?" I asked in my attempt to clarify both itinerary and intent.

"I will drive you into the city to do whatever, go wherever, and eat whatever you want. I don't dance and this weekend will be no exception to the rule. And I thought it was customary for a man to pay for a lady?" he said as though this should have all been very obvious.

"So it's a date?" I asked. I didn't do dates. I had never had luck dating in the past and did not want to revive that part of my life just because I gained visual input. Being able to see made the whole situation even more confusing than it was before. There were fewer options to weigh then.

He started to chuckle. That chuckle slowly became laughter, which then escalated quickly into a deep rumbling hysteria. Apparently, I once again didn't see the comedic value in what he'd said. In fact, I became more incensed as his shenanigans continued, as if my observation about it being a date was so off-base. He couldn't have been trying to take me out?

Asshole.

"If you're quite done assaulting my self-esteem now, it

would be awesome if you'd just give me a definite verbal answer. Apparently, in your pristine upbringing, you weren't taught that laughing at someone could be construed as extremely rude, and, quite frankly, a dickhead move," I shot at him. I felt tears threatening to well up in my eyes. I was used to having the occasional insult thrown my way while growing up, but this was different. It was never by someone I liked.

He seemed to pick up on my distress, as if that took a massive IQ.

"No, Ruby. It is most certainly not a date," he said.

Good to know.

"I think you could have made that point clear without the theatrics. Next time it would be *really* super if you could refrain from undoing years of therapy in the process," I choked out, turning quickly away from him for fear that my eyes would betray me.

When I was certain I had myself composed, I turned back to see that his face went from amused, to serious, then to grim. His forehead actually furrowed and his eyebrows were in danger of swallowing up his eyes.

"I did not intend to hurt your feelings. It just struck me as funny. It's sort of an inside joke with my friends. You wouldn't get it. It's not really you that makes it funny," he said.

"Well, since I don't see your friends here, there isn't really an inside joke to be had," I stated. "Don't ever do that again."

With that, I turned and stormed out of the shop to the back room and slammed the door. I banged some things around like a five-year-old having a moderate tantrum until I felt better. I grabbed a necklace I'd been working on and started tinkering on it without real purpose. In my mindless futzing, I realized that I never actually agreed to go, so I pondered for a few moments whether or not I still wanted to. *That really was a dickhead thing to do to me.* However, after some thought, I decided to give him a second chance. We were making progress on the normalcy front, and I did need to learn not to let my sensitivity about my past get in the way of a potentially fun weekend in my immediate future.

I went back into the shop to tell him, but when I peeked around the door, I saw that he had already gone. I walked over to the register and saw that he'd left me a note pinned to the desk with one of my various pointy tools.

RUBY,

I'm very sorry that I caused you pain. Sometimes I forget that you haven't had an easy past, and that some of the things I say could be more hurtful to you than they would to someone else. It was never my intention.

I'm enjoying our friendship (?) very much and I do really want to share the day in Boston with you. If you do not wish to go, I'll understand completely. If you never wish to speak to me again...well, I won't really understand that, but I'll just have to go with it until you see the error in your judgment (and yes, I'm being a smartass. I know).

If you do decide you want to go, I'll be at your place at eight a.m. on Saturday morning. Be waiting for me outside.

If you're not there, then I'll know where things stand (for now).

Sean

WELL SHIT. Now I have to go.

I almost smiled while I stood there holding the letter. He

may have been capable of being an unmitigated ass at times, but his apology was both sincere and entertaining. I knew at that moment I'd be down there bright and early awaiting my pickup, though I'd make a point not to look too happy about it when he rolled up. I once heard Ronnie say that it was good to make men squirm a bit—that it gave you the upper hand. When Sean was involved, that wasn't an easy thing to manage.

I'd take all the help I could get.

10

He rolled up precisely on time, wearing the expression I knew he would; that Cheshire cat routine was getting old. I turned my pouty and wounded face up to a ten, and watched all that smug happiness drain from his face. *That's much better.* He pulled up right in front of me and jumped out of the driver's side as I was opening the passenger door. He made a disapproving face, and I hopped in, smiling at my apparently annoying feminism.

His BMW 6 series coupe was fully loaded and totally decked out with custom improvements. I was no stranger to the pros of luxury cars, having had a father who would rant incessantly about the wonders of German vehicles and bought nothing less than an Audi on principle alone, but Sean's ride was the shit. The leather was softer than a baby's bum and the interior was posh. The jet-black seats and dash contrasted beautifully with the exotic wood grain and occasional chrome detailing. It was nothing less than a work of art. The console was crazy, having only a flat screen and a knob; apparently buttons and gauges were for poor people. The magical knob controlled everything in the car, from the temperature and volume to the navigational system.

"This is an impressive ride...your Mercedes is too. Tell me, do you just appreciate fine German engineering, or are you trying to make up for personal shortcomings?" I kidded. As was becoming commonplace, my witty comment was met with silence and a glare that could combust internal organs. "I'll take your silence to mean it's the former."

It may have been a bit of a low jab, but I did secretly enjoy that I could get him going so easily. The results I could get were amazing when I knew which buttons to push.

"So, did you figure out where you wanted to go today?" he asked, as though no longer fazed by my earlier comment.

"I did. I think I'd like to go to the zoo. I've never seen wild animals anywhere other than TV and photos, and I think I'd enjoy them very much," I said, feeling a bit like an overexcited kindergartener on a field trip.

His lips pressed to a thin line

"The zoo it is."

Guess he's not an animal lover...

We took the trip at a reasonable pace, only exceeding the speed limit by five miles per hour. He never once put the radio or iPod on. The windows and panoramic sunroof stayed closed. He seemed withdrawn and especially contemplative. It made for a very exciting start to the trip.

"Can I ask a question?" I queried.

"Aside from the one you just asked, yes."

"So you have this sweet ride that's got a crazy sound system, wicked sunroof, and an engine that goes balls to the wall in like two seconds, and you choose to drive it like a ninety-year-old woman on her way to church on Sunday?"

Without a single word, he hammered the gas and

started driving like his ass end was on fire. We got up to 120 miles per hour easily, and he showed no signs of slowing. He wove through traffic like a stunt driver in a big-budget action movie. He then rolled all the windows down, sunroof included, and cranked the stereo so loud that I felt the bass reverberating through my chest. It took a minute or two to remember how to breathe again. When I finally did, I looked down at my fingers as they attempted to carve out a place in the armrests, amazed they weren't bleeding from their efforts. I turned to see what had gotten into Sean and was met with a mischievous grin.

"Is this more to your liking?" he asked, looking way too much at me and not nearly enough at the road.

"Yup. Super. Wanna keep your peepers on the road and potential victims ahead of you, please? And possibly ease off the gas a bit?"

With that, he began to slow the car to a much more amenable speed of eighty miles per hour. His point was well-made—no backseat driving in his car.

The atmosphere eventually lightened in the car and my chest, and we enjoyed some witty banter on our way to Boston. I was so excited to finally see the animals that I had been unable to for so many years. However, it seemed selfish to want them caged up just so they could be on display for me. My love/hate relationship was why I had put off going for so long, but I pushed my hang-ups to the back of my mind when we arrived and prepared for an excellent day of exploring and learning.

The day was perfect for being outside. It was seventy-five degrees with no humidity and only a few clouds. Being somewhat pigmentally challenged, I didn't enjoy the sun as much as others seemed to. I doubted very much that the blazing orb in the sky was a problem for my companion, Captain Mediterranean, and his light olive complexion.

Some people really do have all the luck.

When we walked through the main entrance area, I was instantly overwhelmed. The zoo was enormous, and I had no idea where I wanted to start. As if sensing my dilemma, Sean sighed and grabbed my hand, heading off to some exhibit on our left. Not sure exactly where we were headed, my anticipation built with every step. When we came upon the gorilla enclosure, I almost leapt out of my skin. They were my favorite. From the first moment I saw them on the National Geographic channel, I fell in love with them. There was something so strong and majestic about them, with an intelligence that was clearly visible; their eyes held wisdom in a way that was unbelievably human.

Because the enclosure was a large glass semicircle, there was room to go right up to it. I managed to find my own little spot away from all the other onlookers, to sit and marvel at what I was seeing. I focused on their behavior and dynamics, and could easily tell the hierarchy amongst them. The young ones played as their mothers watched, all the while being supervised by one massive silverback hiding along the back wall.

He must have sensed me observing him because he turned and looked directly at me. It was glorious. We shared a moment of eye contact that felt like an eternity, and then it happened. He ambled over towards the glass directly in front of me. We were so close that I could see every detail on his face. He slowly put his right hand up to the glass and looked at me—*really* looked at me. I returned the gesture by placing my left to the glass, directly over his. He then placed his other on the glass, and I again followed his lead. To my continued amazement, he placed his forehead against the glass and lightly grunted at me to do the same. I obliged. We stayed like that for at least one minute before he snorted loudly and ambled away. I felt oddly connected to him in a way that I couldn't make sense of.

As the day went on, I felt that same strange connection with the animals repeated over and over again.

11

"I'd planned on doing more with you today in the city, but I didn't expect you'd be so enthralled with the zoo," Sean said casually.

"Sorry," I replied sheepishly. I was embarrassed by how long I was able to stare at the polar bear exhibit without blinking.

We'd spent the entire day wandering the zoo, sometimes seeing the same animals over and over again. Sean indulged my every childlike request without complaint and never urged me to move along. I didn't pay much attention to him while we were there, but I did catch him looking at me in the reflection of the sea lion aquarium. He looked so amused, the way a parent looks at a child when they're having a new experience.

"No need to be. It was fun. Perhaps the circus next time?" he asked with a curl at the corner of his mouth.

"No thanks. Clowns are terrifying," I replied, shuddering at the thought.

The other corner of his mouth followed suit, and a full-on grin crossed his face.

"I'm sure I could keep you safe," he said dryly. I didn't doubt that for a second.

Wanting desperately to change the subject, I asked where we were going for dinner. He said nothing, but turned up the wattage of his smile and placed his hand on the small of my back, guiding me down the street. We were both silent as we walked; I soaked in the city lights, and he did whatever it was he did when he was quiet. It was surprisingly comfortable and easy.

I was gazing off at a tall building in the distance when he ushered me to my right, off of the main street. My pulse quickened a little in direct proportion to the increasing darkness of my surroundings. We were walking down what appeared to be a poorly lit alley, and to say it was ominous was an understatement.

Stacks of wooden palettes lined the brick walls, narrowing the passable space and offering cover for the types of people inclined to lurk around in the darkness. Broken bottles littered the ground, their shards crunching loudly underfoot as we made our way further down. When the dumpster just beyond us rattled, I shrieked, turning to dart back to the safety of the street. Before I could, Sean grabbed hold of me, pointing me to face a large red door with no signage or address.

"Are you ready to eat?" he asked calmly, with that damned smile on his face. Again.

"This is dinner?" I asked, looking dubiously at the crimson entrance.

"So judgmental, Ruby," he said with a joking hint of condescension, "It's the best food you'll ever eat."

With the small of my back captive again, I was firmly guided through the entrance as he held the door. *Ever the gentleman.*

"How on Earth did you know about his place? How does anybody know about this place for that matter? You'd think they'd hidden it on purpose."

He smiled down at me as we approached the host.

"Exclusivity is easily kept through camouflage, Ruby. Some places are better kept a secret."

The owner smiled as we entered and sat us back at the "usual table." I'm not sure exactly whom it was usual for, since I'd never been there and Sean lived in Portsmouth, supposedly busy teaching at the college. I blew off the comment to peruse the menu. What I loved most about mom-and-pop style restaurants was their remarkable ability to keep the food simple and familiar, but deliver it in a way that far surpassed your expectations. The red door place was no exception to that rule.

"You should really try the crab cakes...best in New England," he said bringing me out of my indecision.

"Um...sure. That sounds great, but," I stammered, trying to explain myself, "I...um...I've never had one before."

"How can you live on the east coast and have never had a crab cake? Did your parents keep you in a cage?" he asked jokingly, clearly trying to drive home his utter shock and confusion. I stared silently at my menu as his laughter slowly faded to nothing, matching my soundless state. He continued to say nothing, waiting for me to somehow explain why that comment had drawn such a reaction. When I finally had my emotions in check, I raised my head enough to see his mouth, but not meet his eyes.

"Cages come in all sorts of sizes, shapes, and styles," was all I could utter softly under my breath.

He seemed to pause, thinking of what best to ask next for clarification.

"And yours?" he asked gently.

"Mine was forged by my parents' insecurity, fear, and overprotection. We lived in a tiny, rural town not far from where my parents worked. I was homeschooled with a private tutor. I had few friends growing up and was never allowed to do the normal kid things. They worried about myriad things that could happen to me if I left the house: get hit by cars, wander off, be made fun of, break something, be mugged...or worse." I drifted off after that sentiment, trying to banish the memory of the woods that instantly flickered in my mind. "There were no playgrounds, birthday parties, sleepovers, movies, and never any boys. As I got older they became more desperate to control things. They became dietary fascists and very strict vegans. So, long story short, I've never had a crab cake. I don't remember what meat tastes like. I don't enjoy being vegan, but it's how I've eaten for so long that I just stuck with it. I feel like I'm honoring something that they valued, even though it's not really me, and not especially easy or enjoyable for that matter."

"Well," he said, "that explains why you're so thin; you haven't really eaten for years." He instantly started to laugh his hearty laugh, and I couldn't help but smile when I heard it. My mood instantly improved with his energy. "I'm not trying to push you off the wagon, but if you're into trying it, I think you'd love it."

I smiled in response to his reiterated suggestion. As I looked down again at the menu to see what the crab cake entailed, something about his energy changed. His hand reached across the table and grabbed mine with moderate intensity.

"You need to understand something. People are not meant to be locked up and hidden from society...especially not children."

His eyes were fierce and the energy that roiled off of him made it hard for me to breathe. He paused for a moment, shutting his eyes as if trying to expunge something from his mind. Taking a deep breath, he reopened them slowly. The intensity in his candlelit eyes was disturbing, and I swore it made them darken.

He spoke his next words slowly and succinctly.

"You will never be caged again."

Not knowing what to say, and horribly uncomfortable with our contact, I smiled sheepishly while trying delicately to pull my hand away. His grip instantly tightened, not to the point of discomfort, but to let me know that he wasn't letting me off the hook that easily.

"Look at me, Ruby," he said, giving a tiny squeeze.

I put my menu down and lifted my eyes up to meet his gaze. It burned through me like flame through paper.

"You will *never* be caged again."

"I know" was all I could say. The whole interaction was such a strange thing. I couldn't figure out why he was so concerned. He looked tortured as he told me this, as if he had an understanding of my life and was trying to somehow convey that message without actually saying it. Or he just felt sorry for me; I knew a lot about that. The thought of his sentiment being pity angered me.

"New subject. Now," I blurted before my anger could creep to a more dangerous level. I hated pity more than almost anything else in the world. I lived surrounded by it for years. I wasn't interested in any more.

"Okay," he said cautiously. "Care to tell me how you got into the jewelry business? It seems like an odd calling for you."

I laughed inwardly at his remark. He had no idea how odd it was.

"My parents pushed me in education when I was growing up, always wanting the best for me. They were adamant about me having a strong education and well-paying career. They constantly stressed that I couldn't rely on someone else to take care of me...that nobody would want to sign on for that responsibility," I said, fiddling with my silverware. "My parents were a study in contradictions. They did everything they could to make sure that I wasn't capable of being on my own, but then stressed me out about being able to be. At any rate, I went to school for biomedical research. I couldn't use the microscope, but I was a whiz at chemistry and spent the better part of my college years researching various formulations for medications to cure autoimmune diseases. After my parents died, I decided that it was more their calling for me, and that I never really enjoyed it. Having my sight allowed me to explore my more artistic side that my parents tried their best to stifle, saying that it could never get me anywhere in life, and that such things should not be indulged by those who couldn't afford to.

"I took time after their deaths to contemplate what I wanted to do...where I wanted to go. I knew I couldn't stay in the house I'd grown up in and sold it a month or so later. I needed change, but I didn't want to wander too far from home, so I somehow settled on Portsmouth to live. After weeks of walking around, deciding what part of town to buy in, I realized that I was always drawn to the shop windows of the handmade art, pottery, jewelry—anything artisan, really. I love the idea of recycling and re-purposing, and really love accessories; it seemed a good fit. I like to think I'm pretty good at it too...well, at the designing, at least. Running the business is a whole other story."

"I thought you said your parents let you dance as a kid?"

he asked, seemingly perplexed. "You just said they didn't let you indulge in such things."

"That was the only thing they ever conceded to. I begged for two years straight, then they finally hired me a private instructor and built me a studio in the basement, sans mirrors of course."

The waiter came and took our orders: two crab cake entrees and a bottle of Merlot. I knew we weren't on a date, but it started to take on a decidedly date-like tone. More likely than not, I was just over-analyzing.

"What were we just talking about?" I asked, not waiting for a response. "Oh yeah, dance. So I started with my instructor when I was eight and never stopped."

"Is it different now?" he asked quietly.

"Different? Why would it...oooooh. Hmm. Well, it's easier to do self-correction, that's for sure," I said laughingly, hoping to set him at ease. He looked as though he was treading on offensive ground.

"No, really. Please. Tell me how it's different...I just can't imagine."

He looked truly curious, so I thought about his question at length before answering.

"Well. There's the obvious answer to that question. It's easier to learn something new, and far faster to pick up on choreography, etc. I also now have a sense of whether or not I'm any good. I think, in some ways, it made it much more pure without sight because I wasn't influenced by what I saw around me or what I was told was good. I just did what felt right to me." I realized I'd been looking down at the table as I answered his question, and I shifted my gaze up to him. He looked absolutely riveted, as if what I was telling him was the most fascinating information ever. I was pretty certain that it wasn't, but that didn't seem to matter to him.

"Now...now it's totally different. At the risk of sounding vain, I love to watch myself in the mirror. I have a studio above my apartment and I use it all the time. Dance has always been an outlet for me for emotion of any kind. That hasn't changed. But the ability to see what you're feeling translated into movement that tells a story is so beautiful. It's such a gift, and it's way cheaper than therapy."

"I'd love to see it sometime," he said emphatically.

"I'm not much for performing. I prefer to dance for me. I guess that's changed too because I never knew if I was performing or not before."

"Shy?" he asked.

"Self-conscious."

"Reasons?"

"Not sure."

"Truth?"

I sighed.

"I don't like being the focus of others' attention. It makes me horribly uncomfortable."

"Like now?" he asked.

"Like now."

In our following silence, the wine was presented and poured. I feigned deep interest in the glass and swirled the wine around and around. He pretended not to realize what I was doing. The quiet remained as our dinner was served— and eaten. The check came and went without a sound. We rose to leave in perfect unison and walked out into a chilly Boston evening filled with the sounds of the city.

We contributed none.

Inwardly embarrassed that my shortness had once again ruined a perfectly normal and personable conversation, I moped alongside Sean. I was certain that he couldn't wait to get away from me, the ungrateful and ill-mannered ass who had not only ruined a perfect day in the city, but also hadn't thanked him for the dinner he'd just taken me to or for the stellar recommendation of crab cakes. They were amazing.

I opened my mouth to thank him for ending my vegan career with his enticement of crustaceans, but quickly snapped it shut. The only thing I seemed capable of at that moment was further digging a hole.

I wasn't interested in being six feet underground.

12

When Sean turned to enter the gorgeous apartment building downtown, I was thoroughly confused. I'd thought we were heading for the car to go home after a disastrous ending to a perfect day.

"Where are you going?" I blurted out.

"*We* are going inside to get changed. The day isn't over yet."

"It's ten p.m. Doesn't that inherently make the day over with?" I retorted.

He paused and looked at me sideways, then made an odd snorting sound before continuing on his mission. I chased after him like a child.

"No, seriously...where are we going? And what do I need to get changed for?" I asked with an ounce more decorum than my previous interrogation.

"Out," he said.

"Out?"

"Yes. Out. It'll be good for you to be social for once," he

said to me before muttering under his breath, "I'm not sure it'll be good for everyone else though."

"I heard that," I shouted.

"As was expected."

I crossed my arms over my stomach and stomped through the foyer of the building, which was massive and contemporary with an industrial edge. Everything was stainless and granite, with clean lines and angles everywhere. *Dwell* magazine would have been proud. Decoration was sparse, but there was a line of Dendrobium orchids occupying the shelf along the wall that led to the elevator. We got in and Sean reached over to press the "PH" button.

"Penthouse?" I asked incredulously. "That's an awfully impressive place to own on a teaching salary."

"It's a friend's place. He lets me borrow it on occasion if I'm in the city."

"What if he's around? How do you borrow it then?" I asked.

"He's never around, so it's never a problem," he replied.

I figured it must have been some rich friend's second or third home and just dropped the subject altogether. Sean didn't appear to want to elaborate much, and I'd done enough poking of bears with short sticks in my time to know when to stop. For the most part.

"Wait...you said I have to change. I don't have any clothes here," I stated, thinking this would get some information out of him involuntarily.

"Yes, you do. I took the liberty of having Ronnie pick some things out and ship them down here. They're waiting for you upstairs. She said you'd love them...shoes and all," he said with an air of satisfaction. He plainly enjoyed torturing me with his secrecy. *Sadist.*

"Fine. But I'm not going anywhere until you tell me where we're going."

With that, the elevator dinged, telling us we'd arrived at the penthouse. We took a brief walk down the hall, which looked remarkably like the foyer, to the black door marked 'PH'. Sean took a key out of his pocket and unlocked the door before throwing it open, exposing the most gorgeously decorated apartment I'd ever seen. He waited for me to soak it all in before entering and actually had to call me in like a dog to keep me from gawking at it from the hall all evening. I guessed that wasn't what he had planned.

He gestured me towards a bedroom that had a fabulous pair of shoes awaiting me inside of it. The outfit he'd had sent was laid out neatly on the bed. I could tell from afar that Ronnie had outdone herself this time. The skinny jeans were by Paige and the top was clearly a vintage piece. I didn't recognize it from the shop, so I assumed it was something that had just arrived when Sean put in his odd request. It didn't matter because it was a fabulous V-neck, no-sleeve, tunic-length tank top in a deliciously faded magenta. She'd accessorized for me, pairing it with a chunky, jet-black necklace, which also appeared to be vintage. The crowning glory of the outfit was naturally the shoes, or in this case, shooties: black, ankle-height, suede, and straight out of the eighties. I turned to Sean, grinning like a kid on Christmas, only to see that he was clearly amused by the whole situation. In that moment, I didn't care that he found me entertaining; my fashion buzz was *way* too strong.

I all but ran to the bed to further inspect my garb for the evening. When I heard the door close behind me, I turned to see that he'd left me alone to get dressed without a word. I walked over to lock it, then hurled myself at the clothes. I was in my new outfit in seconds; I loved it! It dawned on me that I'd overlooked a coat draped across a very expensive chair in the corner of the room. She really had planned for everything, and I was glad because I certainly wasn't throwing my Ibex zip-up over that ensemble.

I admired myself in the full-length mirror for awhile before heading out into the living room. I thought I'd changed quickly, but there, on an exquisitely modern and very expensive couch, sat Sean, looking every part the GQ cover model. His normally tousled, black-brown waves were managed back into a more structured style. Undoubtedly, he had used a product of some sort to accomplish it. He was wearing a tight black V-neck T-shirt and a pair of Diesel jeans. His shoes were clearly Michael Kors and were a plain black, Euro-style slip on. To complete his look, he had a smug, satisfied look on his face, as if he'd won the getting-dressed race that I was an unknowing participant in.

He motioned for me to come sit by him on the couch. In my most unobliging fashion, I sauntered over to the uber-expensive coffee table in front of him and planted my ass there instead. His grin spread wider.

"I see that everything fits," he said, with elevator eyes scanning my new clothes.

"Ronnie knows my size well. I give her a lot of business."

"Mhmm. Indeed she does and apparently you do," he said while rising slowly to his feet. His eyes never left me. "Ready for the last stop?"

"Where are we going exactly?" I asked hesitantly. I hated going somewhere unfamiliar, especially not knowing if my attire was appropriate.

"I thought I'd take you somewhere you could dance," he answered, pausing briefly. "I figured that if I chaperoned, you could only get into a minimal amount of trouble."

"That's funny. To me it seems that trouble always happens when you're around," I said, feeling mildly insulted by his condescension.

"That's because I'm always the one bailing you out of it. There are two sides to that coin, Ruby," he said, hovering over me as I sat defiantly on the table. I was proud of myself for not shrinking under the weight of his stature. Instead I slowly peeled myself off of the table and uncurled my five-foot-nine-inch frame to stand only inches from him—toe-to-toe so to speak.

He stared down at me with an angry curiosity. I wondered if he was used to people cowering away from him when he was like this. I'd never seen this side of him before, but it mattered not at all. I didn't back down.

His expression lightened after a minute or so of the unspoken duel we were having. I was right, he was wrong, and apparently he caught on to that. He laughed inwardly and asked if I was done with my pissing contest so that we could go. "Yes" was my only response.

It irritated me to no end that he always looked amused by my anger, frustration, impatience, etc. That occasion was no exception.

He turned towards the door and made his way to it with a cocky swagger that only he could pull off. It made me madder that it was impossible not to stare at his ass while he did it.

"The party isn't coming to us, Ruby," he called out over his shoulder as he swung the door open. "It would be such a shame to waste that outfit on this apartment all night."

I silently walked towards him, giving him no response at all other than the obvious. He was right; it would have been a terrible waste of such a great outfit.

It annoyed the shit out of me when he was right.

13

"**V**ain? That's it? That's the name of the club?" I asked with very dubious inflection. "Have you even been here before? How do you know it's any good? This looks way out of my comfort zone."

The line to get in wrapped around the corner and the inhabitants of it, at least the female ones, were on the near side of naked. I hadn't known skirts came in that length, if they could be called a *length* of anything. The undergarment policy appeared to be quite loose as well.

I turned to look at him with my "hell no" face, but was met with a huge shit-eating grin. *He's enjoying this!* He knew I was preparing to flee the scene.

"Everything is out of your comfort zone, Ruby. Learn to adapt," he said, walking towards the massive building.

"I think we should go somewhere else. It's pretty obvious that we'll never get in anyway. Look at the line. We'll be out here all night," I said, desperately trying to plead my case.

"I know for a fact that we'll get in right away," he said before doing something completely unnerving. He leaned in very close to me and whispered right in my ear. "There's no need to be concerned about your apparel. You look just fine. Amazing, actually."

What the...

"Why do you think I'm concerned with my clothes? How I look?" I asked defensively. I wasn't worried about what *I* was wearing, but rather the lack of clothing that *others* were wearing.

"You need to work on your poker face, Ruby. I can read your every thought," he said matter-of-factly as he proceeded towards the front entrance. He didn't even pause as he unclipped the velvety red rope and moved it aside. He looked back at me and scoffed at my hesitation, but then gently grabbed my arm and ushered me through without so much as a glance to anyone working the door. They all nodded at him as he passed, but didn't acknowledge me at all, unless I considered hostile stares acknowledgment—no doubt a statement of disapproval of my wardrobe choice for the evening. In my defense, I hadn't known that we were going to that type of establishment, but prior knowledge would not have led me to wear anything more appropriate in their eyes. I pinched my eyes shut for a moment and reminded myself that sexy wasn't about how much skin you flashed. Sexy was about flashing as little as possible to make someone want to see more. At least that's what my fashion magazines told me.

Guess the girls in line don't read Cosmo...

I was quickly pulled out of my ruminations when we entered the main club area. It was enormous. Enormous like basketball-arena enormous. I think my jaw actually hung open until Sean's voice snapped it closed.

"Welcome to the big city," he said. I didn't feel very welcome.

I felt assessing eyes looking me over—men to see if I'd

meet their sexual desires, and women to see if I was competition for those men. Some of the women actually looked at me in a confused manner, though it took me a while to figure out why. I guess it wasn't every day that you saw an amazingly hot guy bringing a pale, lanky girl to that kind of place.

Are they jealous? Can't be. They have to know that he's not with me.

At that moment he reached back and took my hand in his to draw me through the crowd. When their faces scowled, I realized that they wanted me dead and Sean however they could get him. I smiled, even if their aggression was misplaced. I was going to live their jealousy up as much as possible. Ruby 1, pretty girls 0.

We slowly made our way over to the bar. The crowd was thick with sweaty bodies gyrating in positions that I was pretty sure wouldn't have made their parents proud. I must have looked a little shell-shocked when we made it to our destination because Sean laughed and quickly got me a vodka cranberry to take the edge off of my anxiety. He spoke to the bartender as though they were old friends, though he later denied that they were. He wasn't drinking, either.

"Are you trying to get me drunk?" I asked nervously. Humor and sarcasm were going to be the order of the night to get me through my growing discomfort. Instead of laughing, he looked at me rather heatedly, his eyebrow cocked ever so slightly.

"Would you like me to?" he asked, leaning forward so that I could hear him better.

I took a tiny sip of my cocktail and placed it back on the bar. That made him laugh.

"Point made," he said, leaning his elbows behind him on the bar-top.

I kept my eyes off of the dance floor while we talked mindlessly about the decor, my drink, and the random people surrounding us. Eventually, I did get up the courage to ask how we got in with no difficulties at all, assuming that he would be vague and evasive with his answer. I was surprised when he said that he knew the owner. When I tried to pry a bit and find out more, he suddenly looked very distant. And not very happy.

"I think you have an admirer," he said, still looking out into the crowd of moving bodies. He actually growled for a split second after he choked the comment out.

"What are you talking about?" I asked, trying to figure out who he had in his line of sight. "And why do you look like you're going to kick somebody's ass?"

"I don't like how he's looking at you," he said, voice low and threatening. "He looks like he's starving and you're lunch."

"You don't even know that he's looking at me. This place is full...he could be looking at anyone in this direction!" I argued.

"No," he said convincingly. "It's you he wants."

I turned to see who my potential admirer was, hoping I wasn't going to have a rerun of the "Creeptastic" adventure. I scanned the vast crowd, unable to find who Sean was all in a twist about. I was about to turn and tell him how crazy he was when my eyes fell on an elevated section of the dance floor. There were about fifty people up there, but my eyes landed on *him* instantly. They were drawn to him, and I was unable to pry them off.

His honey brown eyes were undressing me from twenty yards away, and I liked it. I wanted to touch the face that so beautifully framed those eyes, along with a few other things. I felt myself start to walk in that direction when Sean grabbed my arm and whipped me around. My head felt funny instantly, but I assumed it was the lingering effects from the centrifugal forces I had just experienced.

He looked angry at me.

"Just what do you think you're doing?" he asked, his voice rumbling through me.

I cocked my head to the side in an unfamiliar gesture. "*I'm* going to dance."

"You have no idea what the guys here can be like. It's not safe for a girl like you," he said, looking somewhat genuinely concerned under all that rage.

A smile that I'd never smiled before crossed my lips. "I don't think you have any idea what kind of girl I am."

I watched his eyes flash something right as I pulled away from him and strutted through the crowd to the driving beat of the bass. The mass of club-goers parted before me as I crossed the floor. I felt pulled to him, as though my body moved through no volition of my own. He was no longer dancing, only standing, staring as I approached.

I couldn't get there fast enough. When I finally reached him, I stopped just inches away, our faces nearly pressed together. His caramel eyes were fierce and burning, and I loved them. He smelled rugged and fresh, like ocean and forest, and I had to work hard not to bury my face in his chest and breathe him in. I looked over his body to enjoy its magnificence. He was all man—strong, lean, tall, and he exuded sex and danger. I wanted whatever it was he was selling.

His style was understated: a simple white T-shirt that was practically painted onto him, dark jeans that were tight in all the right places, and bright white Pumas with a lime green arc on the side. The only standout piece was a silver necklace that hung close to his neck with a pendant of some intricate design, all curves and angles woven together. I was fascinated by it, but not enough for my eyes to linger there for too long. His face was the showstopper and his eyes were all for me. They looked beautiful surrounded by his "café con leche" skin. There was no hair on his face or head, leaving it completely smooth, and I had an uncontrollable urge to run my hands over both but managed to gain some composure as I saw my hands starting to drift towards him.

The music at the club managed to save me from myself. The next song came thumping through the speakers with an animalistic beat, and before I could think, the two of us moved as one on the floor. I was consumed by him, unaware that anyone else was there. I wanted to be alone with him.

Though our bodies were glued to one another, we managed some semblance of decorum. We weren't having sex with our clothes on like I'd seen so many others doing that night. It was far more intimate and intense than that; we were one. Music moved through us and played us like we were the same instrument.

His face was close, breathing my air. Every time I made eye contact with him, I lost myself in the most literal sense. I said things I'd never said before and did things I would never have done; I was a completely different person. I was so influenced by his energy, his power, as if it were seeping out of him and into me. I knew I could sense the feelings of others as well as I could my own, but this was entirely different and new. The feeling was heightened exponentially with eye contact, so I tried my best to avoid it. I did an amazingly poor job of it.

I heard a voice from behind me but didn't acknowledge it until a hand clamped down onto my arm and jerked me around in a not-so-friendly way. Sean's look was murderous. He was visually communicating his desire to creatively remove certain body parts from the guy he'd just peeled me off of, making sure the process was intolerable. There was something personal about his stare, like the two had been at a crossroads before.

"Do you two know each other?" I asked, not really expecting an honest answer. I needed to defuse the situation before the pissing contest got any more heated. The man laughed and said nothing. I abruptly turned to look at Sean, not sure how he would react to the man's expressed humor with the situation. He did nothing but stare him down.

"You never truly know anyone, Ruby," he said calmly. "But, no. I don't know *him.*"

Sean's emphasis on the word "him" seemed strange, but so was Sean sometimes. I shrugged as I audibly exhaled. *Boys can be so trying.*

I looked back at the man causing such a clear air of tension between them. I wanted to know who he was. However, as soon as I looked at him, I no longer cared; I just wanted to be with him regardless of the cost.

"I'm Eric," he said without being prompted.

"Ruby," I managed as I struggled against Sean's very strong grip to get closer to Eric.

"We're leaving," Sean stated as he whirled me around and marched me towards the door. My feet barely made contact with the floor, and I realized he'd picked me up around the waist to drag me out of the dance hall. Eric followed closely behind with a wickedly amused look plastered all over his face. The situation was more personal than either of them was letting on, and I was furious at being in the dark about something that so clearly involved me.

Sean stomped through the lobby, pushing through innocent club-goers with no regard. As we broke through the front door, Eric slipped a small piece of paper into my hand as Sean continued on towards the parking lot. He didn't see me take it, so I managed to quickly slip it into my shirt and down my bra even with the restricted range of motion I had in my arm. I doubted that Sean would strip-search me to find it even if he had seen what I did. Eric slipped out of sight into the bar while I continued to be hauled away like luggage to the car.

"I'm quite capable of walking, you know," I said with as much ferocity as I could muster.

"I've seen what you're capable of tonight," he scoffed.

"Why are you so angry with me?" I asked, trying desperately to figure out what offense of mine he'd suffered.

"It's nothing," he answered.

"Nothing? This is how you act about nothing? Remind me never to do *something* to you, then, because I shudder to think what your reaction would be to that," I said, trying to wiggle away from him.

He had no reply.

We made our way to the car, me tucked under his arm and Sean still pissed off. When we got to the BMW, he put me down right in front of him and bent down so close to me that I could see the tiny scar just above his left eyebrow.

"I'm angry because you don't know what the hell you're doing and you're going to get yourself hurt one of these days. You know nothing about that guy, and yet I barely managed to get you out of there while your clothes were still on," he said with an ever-increasing volume. "You looked like a bitch in heat out there. Do you have any idea what he's capable of?"

"No, I don't," I yelled, feeling insulted. "Apparently you do though, so why not be a peach and share some of your vast knowledge on the subject?" I asked angrily.

"All you need to know is that guys like that are trouble.

They care about only one thing in life and that's them," he said, his eyes flashing hatred. "They are always their own bottom line...everyone and everything else is assessed as to whether or not they can improve that." In the dim lighting the streetlamps provided, I could have sworn his beautiful green eyes were swallowed by a black so deep it appeared endless. "Any more questions?"

I hadn't noticed how tightly he was gripping my arms, and I tried to pull them out of his grasp before they were bruised.

"Why do you even care?" I asked, finally freeing myself.

I knew it had been a low blow when I said it, but I was so infuriated that it didn't seem to matter at the time. His expression softened slightly, but I felt his anger and anxiety coursing through me.

"If you have to ask that question, then you really aren't the person I thought you were," he said, opening the car door. I sighed, walking around to the passenger side to get in. We both sat in darkened silence for a few minutes; he hadn't even started the car. I felt the growing tension in the air and knew I wouldn't be able to take it for too much longer. I knew he was angry and clearly distraught at my behavior, but there was something else coming off of him, something that I couldn't place.

Is he...hurt?

He finally broke the silence.

"I'm sorry," he said as he turned to face me. "I have no right to judge your behavior or your choice in...men." The last word came off his tongue like it was bitter, offending his mouth.

I sooooo wasn't expecting that.

I wasn't sure what to say. The truth was that I didn't recognize my behavior that night any more than he did. I'd felt strange from the moment I laid eyes on Eric. That sensation seemed to only increase with my physical proximity to him. As soon as he went back into the club, it was like I slowly came down off a high and more into myself. With that came the embarrassment and shame of my uncharacteristically whorish behavior. I was even more ashamed that Sean had been there to witness it, and, to add insult to injury, had to save me from the whole debacle.

He owed me no apology.

"Don't be. I was being defensive earlier. I...I don't know what happened. I've never felt like that before, and I certainly haven't acted that way either. What's really weird is that the feeling seems to be fading. Do you think somebody slipped something into my drink?" I asked while I grasped for something to rationalize my behavior.

"Yes," he said, firmly. "I think that's exactly what happened. I'm going to take you home now, and I'm going to stay over to make sure there aren't any ill effects from whatever got into your system tonight." He fired up the engine and backed the car out onto the street. "No arguments, either."

I saw no point in challenging him and surrendered to his plan, falling asleep on the car ride home. Before I reached the point of dreaming, I awoke with a shooting pain in my head, courtesy of the wall it was banged against in my stairwell.

"OUCH!" I groused.

He grinned impishly.

"Sorry, I didn't gauge that corner very well," he said.

I closed my eyes and rubbed the growing knot on the top of my head. He gently put me down in front of the apartment door and unlocked it. I dragged myself across the threshold and headed down the hall, stopping at the linen closet to get extra blankets and a pillow for Sean's rendezvous with my sofa. I walked back into the living room and placed them on the coffee table before immediately heading back down the hallway to my room. There was no stop to use the bathroom or brush my teeth. My clothes remained where they were when I collapsed on my bed, too exhausted to stand any longer. I didn't care about anything but sleep.

I heard his footsteps coming down the hall to my room and knew without looking that he was paused in my doorway.

"I just came to say goodnight," he said softly. I managed to grunt in response as I lay across the bed on top of the covers. He moved closer, making his way into my room uninvited. My pulse started to quicken. My body went rigid.

"Shhhhhhhhhhh," he said, seeing the anxiety he was causing me. "I just wanted to make it better," he said, leaning over to place a whisper of a kiss on my head where he'd bumped it against the wall. "Sleep well, Ruby," he said softly as he walked out of my room, closing the door behind him.

14

I awoke the next morning feeling much more like myself. The effects of the drugs had worn off completely.

I did a quick scan of my body, making sure that all the appropriate bits were functional and accounted for. Sitting up cautiously, I paused when I reached a full upright position, unsure if there would be a bass drum playing in my temples from the previous night's shenanigans. Luckily for me, there wasn't, so I proceeded to get up and go see what I could wrangle up for breakfast.

I sauntered down the hallway, passing the bathroom and kitchen on the way to the living room to see if Sean was awake and ready for some food. When I arrived, I saw an empty couch with a neatly folded stack of blankets on top of it, but no Sean. There was, however, a note atop the pile.

RUBY,

I looked in this morning to see that you were okay. I had to leave to go grade some awfully written term papers—didn't want to wake you to say goodbye. Will stop by the shop later today to make sure you're doing well.

    Sean

No longer needing to cook for two, I opted for a banana and a water to go. I'd been neglecting the business part of my business for too long, so I had a hot and heavy date with QuickBooks to rectify that situation. I grabbed the stack of blankets and took them to the linen closet, neatly placing them on a shelf before continuing down the hall to my room. I needed to grab a jacket but couldn't find one in the mass chaos of my bedroom, so I settled for a black Nike hoodie that I found buried in the back of my closet. I also grabbed a bandana to pull my hair back with so it wouldn't drive me certifiably insane while working on the books.

As I turned to leave, a small piece of black paper lying innocently on my bed caught my attention. It was slightly hidden by a fold in the covers so I didn't recognize it immediately. I knelt down on the bed and reached across to retrieve it from my wadded-up comforter. The second I touched it, a rush of heat went through me and I knew exactly what it was. *Eric.* It was his card, which was really just his name and phone number—no business, profession, address, or last name.

I felt compelled to call him that second, and it took more restraint than I thought I possessed not to do it. *Don't want him to think I'm fatal attraction material.* I sighed and stuck it in my back pocket. Maybe out of sight, out of mind would prove true.

AFTER HOURS of filing through bank statements and invoices and reconciling the accounts, I came to two very distinct conclusions: that accountants were certifiably insane, and that I was the world's worst businesswoman. The biggest challenge for any self-employed craftsman was that being great at your skill did not equal business success. I needed to get my bookkeeping shit together before I failed, as that possibility was becoming all too real to me. I really needed help.

Torn between my desire to face the situation and run away from it altogether, I decided I would organize the back studio and put my frustration into that task for a bit. On my way around the counter, I reached my hands to the small of my back to force a low back stretch; computer time was proving terrible for my body. As I slid my hands down, they eventually landed in the back pockets of my jeans. My right hand flared like it was on fire when it touched the little piece of black paper I had tucked away so strategically. I pulled it out just as I crossed paths with my office phone. The compulsion to pick it up and call him was all-consuming and undeniable. I was clearly no match for it.

The receiver was ringing before I even realized I'd dialed him.

"Hello?"

15

When I hung up three hours later, I realized that I had no idea what had just happened. I knew we talked, flirted, and made plans for the night, but I would have sworn that the person talking just wasn't me. It was as though I'd been in some sort of weird fugue that I snapped out of as soon as the receiver clicked off, leaving me with the gist of what had been said and done, but no sense of ownership of the words or actions—a real out-of-body experience. I'd never sounded so self-assured and confident talking to a guy before, but, with Eric, everything seemed so natural, so effortless, so right. I didn't have to try, I just was, and it was a feeling I really started to like.

He had asked me to go to a party that his friend was hosting—nothing too formal, but not exactly a college kegger either. It was at a downtown apartment building in Boston, in the penthouse. Apparently his friend had recently acquired the place and wanted to christen it. Normally I was intimidated by events like that and would have found a way to weasel out of it, or suggest something else, but I didn't. Somehow knowing that I was going to be with him made everything okay.

We agreed to meet at *Vain* since I actually knew where that was. Boston wasn't known as an easy city to navigate when you weren't from there, and I didn't want to be late because I was driving aimlessly through downtown streets. That being said, I was a cautious woman, and I knew enough to pick a neutral place to meet. The world wasn't safe for a single girl, and I'd watched enough *Dateline NBC* to know that to be true. I may have picked up amazing vibes from Eric, but I didn't know him and I didn't want to end up dead in a gutter somewhere because I surrendered common sense because of the warm fuzzies he gave me.

Once all the details were ironed out, he let me go to get myself ready for the party. He seemed to sense that I was about to have a meltdown of epic proportions, though I was certain he was unaware that it was regarding my wardrobe decision. Regardless, his polite dismissal allotted enough time for that to occur. I couldn't for the life of me think of something fabulous to wear. I needed my fashion consultant, a.k.a. Ronnie, to hook me up, but her store was closed, so I was on my own.

I flew upstairs and tore into the apartment, barely remembering to close the door behind me. I continued straight into the bedroom, directly to my walk-in closet. I stared blankly up into the u-shaped racks that lined the walls, the two tiers of clothing spanning from floor to ceiling. Building that closet had been the best money I'd ever spent. I may have lost square footage in the guest bedroom, but I didn't care. My clothes needed a good home.

Surrounded by the all those garments, I knew that, logically speaking, there had to be something appropriate to wear, but I felt strangely at odds with everything I grabbed.

Even old favorites didn't do it for me, and they were my fail-safe, go-to ringers.

I tore through that closet like a wardrobe-challenged tornado, tearing every piece of clothing off of its hanger until every last article lay strewn across the floor. I stood amid the aftermath, ankle-deep in the sea of fabric I had created, wearing only black bikini underwear and a matching demi-bra. Wading through the mess to grab a pair of jeans, I caught a glimpse of myself in the antique mirror I had propped along the wall. For the briefest of moments I had the most bizarre and disturbing thought.

This could work...maybe with a slip over it?

I struggled to make sense of the thought, shaking my head while rummaging through my shelf of shoes. If I couldn't be inspired to build an outfit out of my clothing, I hoped that maybe I could with a great shoe choice. I wanted to make a great impression on all of Eric's friends and be comfortable at the same time, and that was a tall order for any shoe. It was hard to look sexy with bloody feet from rubbed-off blisters, walking like you just got off the horse you'd been riding for a week straight. I eyed the perfect pair to fit the bill.

I'd spent a small fortune on them after seeing them in a *W* magazine that Ronnie had lying around her shop a month or two earlier. They were impossible to resist, and, frankly, I didn't want to. Everything about them was perfect: royal purple satin stilettos with a faux platform and jeweled toe embellishment. Christian Louboutin really knew a thing or two about designing shoes.

I screeched in an all-too-girlie way when I found them and slipped them on to wade back through the mess I'd made. I was literally hoping to stumble across the perfect accompanying pieces when I saw myself in the mirror again.

He'll love it.

Immediately after thinking it, a flush of heat went through my body like nothing I'd ever experienced before, and, God help me, I reached for a coat as I walked out of the room.

What's wrong with me?

I was rapidly turning into a therapist's dream. My chart would have read: "patient suffers from delusions and distinct breaks with reality, along with a complete lack of social understanding and assimilation...and she's a ho."

Frustrated and horrified with myself, I looked back into the room and saw something sparkle from under the pile. I snatched it and held it up. *This will work.* I tossed on the pewter, sequined racer-back tank and slipped my bra off; bra straps should never be a visible part of an outfit. I found the appropriate pair of dark-wash super-skinny jeans to complement the looseness of the top. A few bangles and hoop earrings later, and I was ready to go. I grabbed my cropped leather jacket as I headed out the door and slipped it on as I ran down the stairs.

I locked up the building behind me and headed for my car. Once in, I made sure the iPod was cued up and ready to go with my best party music playlist, checked the gas, fired her up, and headed off to 95S. It promised to be a great night, pending my ability to keep my libido in check and my clothes on.

I pulled up outside *Vain* just shortly after 10pm. I called him when I was twenty minutes out of town so he could drive down to meet me there. He was perched in a very masculine way against the brick wall of the club, looking like a god. He had so many amazing features, but his skin blew me away. Such a contrast to my own, the milky brown looked like something I wanted to eat. Maybe I did.

He smiled at me when I pulled up next to him.

"Hey sugar, you lookin' for a date?" he asked as he approached the car.

I smiled in response. Nobody could out-quote me when it came to *Pretty Woman*.

We bantered through the lines of the pick-up scene for a minute or two until he leaned his butt against my passenger door, waiting for me to cave.

"Get in!" I demanded, laughing hysterically at the scenario. "I bet you're the only straight man that can quote *Pretty Woman* with that kind of accuracy. You are straight, right?" I asked jokingly, wiping the tears from my eyes.

He leaned across the console towards me, stopping only inches from my face. His face was serious and sexual. Thank God my seat belt was on, or I'd have jumped him right there in the car surrounded by club-goers.

"Do I throw you the gay vibe?"

I gulped.

"Nnnnnnno...uh, no. Not a bit. I was just kidding...I..."

He pressed an index finger gently across my lips.

"Do you always ramble when you're nervous?" he asked.

Apparently.

I chose not to respond and turned eight thousand shades of red instead. I was glad that he wasn't aware of the effect he had on me, and even more so that the car's interior was dark enough to hide it. I drove while he dictated directions, keeping my eyes firmly affixed to the road ahead of me. I didn't think "raging hormones" would be an adequate excuse for any accidents I caused, though I'm sure the employees at traffic court would have enjoyed the story.

Vain was only a few blocks away from the party destination, which thankfully didn't give us too much time alone in the confines of my car. I couldn't be trusted with him alone. I needed a buffer in the worst way.

"This is a pretty sweet car," he said, stroking the dash admiringly. "And I'm glad to see that you drive stick. Frankly, there's nothing more annoying than people with automatic sports cars...such a waste."

"Thanks. It was my dad's car. He bought it shortly before...," I started before pausing. "He bought it about a year ago. He loved it."

I could feel him looking at me. I didn't know what to say to break the awkwardness that I had so adeptly caused.

"Make a right up here," he directed. "You can park in that lot over there."

I did what he said, and we got out simultaneously in silence.

"Which building?" I asked, walking away from the car.

"So if he loved it so much, why did he let you have it?" he asked, ignoring my question. "An Audi TT is quite a present."

I stopped walking but didn't turn to look at him. I heard him coming up behind me.

"I inherited it. It's one of two things I kept, besides the money," I said solemnly.

"So what's the other?" he asked as he reached down and took my hand in his.

"My ring."

He lifted my hand slowly, inspecting the hand he had just acquired.

"This one?" he asked, looking at the platinum band.

"Yep, it's a family heirloom. It's the only thing I have from my childhood that really means anything to me."

"What about pictures of your parents? You didn't keep those?"

"No point," I said, staring off at nothing, "I never knew what they looked like in life. I didn't see a point in keeping photos to remember them."

"So both your parents are gone?" he asked.

"Yes," I whispered.

"What do you mean 'I never knew what they looked like in life'?"

"Look, it's a long story," I snipped, pulling my hand away from him. "I was born blind. I can see now. That's the short of it."

The silence between us felt heavy. He cautiously took my hand again and gave it a little tug, encouraging me towards the building. Again, I felt his stare on my face but couldn't bring myself to look at him. I was with a man who rattled my every cell, and I was ruining it by bringing up my family baggage and being a bitch about it to boot. I was disgusted with my behavior and wondered if I'd ever get past the social stupidity I was cursed with.

Not paying attention to what was going on around me, I hadn't realized he'd stopped just short of the front steps. I ran into him with all the elegance of a battering ram. He captured my face, cupping it on both sides, and kissed me like the world was coming to an end. I was pretty certain that if it had been, I wouldn't have cared—I just didn't want him to stop. My body temperature spiked so high that I was certain my proteins were denaturing as I stood in the street making out with Eric.

He pulled away abruptly, leaving me leaning towards his retreating lips.

"I just wanted to apologize for killing the mood," he said, smiling.

"Is there anything else you want to apologize for?" I asked, my voice husky, panting for breath.

"I'm sure I can come up with some affront to make up for by the end of the night," he said, guiding me up the stairs into the building.

"You'd better," I countered as I walked past him into the foyer. "You'd better."

16

I did my best to get a hold of myself on the elevator ride up to the penthouse. Eric seemed greatly amused by my obvious efforts, and did nothing to make it easier. He did not, however, kiss me again, and I was oddly thankful for that.

When we reached the door of the apartment, he stopped quickly and turned to face me. "I want you to stay near me tonight," he said, his face serious. It seemed like a strange request, but I was happy to oblige. Hell, I'd have been happy if he wanted to paint me onto him and wear me around like clothing for the evening.

"Okay," I said without questioning him.

"Good," he replied with a tight nod of his head.

He tightened his grip on my hand as we approached the apartment. He didn't bother to knock, just opened the door as if it were his own place. *I guess they're really good friends.*

I caught a glimpse of the place before entering and almost fell over. It was like nothing I'd ever been in before. It was the Taj Mahal of apartments, massive in every way. "Penthouse" implied a certain grandiosity, but I'd only been in one before, and Sean's friend's place didn't even come close. This one even beat the hell out of Richard Gere's in *Pretty Woman.*

The ceiling was vaulted, with an occasional ornate column anchoring it to the floor. Those columns were clearly original to the building and stood imposingly throughout. The wall of windows on the far side of the space was so extensive that it covered virtually from floor to ceiling. The lighting was original leaded-crystal chandeliers, giving the impression of a reception hall more than a home. The entire abode was exquisite, and I felt horribly under-dressed to be in such a palatial apartment. When I looked at the people surrounding me, it didn't help that feeling at all.

I was irritated that Eric hadn't accurately described the event, downplaying the formality of the 'housewarming party.' Perhaps if he'd used the word 'soiree' when he informed me of our plans for that night, I'd have been far better apprised and able to make the appropriate wardrobe selection. Not that I owned anything fancy enough to be appropriate.

All eyes were on us, and I felt like shrinking into the glossy parquet flooring. The only thing that could have made it more of a B-movie moment would have been the music coming to a screeching halt. I clenched my jaw and waited for that shoe to drop.

I looked at Eric, panicked by my fashion faux pas, and it was only then that I really noticed his attire. He wore a black custom-tailored suit with a crisp, white button-down shirt, sans tie. He looked like he had stepped off of an Armani runway. Maybe he had. He was surely mortified at my out-for-drinks attire, and more so to be seen with me.

He watched as I panned over his outfit, a grin plastered

to his face. He then returned the favor, his eyes sliding up and down every part of me. I watched in horror as he assessed my garb.

"Are those Louboutin's from fall or winter last year?" he asked.

"Fff...fall," I stammered.

"They're amazing. You look amazing in them. By far the best pair in the room," he said matter-of-factly. "Even better than mine."

"How did you know that?" I asked, revisiting the gay issue in my mind.

"I know *all* things expensive and exquisite, Ruby. It's important to me," he replied, eyeing me strangely.

Duly noted.

I hadn't noticed that the party had resumed while we were doing our reciprocating wardrobe checks, nor did I notice that we had been approached by a very handsome but intimidating-looking man.

"Am I to assume this is your mysterious lady, Eric?" the gentleman asked.

"Yes...so sorry, Marcus. This is Ruby."

"Indeed she is. Highly valuable and precious would describe someone of this beauty. Such a well-suited name," Marcus said, honey rolling off of his tongue.

I extended my hand to shake his. Instead he took mine and gently brought it to his lips, brushing it ever so slightly with them. He spoke with an accent that I couldn't quite place: European, but muddled somehow, making it hard to pinpoint.

"Thank you for attending our little get-together," said the distinguished-looking blond.

"Thank you for having me."

"You'll have to excuse everyone here. Their manners are

an atrocity. I've been trying to improve them, but you'd think they'd been raised by a pack of wolves."

He and Eric laughed heartily at the comment and I joined in, not wanting to be left out as usual. When the laughter broke, Marcus gingerly took my arm and wove it under his.

"Eric, I think a few drinks are in order. Ruby, what will you have?"

"Um...whatever you're having," I said to Eric.

"Excellent then. Three champagnes please, Eric," Marcus said, dismissing him with a wave of his hand. "While he does that, we'll have a chance to get acquainted."

I looked at Eric quickly, searching his face. He'd told me to stay near him.

"It's okay, Ruby, I'll be right back. Enjoy yourself," he said, kissing me lightly on the forehead before walking away. As I watched his head disappear into the crowd of strangers, Marcus redirected us towards the windows and slowly paced us off.

"Eric has told me how you two met, so now I'd like to hear something specifically about you, dear. Tell me, where is your family from?" Marcus asked.

"I grew up in New Hampshire; both of my parents taught at Dartmouth College."

"Oh, how excellent," he replied, "academics! I do appreciate people with learning." He leaned against one of the enormous windows, momentarily gazing outside. "Was it beautiful there? That's in the Green Mountains, no? Fall must have been exquisite."

"I...I wouldn't know," I fumbled. "I know it is where I am now though."

"I'm not sure I follow, dear. Did you never spend fall at home? Ah! You were at boarding school, no doubt."

I hesitated, trying to find the best way to explain my visual history. I was really hoping Eric would reappear and save me from the whole line of questioning entirely, but I had no such luck.

"No. No boarding school," I replied, playing nervously with the hem of my shirt. "It's a strange story really. The short of it is that I was born blind. I never saw the fall. I never saw anything." Marcus looked stunned and taken aback. "It's okay," I said, trying to save the conversation. "I gained my vision after a trauma. The doctors call me a miracle."

His expression changed to one of intrigue.

"Trauma, you say? How old were you?" he inquired.

"Twenty-eight."

"Interesting," he said, pushing off of the window. "What happened?"

He seemed oddly persistent in his inquiry and it was slightly off-putting—not conversational at all. It was more of a fact-finding mission and it made me uncomfortable.

Where in the hell is Eric?

"My family...we were attacked in the woods. My parents were killed. I don't like to talk about it," I responded, unable to keep some of my change in mood in check.

"I'm so sorry, dear. Of course you don't," he said, his face softening. "Have they been gone long?"

"Not even a year," I said with a hint of sadness.

The subject quickly changed to something more generic and lighthearted. I couldn't put my finger on it, but something about his apology just didn't seem sincere, and it was really bothering me. He professed it a couple of more times before Eric's return, but I couldn't shake the feeling that he was distracted, mentally piecing something together. His gaze was studious, and the energy he put off was no longer friendly, but frustrated. I did my best to hide my suspicion with my lack of poker face.

Eric returned shortly thereafter and the three of us chatted for a bit, but something was becoming more and more off in the room. I sensed a growing wave of hostility and aggressiveness, which seemed to correspond directly to my increasing discomfort. I slammed the rest of my drink down my throat and tried to excuse myself to go outside and get some air. Eric wasn't far behind me.

I wove my way through the mass of bodies as my need for escape increased exponentially. I was nearing the end of the crowd when a huge male stepped directly in front of me, causing me to bounce off of his chest and stumble backwards into Eric, who quickly shielded me behind him and stepped up to the wall of man.

"Do you have a problem, Duncan?"

The massive man laughed heartily before bending down to speak directly into Eric's face.

"How could you bring the dessert and not expect to share it?" he asked.

Is this guy high? What dessert?

The room was suddenly so silent you could have heard the proverbial pin drop. All the men at the party were encircling us, closing in. Testosterone flooded the air. They wanted, or expected, a fight, and had the energy to fuel one.

"Back off Duncan, she's mine," Eric said, sounding far more menacing than I'd expected.

"I'm within my rights and you know it," he replied calmly, inching closer to Eric.

"Ruby," Eric said calmly, "I want you to follow me to the door. Hold onto my waist and don't let go."

I said nothing but latched onto him like a vise.

"She's not leaving with you, Eric. She's going to stay and

play, aren't you, sugar?" Duncan asked, staring me down over Eric's head.

I felt his body coil, ready to swing if Duncan came any closer.

"ENOUGH!" Marcus yelled. "Let them leave, Duncan. Your manners are appalling and we shall discuss them later."

Duncan looked at Marcus in the back of the room in utter disbelief. Eric hustled towards the door, dragging me behind him without resistance from a single person there. He said nothing to me as he hauled me to the elevator. He continued his silence in the elevator and on the way to the car, despite my attempts to interrogate him.

When we reached the car, he opened the door and literally put me into the seat and turned it on for me.

"Do you know how to get back to your place from here?" he asked frantically.

"I...I think so."

"Go. Go now. Don't stop for anyone or anything."

"I don't understand what's hap—"

"JUST GO!" he screamed at me. "I'm so sorry, Ruby, but you need to go now. You must call me the instant you get home, do you understand me?"

"Yes, but I—"

"GO!" he yelled before quickly kissing me and slamming the door.

I pulled out and gunned it down the street, hoping desperately that I'd turned the right way. I drove like a maniac through the city, fleeing something I didn't comprehend. I tried not to think about it while in town, but as soon as I hit the openness of the highway, my head was reeling from the questions that were left unanswered.

I heard my phone vibrating in my purse and tried to dig it out in time to answer. There was a message left for me.

"Ruby, it's Eric. Look, I'm so sorry and I'll explain everything, but I need you to call me so that I know that you're alone and okay."

I was too flustered to call while driving, so I tossed the phone aside. I would call him when I got back. With my increasing distance from the party, anger started to build. I felt cast out and abandoned, left to drive home scared and alone. The night had come up *way* short of what I'd hoped for, and I couldn't wait to be home so I could sleep it off.

Eric had some major explaining to do, no matter what effect he had on me and my undergarments. No amount of infatuation was going to override that. At least that's what I kept telling myself.

I pulled up to my apartment, nearly slamming into the car in front of my spot. I collected my things from the car and hurried out, wanting to hit my bed ASAP. I unlocked the front door without looking at it, and pulled it open. As I went to lock it behind me, I noticed a note taped to the outside. I opened the door enough to reach around and take it down, closing and locking it behind me. As I climbed the steps, I opened and read it.

Ruby,

I stopped by to see you tonight. Just wanted to know what you were up to. Call me when you get in so I know you got home okay.
Sean

I WALKED into the apartment and threw my things down on

the floor as I made my way down the hall to my bedroom. I wasn't going to call either of them. I texted a generic message and sent it to them both: I was fine, I was home, and I would talk to them later.

My home phone rang instantly. I looked at it dubiously before unplugging it and every other one in the house. I turned my cell off before either had a chance to ring that one and slumped into bed. I'd had enough adventure for the evening.

I had no intention of starting any more.

17

I dreamt of the party, my mind deeply immersed in reliving the events of that night. Eric and I were dancing dangerously close together amid the crowd of people, and I could see Marcus on the far side of the room staring at us. I couldn't tell why. His gaze was neither angry nor malicious, but it was very firmly affixed on us.

I looked over Eric's shoulder as our bodies molded to one another, wanting to observe the crowd, but all their faces were turned away from me. I tried to move around to catch a glimpse of even a profile, but did not succeed.

Suddenly, there was a high-pitched screeching, buzzing sound going off in the penthouse. *An alarm*, I thought to myself. The chaos was immediate, and Eric worked hard to rush me through the crowd to the door. Again, I tried to look upon the faces of those I passed, but they were always blurred, as if our movements were too fast to allow me to focus on them.

I was forced out the entryway by Eric, who did not follow. The door was closing when I turned to face him, and in those fleeting seconds before it shut for good, I caught a glimpse of him.

And his face wasn't human.

I shot out of bed, realizing that the alarm I heard wasn't in my dream. My godforsaken doorbell/buzzer/most-annoying-sound-in-the-world was going off in high fashion. I sprang out of bed and stumbled down the hall. The microwave's neon-green clock cast an eerie glow on the hardwood as I passed by the kitchen. *4:17am...I swear to God if it's some asshole pot smoker with a fast watch I'm going to get absolutely medieval on someone...*

"WHAT?" I screamed into the intercom, hoping to scare the living daylights out of the unlucky recipient.

"Ruby? Are you okay in there?" the voice asked.

"There are stalker laws in New Hampshire, you know," I growled into the box on the wall. "I got *all* your messages, and I sent you one back. Now I'd like to go to sleep, so leave me alone!"

"I tried calling you after your text, but your machine didn't pick up and your cell went straight to voicemail. I wanted to make sure you were okay. Can I come up?" he asked.

"NO!"

"Are you sure you're all right? I just need to know you're in one piece," he pleaded.

No, everything is not okay. I had the night from hell, the dream from hell, and now the lack-of-sleep-experience from hell...

"Will it make you go away?" I asked.

"Of course."

"Then fine," I replied before opening the door. Instead of buzzing him in, I stormed out of the apartment, flipping the hall light on, and proceeded to descend halfway down the stairs. I then did a dramatic little spin, clearly displaying that both my front and back sides were all accounted for and unharmed. I was met with a most dissatisfied look coming through the windowed door.

"For the love of all that's holy...," I muttered under my breath.

I completed the trek down the stairs to the door, then unlocked and opened it just enough to stick my head through. That concession did not appear to be enough for him, so he forced the door open the rest of the way in and stepped into the foyer.

"Sean, seriously, what is your damage? This is truly unhealthy behavior! Stress is the number one cause of disease, and you are one step away from an ulcer, my friend..."

"Where were you tonight?" he asked, eyeing me intently. "Nice jammies by the way. A little flashy for bedtime, don't you think?"

I looked down and realized that I hadn't changed out of my party outfit. I supposed he had a point there. I scowled before responding, not exactly in the most friendly of moods to begin with. I wasn't much of a morning person, and it was very, very early in the morning.

"I went out, though I'd have thought that was child's play for your keen sense of deduction since I don't exactly parade around in this outfit often."

"Where?" he asked, folding his arms over his chest.

"Boston," I replied, mimicking him.

"With?"

"Someone."

"For what?"

"A party."

He cocked an eyebrow and pressed his lips tightly together.

"Whose party?"

"I doubt you know him. Contrary to popular belief, Sean, you don't know everybody."

His face hardened for a moment before he continued. He looked hurt and angry, but he was controlling it well, considering how badly I was baiting him. His breathing was slow and deliberate, as though he were trying to defuse his rising temper. He massaged his forehead, rubbing tiny circles on it with his thumb and index finger.

"Listen...," he began with a pause. "I know Eric. I know he's bad news. You need to stay away from him, Ruby."

Busted.

"So you admit it finally? You two *do* know each other."

"Yes," he said simply.

"That's it? Just 'yes'?" I prodded.

"Yes."

"Awfully tight-lipped for someone who expects me to spill the beans about my evening."

"Some things are just better left alone, Ruby," he said as he walked past me up the stairs.

"Ummmmmmmm, excuse me? I don't believe I asked if you wanted to come up."

"No," he said, hesitating slightly at the top stair. "No, I don't believe you did." He took the last step slowly before stalking into my home.

With a sigh, I climbed up the stairs and walked into the apartment to find him rummaging through the fridge for an early morning snack, his butt sticking out from behind the door. It was hard to stay angry at an ass like that.

"I'm going to bed," I said wearily.

"That's fine. I'm going to hang out."

"And eat all my food?" I added.

"That too, though I have to say your selection is really going downhill these days."

"Whatever. Back to dreaming for me."

"Were you when I came?" he asked, sounding far more interested than expected. "I wondered what was taking you so long."

"Did you expect me to just pop out of bed and come running?" I asked, closing the refrigerator door on him.

"No, not really. Nothing is ever that easy or convenient with you."

"Whatever," I scoffed, turning to leave. "I'm going back to bed."

"So what was this dream about?" he asked as he walked towards me with a box of leftover Chinese in one hand and chopsticks in the other.

Back to Interrogation 101...

"I don't know. It was sort of a strange version of my evening, but it left off...," I said, cutting myself off. How could I explain something that I couldn't even fully wrap my head around? "It ended weird."

"How so?" he prodded. "Define 'weird'."

"I don't know, Sean. It wasn't exactly crystal clear," I started, feeling my irritation with him growing. "I turned to see Eric, only it wasn't him. His face...it was...it was all wrong."

His chopsticks never faltered.

"Like it wasn't him?" he asked, shoveling lo mein into his mouth.

"No... no, it was him, but at the same time, it wasn't. He didn't look human. But whatever, it was just a dream," I told him dismissively. "It was a really long night and it didn't mean anything. Last night I rode a tricycle down Madison Avenue in a bikini. I doubt that has some greater meaning."

"You did, eh?" he asked, cocking his damned eyebrow again. I started to think that thing had a mind of its own.

"In my dream, you ass. In my dream," I said with exasperation.

"Oh. That's too bad. I would have liked to have seen that," he said, winking at me. He turned, heading back to the living room, and I watched him walk away, all strength and confidence wrapped up in one tall, dark package.

"You don't think it means something...do you?" I asked as he nestled onto the couch.

"Go to bed, Ruby," he replied without looking at me. "Get some sleep."

In a rare act of compliance, I went to my room and did just that.

18

My dream never returned. Instead, I woke up hours later to the smell of breakfast being made, accompanied by classical music. *If only all mornings started this way.*

I floated up from my bed and continued down the hall to find Sean in the kitchen making pancakes and fruit salad while boiling water for tea. He had clearly gone to the store, since I had none of the provisions required for such a meal.

"You're going to be such a good housewife one day," I sighed as he flipped the pancakes gracefully.

"At least one of us will," he replied, lifting only his eyes up from the griddle. It was enough to see the sparkle in them, and I knew instantly that his mouth was curling up at the left corner in an effort to stifle the laughter his little comeback had created.

"Were you up all night?" I asked casually.

"Yes."

"Why?"

"Why do you insist upon asking questions that you don't

really want the answers to?" he asked with the slightest hint of irritation.

"But I *do* want to know why," I countered.

"Fine. I was waiting to see if Eric would show up," he said.

Weird...

"Why? Why would he? That's really messed up, Sean," I replied with my own injection of irritation this time.

"No, it's not," he said as he cleared the griddle, preparing it for the next round.

"Seriously, you're starting to sound crazy. Paranoid even," I told him.

"Listen!" he shouted as he slammed the spatula down on the counter. I'd forgotten I even had one of those.

"I got a call from my buddy, who bounces at *Vain*. He mentioned that he'd seen you drive up to the club and pick Eric up. He also mentioned that, a couple of hours later, he saw you go flying by in your TT. Alone. He thought something might be up so he let me know," he explained.

"So you're spying on me?" I said accusingly.

"No, but Eric is a regular at the club, and the guys there know how he is. They also know how important you are, so they were checking in to be sure I knew what was up."

"So the note and your little inquisition were all for show? You knew where I'd been and *who* I'd been with the whole time?" I shouted, lunging towards him. "Why the theatrics? Is it too much to get some honesty from people these days?"

"You want to lecture me about honesty?" he growled down to me. "Get off your high horse, Ruby. Talk to your little boyfriend about honesty. I doubt he could even define it."

With that he grabbed a handful of pancakes and stalked towards the door.

"Enjoy your fucking breakfast," he said, slamming it behind him.

The whole situation seemed to escalate abnormally quickly, and I was left wondering what I'd missed. Reading between the lines required knowledge of what page you were on; I wasn't even in the right book.

I picked up a pancake, flopping it around back and forth over my hand for a moment before taking a big bite out of it. The boy could cook, that was for sure. What he couldn't do was be up front about things. He was always so secretive and mysterious. The way he always just popped in when I was stressed out or in a bind, saving the day. The way he always did things so easily while I struggled. The way he evaded questions, but demanded answers like he was used to complete compliance from others, and the way he clammed up at the mere mention of Eric's name.

I'd had it. I was going to get some answers for myself. Major answers.

I finished up everything that Sean had made, seeing no sense in letting good food go to waste. I thought it was odd that I hadn't heard anything from Eric yet that morning until it dawned on me that all my phones were still unplugged and turned off. I ran through the house plugging them back in. I grabbed my cell from my nightstand, flipped it open, and powered it up. There were thirty-two new voice-mails. I started to listen to them: one from Eric, one from Sean, another from Eric, again from Sean. It went back and forth for about the first eight messages, then it was only Eric. He sounded positively desperate. I instantly felt guilty for letting my anger get the better of me, causing him to have a sleepless night of worry. I was getting out of my messages to call him when a beep came through; he was on the other line.

"Hello," I said, looking at the mess of clothes that still covered my bedroom floor.

"RUBY!! Are you okay? Why the fuck haven't you called me?" he yelled. I had to hold the phone away from my ear to avoid the deafening sound. I was once again angered for a brief moment. *Why is he yelling at me?*

"I think you ought to take that down a notch if you expect me to stay on the line," I said sternly.

He started backpedaling immediately.

"I'm sorry, I'm sorry, you're right. I was just so worried."

"I texted you and told you I was fine. I don't see what the big deal is."

"Anybody could have sent that text using your phone, Ruby. I didn't know it was you," he said with deep concern in his voice.

"What is with you guys? Everybody is so freaking paranoid. What did you think happened? Someone jumped me going ninety miles per hour down the interstate? Not likely," I said.

He paused for a while, his deep breathing coming across the phone with increasing volume.

"You guys?" he inquired, trying to stifle the growing anger in his voice.

"Yes. You guys. Sean was just here and equally paranoid. He showed up at four a.m. to make sure I was okay," I told him. "Apparently he knew where I was last night because he has his buddies at the club keeping an eye on me. They saw me pick you up."

Again, the breathing was all that I heard through the phone. That was until I heard a muffled man-scream, followed by the crash of something very large, like furniture, being broken in the background.

"I'm coming over. I need to talk to you...explain some things. What time?" he asked.

It was already early afternoon. I had some things to do at work and apparently, according to Sean, I needed to get some groceries too.

"Five would work...but—"

"I'll see you then," he said quickly, and I thought he'd hung up the phone until his voice returned, much softer, somewhat pleading.

"Ruby?"

"Yes?"

"Do me a favor? Please?" he asked.

"I guess."

"Stay away from Sean," he said.

"But, Eric, he's my frie—"

"I know, I know. Just stay away from him at least until I can meet with you."

I sighed deeply aloud.

"Okay. I don't understand, but I'll do it," I said with the returning need to please him.

"I'll see you soon," he said, and hung up.

All my life I was virtually without companionship, especially the male kind, and now I was being torn between the two men in my life. I felt as though I would eventually have to make a choice between the man who saved me and the man who made me need to be saved from myself.

Always between a rock and a hard place...

19

I mindlessly ran errands and tied up some loose ends at the shop, but it was impossible to focus on anything other than seeing Eric again. There was a constant swirl of emotions running through me, and my frontal lobe was too busy sorting through the sensations to make room for much else. I knew that, when I saw him, I'd be hit with the wall of heat/attraction/belonging that I always was, but it seemed to be a little less pronounced with each encounter, and for that I counted my blessings. On the other hand, my hurt and anger was still very much alive, and the only way to abate that was answers, and lots of them. I hoped he was in the caring and sharing kind of mood when he arrived.

When I returned home, I set about doing a few more menial tasks to kill time before his arrival. He had texted to say he would be arriving in about fifteen minutes, and it was all I could do to keep from spontaneously combusting. It sent me into a frenzy, and I was positive my apartment had never been so clean.

Suddenly, the most-annoying-sound-in-the-world went off, and, like Pavlov's dog, I flew to the intercom to buzz him in. He had the good sense to look sheepish as he climbed the stairs to my apartment and pulled from behind his back the most glorious bouquet of flowers. There were bursts of magenta Dendrobium and Cymbidium orchids, citron and chartreuse lilies with pockets of mandarin-colored pod-like blossoms that I didn't recognize. They were exotic and expensive—the best. They by no means made up for his actions of the previous night, but he was working hard to make up for it, so I had to give him points for that.

"Ruby, I don't really know where to start," he said apologetically. His eyes were downcast, his posture submissive.

"I have an idea," I said calmly. "Why don't you let me ask what I want to know. We can start there." I hadn't wanted to sound irritated, but there was an undeniable tone to my words. I smiled brightly when his gaze met mine to try to cover up the anger seeping through.

"Fair enough," he replied, golden eyes affixed to mine. "Fire away."

I had thought about how I wanted to interrogate him all afternoon, but, when given the chance, I seemed scattered and unfocused on what the really important issues were.

"Good. We can start with Sean," I instructed. "You two have some serious bullshit going on between you and I can smell it for miles. I want to know why you two hate each other so much," I demanded.

"I think I'd rather start with the party, if that's okay with you?" he asked.

Ugggggggghhhhhhhh...

I was instantly annoyed by his question-dodging, when he'd clearly promised he'd let me direct the conversation. That was until he stepped so near me that I could feel the heat radiating off of his body. It was instant forgiveness.

"Fine," I said breathily. "Tell me what happened."

He paced the room, taking his time, seeming to choose his words carefully.

"My friends are a little *different*. It's an interesting group dynamic when we get together."

"That's the understatement of the year," I blurted like a Tourette's sufferer. "Sorry, please continue. Tell me about Marcus," I said, voice softening. "I get a strange read from him."

"Marcus is great. He's the reason I'm in Boston. I met him a while back and he made a business proposition that I couldn't walk away from. We've been really tight ever since," he said with admiration. He stopped wearing holes in my rug for a moment to look me in the eyes. "You didn't like him?" he asked, genuinely surprised. "He seemed absolutely taken with you. You were all he spoke about for the rest of the evening."

"He was nice and all, but something, well...it just seemed off."

"Maybe you just need to spend more time with him," he replied, moving closer to me.

"No offense, but I don't think I'll be up for that anytime soon," I choked out, literally coughing on the words. "What was up with that guy Duncan? He seems like a real *dream*."

"Like I said, some of the guys in the group are interesting, and when we're all together things can get a bit out of hand," he said, fidgeting with his shirt hem.

"Right, but what was *his* deal? Why was he trying to start a fight?" I approached him, trying to steal his attention away from the shirt edge he was fraying.

"He wanted you," he said as his face met mine. The seriousness of his gaze made me think that he wasn't referring to me being Duncan's first choice for dance partner.

"So he wanted me, so what? He was going to fight you

for dibs?" I asked incredulously. "Do people actually do things like that?" Eric said nothing in response, but the look on his face was plain enough for even me to read. I'd hit the nail on the head. "So he fights you...then what? He wins and carries me off into the sunset? The nearest bedroom? There are laws against shit like that, you know?" I said, my voice rising.

"Yes. I'm quite aware of human law," was his only response.

Human law?

"Well, we're not in Marty Stouffer's Wild America, so human law would be what I'm referring to. Is Duncan some kind of sociopath or something?" I asked, stepping closer still.

"No. He's got an alpha personality. They see things a little differently than you do. He doesn't see anything wrong with his behavior," he said, staring at me with empty eyes.

"Apparently your friends don't either, since they were all champing at the bit to see what was going to go down. Hell, they were encouraging it!" I yelled.

"This is what I'm trying to explain to you. The group...they're not like normal people when they get together. They aren't normal people."

"Well no offense to them, but I have no intention of going near those psychos again."

He made a sound in the back of his throat that sounded strangely like a low growl. His eyes glowed as if illuminated from the inside. Anger rolled off of him and crashed into me so hard that it physically knocked me over, and I stumbled back a step or two before regaining my composure.

"They are not *psychos*," he snarled, a tone I'd not heard from him before. "They are my brothers and sisters, and you will *not* insult them."

"Holy mood swing, Batman! I'm only trying to point out that they..."

"Do you know why you have your blackouts, Ruby?" he asked calmly, hijacking my rebuttal. "Did your precious Sean ever tell you that? No, no I don't think he did, did he?"

I didn't remember having told Eric about my blackouts, or how I'd been looking for answers to why they started. Sean knew I had them but had never offered up any suggestions as to why, despite having a PhD in neurophysiology. Furthermore, I failed to see the relevance of the topic at that moment.

"What are you talking about? What does this have to do with anything that happened last night?" I yelled, storming into the kitchen. I needed space. "You're seriously starting to freak me out, Eric," I cried as I slowly backed away from him towards the door. Seeing my fear, he eased his menacing nature.

"But you do have blackouts, don't you?" he pressed, following me into the tiny room.

"Yes, but—"

"And you only have blackouts after *really* stressful events, right?" he asked.

"Yes," I whispered.

"And on rare occasions, you wake up and don't know where you or your clothes are, right?"

"How did you know...," I trailed off, unable to speak, eyes widening.

"Sometimes there's blood on you, isn't there?"

I raised an extended index finger, indicating that only once was that true.

He had moved so near me that the pull to him was there again, but it was so buried by fear that it was hardly noticeable.

"You have no idea what you are, do you?" he asked, placing his hands on my shoulders and leaning his face against mine.

"You're one of us," he whispered, as if that would mean something to me.

I looked at him with desperation so plain that I saw it reflected back to me in his eyes. I had no idea what he was talking about, and my fear was building.

"You're a werewolf, Ruby."

I froze.

"A what?" I asked, thinking I hadn't heard him clearly. Surely he hadn't just said I was a werewolf.

"You're a lycanthrope. A werewolf."

I didn't know what to do. There was no proper course of action to take after being told, in all seriousness, that I was a mythical creature—an urban legend. It was more than I could bear. At first I tried to stifle the laugh that was building, but it boiled over. My body shook until I convulsed and broke out into full-on hysterics.

"Are you high?" I wheezed between gasps for air. "Am I being punked?" I tried to look at him, but his disapproving face was too much and only fueled my laughter. I walked back into the living room to try to pull myself together. "Nice way to ease the tension, Eric."

"This is not a joke, Ruby," he said, clearly finding nothing humorous about the situation. He followed me out, stopping in the middle of the hallway.

"*This is not a joke, Ruby*'," I mimicked. "You sure about that? 'Cause it's the funniest shit I've heard in years," I shouted, still laughing so hard I was afraid I might pee a little.

"You are!" he growled. "I can prove it!"

"Stop, stop," I cried as I rolled onto the floor, holding my stomach. "It hurts...my abs hurt. Please, please show me Wolfman Jack. This I have to see."

I was curled up in pain from the workout he was giving my abs, and it was almost physically impossible to stand up. I'd heard of laughing until it hurt, and I was getting a crash course in it. He started making a ruckus around me, but I couldn't bring myself to look, too afraid that he was only going to fuel my laughter further. Neither my abs nor my bladder could have survived much more.

This guy really wants to make up for last night...

When I heard ripping sounds and occasional pops, I started to wonder what he was doing, but when he cried out in pain, I finally snapped my attention back to him. I immediately wished I hadn't. What I saw was the best cure for the church giggles ever.

It was something that I couldn't really have been seeing. My mind was on the verge of splintering into little pieces as it tried to wrap itself around those images. A very large and very furry beast was before me, and his name was Eric. Apparently he wasn't as funny as I'd thought.

My near pant-peeing experience evolved into a near pant-shitting one instead.

The wolf's eyes were a yellowy gold, but the warmth of his original caramel color was still there. He stood proudly, intimidating me with his size and grandeur, making me wish I'd not been sprawled across the floor in hysterics prior to his change. His thick and luxurious fur was a rich brown, with the slightest hint of auburn at the tips, and his face had flashes of blond. He was absolutely beautiful.

Without thinking, my hand reached out to touch him, wanting to run my fingers through his coat repeatedly. When he moved suddenly to close the distance between us,

I snatched it back. He wasn't exactly petting zoo material, unless maybe you were Stephen King.

I scrambled backwards, pinning myself against the wall, my knees tucked tightly into my chest. As far as escape plans went, it sucked.

I not-so-subtly worked my hand up along the wall, desperate to reach the doorknob, as he prowled towards me, panting. Once my hand found it, I grabbed the handle and torqued it down, using it to lever my body off the floor all in one motion. I wedged myself through the partial opening, trying to slam the door behind me. As far as I knew, wolves didn't have opposable thumbs, so I was banking on the werewolf species not having them either. Then I heard it click shut, immediately followed by a cracking sound. I watched in amazement as the door shuddered under the stress of his blows. It would not hold for long.

Paralyzed by my fear, I stood and watched the door weaken under the constant assault. The wolf wanted out badly, and it appeared as though he would have his way come Hell or high water. I ran up the stairs towards the studio, hoping that if I could get there in time, I could lock myself in and then escape down the fire escape to the back alley. I was positive that he'd have to change form before trying to find me and by then I'd be long gone.

As I rounded the corner on the landing to take the final flight up, I heard the apartment door casing shatter below me. I scrambled faster to make it to my destination. With two steps to go, he was on me, but not in that Hollywood, figuratively-speaking sort of way. He was physically on top of me, having tackled me from behind, driving my lower half into the stairs while my upper body flopped onto the landing. I was just shy of the door I was so desperate to reach.

I wrestled under his weight, trying to wriggle free and

carry out my plan; my actions were the definition of futile. He pawed my shoulder, flipping me onto my back, all the while making sure that just enough of his body weight was on me to keep me from going anywhere. A massive head hung above me, breathing warm, damp air on my face. We were nose to muzzle.

I couldn't pick up on his energy. My empath gifts didn't seem to cross the border between species, leaving me with no way of knowing what he wanted. What he was going to do. My only hope was that he would end it quickly and painlessly. I squeezed my eyes shut and tucked my head, awaiting the killing blow.

It never came.

Instead, I received a slobbery salutation in the form of a full-face lick. It was both utterly revolting and unbelievably welcome. I squinted one eye open just enough to see the wolf hovering over me like a dog awaiting a command.

WTF?

I quickly came to the conclusion that I wasn't about to die, and it was most excellent news for me. He nudged at me with his huge nose, urging me up the stairs and into the studio. I saw no harm in doing what he asked. As he let his weight off of me, I crab-walked on hands and feet up the remaining steps to the door, pushing myself up through a squat position so that my weight was against the door and my hands free. I thought it smart to be ready to defend myself, just in case.

When he never made a move for me, I reached back and turned the knob. His eyes never left mine. I wasn't sure, but I thought he was assessing me. It wasn't how a predator watches prey, but more curious and intellectual than that.

I opened the door cautiously and stepped over the

threshold backwards, facing him. He followed me, step for step; if I paused, so did he. It was a dance of sorts.

He clearly sensed my unease with the situation, which made me wonder if wolves were just exceptionally astute, or if there was more going on in that particular wolf's mind. I wanted to test out my theory.

"I wonder if he'd follow me onto the fire escape? Most dogs hate open stairs," I whispered to myself as I turned my back on him to face the point of egress in question.

I hadn't even taken a step before I got my answer. A flash of fur blew through my periphery and landed directly in front of me, growling. Ruby 1, wolf-named-Eric 0.

So it was clear that he understood me, and had impeccable hearing. Maybe it was still possible to get some answers out of him.

"You understand me?" I asked.

His head bobbled awkwardly up and down in an act of acknowledgment.

"Can you talk?"

He shook his head as though he'd gotten water on it.

I pondered the situation for a moment. He could understand me and answer direct yes/no questions, but details were going to be out of the question. The scenario wasn't what I'd had in mind, but the evening as a whole was off-track, so I had to roll with it.

I found myself unsure of where to start. My original curiosity about his relationship with Sean took a back seat to the recent revelation that both Eric and I were werewolves. I needed to know more. Much more, including how he knew what I was, what it meant, and if he knew anything about how to control my blackouts.

"So...I'm a werewolf?"

It wasn't the most inventive start to the conversation, but

I had to begin somewhere, and the obvious seemed as good a place as any. He cocked his head to the side and stared at me with blank eyes. Taking the hint, I moved on to the next question.

"Does it hurt?" I asked sheepishly, wondering if that was some werewolf taboo that I shouldn't be bringing up. He inhaled deeply, then hung his head in submission and bobbed it up and down slightly, all the while letting out the faintest of whines.

I instinctively reached for him. I didn't like that his Change caused him pain. Without thinking, I lowered myself to the floor in front of him, leaving me face to muzzle. I ran my hands through the thick, wiry coat on his neck.

"Shhhhhh," I whispered. "It's okay."

He nuzzled his nose in the crook of my neck, breathing heavily and warmly on me. Something in my blood ran so hot, so fast, that I thought I would burst into flames. I sprang backward away from him, not knowing what was going on or why he had such a strange effect on me, even while in canine form. I was already frustrated with the bullshit of asking yes and no questions, and I wanted real answers.

Like a good boy, he didn't pursue my retreat.

"Do you control your Change?" I asked, still sitting on the hardwood floor.

He wagged his head *yes* at me.

"Is it dependent on the moon?"

He made a horrible coughing/snorting sound while shaking his head. I thought at first that he was choking on something, then realized while looking into his eyes that he was actually laughing at me.

"I'll take that as a 'no'," I said, sneering at him. I didn't like being laughed at by a wolf, or anyone else for that matter. It wasn't really a dumb question, anyway.

"I want you to change back now," I commanded.

His ears perked to attention and his head stood straight above his vast shoulders; he did nothing else in response.

"NOW!" I screamed, hoping my anger would motivate him.

He stomped back and forth with his front feet and snorted.

With an eerily calm and controlled voice, I played the only card I had left.

"Then I guess I'll have to get Sean over here," I purred. "Maybe *he* can answer some questions for me."

I started to get up and make my way to the door, but my progress was halted by a paralyzing growling sound. It stopped me dead in my tracks. Eric circled around to the front of me in a hunting prowl. He was facing me squarely, with his head sunk down just slightly below his shoulders. His eyes were permafixed on mine. When I tried to take another step, he snarled and snapped at me.

"I gave you a choice. What will it be?" I asked, knowing that he could probably smell my fear and see right through my bravado. Much to my amazement, the growling stopped, but his posture remained. He slowly inhaled, blowing it out in one sharp gust before he backed up a few paces, giving himself room, but never taking his eyes off of me.

His fur rose all over his body, and, slowly, you could see the tiny tremors coursing through his body. They started small and subtle, like the faraway hum of a locomotive. Then they grew and grew, until the wood floors creaked and vibrated beneath him and the mirrors that covered the walls of the studio shook. The violence of his seizure-like movements frightened me. Things began falling from the walls and shelves, and plaster rained down on me from the ceiling above.

We never took our eyes off of each other.

Just when it looked as though his body was going to tear itself apart, he snapped his head back and howled a cry that raised every hair on my body. The sudden release of energy into the room was electric. I, too, threw my head back, inhaling the power.

When I slowly brought my attention back down to Eric, he lay silently on his side, naked and motionless. His body was dimly illuminated, as most of the lights had blown out during his Change. The deeply defined muscles of his back were marked with shadowy lines, accentuating them, and his skin looked richer in the darkness.

There was no blood, no fur, and no sound.

I made my way to him slowly, as if afraid to wake him. I was worried that I had pushed him too far, and that maybe forcing him to Change so suddenly had harmed him, even killed him.

Closing the distance quickly after that thought, I threw myself onto my knees behind him. With trembling hands, I reached for his shoulder. The second our skin touched, he inhaled the breath of a drowning man, launching himself onto his back while propping up on his elbows behind him.

His very human eyes locked on me, and I came undone.

Without thinking, I pounced on him, kissing with a passion that was driven by an inner being I'd never known existed. My enthusiasm was equally matched by his. Before I knew it, I was on my back with a very naked Eric atop me, trying very hard to apply his 'clothing optional' policy to me as well.

That seemed to clear my head.

"Off...OFF!" I yelled as I wriggled to get out from under

him. Somehow, the wriggling didn't seem to improve the situation.

He looked down at me with a predatory grin.

"But *on* seems to be a much better fit, don't you think?" he asked, kissing his way down my neck.

"GET. OFF. OF. ME. NOW!" I said, giving him a shove. It was like trying to move stone. His grin faded momentarily as he pushed himself into a plank position above me.

"Whatever you need...," he said, voice trailing off at the end.

I flipped around like a fish out of water for a few seconds, trying to regain control of my body and get it away from his quickly. My eyes squinted so as not to take in the view I was being given.

Space. I need space...now!

I breathed frantically as I put some distance between us, and managed to slowly wind myself down while Eric lounged around casually on the floor, posed like an ancient Roman sculpture. Modesty seemed not to be of concern.

I turned my body away from him with as much subtlety as I could and pretended to take great concern in the damage caused by his transformation. Eye contact was out of the question for the remainder of our time together.

"Are you feeling better now?" I whispered.

"No, actually. I'm feeling a little *stiff*...as it were," he replied. I didn't need a reminder of that. I chose to ignore his little innuendo and got down to business.

"You promised me answers, Eric," I said somberly. "I need them. Please, tell me who I am. What I am."

I risked a glance in his general direction for effect, being very careful where exactly my vision landed.

He sighed.

"It's like I told you, Ruby. You're a werewolf. A very special werewolf to be exact," he said plainly, voice soft.

"I don't understand...what...why...how did I not know? How did my parents not know? This stuff is make-believe, urban legend, folklore," I protested, my voice starting to waver. "They don't exist."

"*Things* like this are you, my dear. You're going to have to find a way to accept that. We all did."

"But how does it happen? And why me?" I asked, pleading for answers that would make the news easier to swallow.

"Yours was genetic. You were always meant to be this way, but that isn't the case for us all," he said, sounding thoughtful.

"If I've always been this way, how did I not know it?" I asked, turning to see him out of my periphery.

"Genetic weres don't express the gene automatically. There has to be an environmental stimulus, a key to unlock that genetic coding. Trauma seems to be the common link." He paused for a moment before continuing. "Whatever happened to you the night your parents died was more than your mind could handle. The stress forced the expression of the gene. I'm amazed it never happened sooner," he said, pushing himself up into a seated position. He carefully pulled his legs to his chest to tactfully cover what I was so desperate to both avoid and attack. I needed to get my libido in check.

"But why the blackouts? Are you saying that every time I've blacked out since then, it's had to do with...with...all of this?" I said, flipping my hand through the air in an attempt to express my point.

"It seems to be the case, though it's bizarre. That's why I asked Marcus about it. I'd never heard of anything like it before you," he said, sounding truly perplexed by my uncharacteristic behavior.

"And?" I prodded.

"He explained that you were an altogether different creature. Though you are a werewolf, you're an anomaly of the species. 'Special,' I believe he said. Something rare and powerful." He slowly moved toward me. I heard the soft brushing of his skin on the hardwood as I studiously avoided looking directly at him.

"He thinks the blackouts are coincidental, some function of your visual adaptation, but he isn't certain. They could be something else entirely."

"Why would he know so much about me? He doesn't actually *know* me at all," I asked, getting that strange feeling about Marcus at the mere thought of him.

Eric was so close to me that I could feel his breath on the side of my neck as he spoke. I stared at the floor, trying to absorb the information he gave so freely without being distracted.

"Marcus is very old," he said, winding a loose strand of my hair around his finger repeatedly. "He knows about and has seen things that the rest of us have never been exposed to. He said he recognized you at the party, that you reminded him of someone very close to him."

"That seems to be a pretty weak determinant of who and what I am," I countered. "People look like other people all the time. It doesn't mean anything," I rebuffed.

I could instantly feel his frustration, as well as his loyalty to Marcus, crash over me. Marcus was clearly not to be questioned.

"He knows because he's Marcus," he said, his voice low and threatening at first. "If you're hell-bent on further proof, look to your ring. He said it was given to your relative centuries ago. You said it was an heirloom, did you not? Given to you by your parents? One of the few things you valued enough to keep? Tell me that wasn't because you feel connected to it somehow."

He was right. All of it. I rarely, if ever, took it off because it felt wrong to be without it. It was safe and familiar, and my only link to my family.

"So what does this mean?" I whispered to the floor.

"It means that Marcus is right. That you are Rouge et Blanc," he said as he lightly ran his hand down my back in a comforting gesture. My skin flared under his touch, my pulse quickened.

"What is that?" I asked, aware that the literal translation meant red and white, but it still gave me no insight into the implications of that title.

"It's a werewolf of great power, importance, and strength. Marcus believes that you are the only one in existence."

"Okay, so I'm like the Wonder Woman of the werewolf world?" I joked, trying desperately to lighten the gravity of the conversation.

He laughed. Once.

"To be honest, I don't know much about the RB other than your power is virtually unmatched. That your kind was hunted early on to try to exterminate your power from the face of the earth, and that, in wolf form, there is nothing more beautiful..."

"Exterminated? By what? What could take us out if we're so unbelievably powerful?"

I fully abandoned my no-look policy and met his stare, which was only inches from my face. His eyes went blank for a moment before a fire took up residence behind them, a burning shade of amber full of rage and hate.

"Sean," was his only reply.

"Huh?" I grunted, whipping my head around in the room, expecting to see Sean standing there. "What about him? Why are you changing the subject?"

"You asked me a question, Ruby. That's your answer," he replied with a seriousness that instantly stripped my confusion away.

I paled, feeling the blood drain out from my face, as if removing the blood supply to my head would keep me from processing that insurmountable information. I felt my mouth moving, but was certain that no sound escaped.

Eric slowly pulled me to him, pressing my body to his. He spoke softly into my ear.

"He's a murderer, Ruby. I've known him a long, long time. He's capable of unspeakable things, and that's why I left him and the brothers. You were right to think that there was history between us, and if I had known what you were, I would never have left you in such a dangerous spot. I'm so sorry, Ruby," he whispered as he rocked me gently.

I was numb. The blows kept coming and I eventually stopped dodging. All I had left to be answered were "why's".

"Why would he hurt me? Sean's my friend...," I said, my voice sounding hollow and empty. Completely unconvincing, even to myself.

"He would hurt you because it's his job, his calling...his purpose. He's a mercenary—an assassin for the brotherhood. Killing you is what he was born to do."

Ask a stupid question...

20

"Explain," I demanded, folding my arms in front of my chest. He hesitated slightly, as if he was uncertain if he should say anything more. I couldn't fathom why it mattered; the damage was already done.

"The purpose of the brotherhood is to regulate the werewolf population, and to keep a distinct divide between the supernatural and human worlds," he said before pausing. "But Sean's role in that took on a more specific task...to kill RBs. All of them."

The emptiness I felt was endless. I was such a fool. Sean had not only been lying to me, stringing me along, but also waiting for the perfect opportunity to carry out whatever plan he'd concocted. I then learned how sharp the sting of betrayal could be. To know that he would eventually kill me was painful enough, but the real torture was that he'd played me, building up a phony friendship to heighten the climax of my death.

My face betrayed my every emotion, judging by Eric's response. He looked as though he pitied me, but there was an undertone of what appeared to be satisfaction. Satisfaction in knowing that, in some small way, he was going to stick it to Sean. It was petty, but understandable. I could have, however, done without the pity. I abhorred pity. I didn't need it.

"So he knows what I am?" I asked, trying to regain my composure.

"Yes," he whispered. "It would appear that way."

"So why wait? Why not kill me already?"

"I'm not sure. Marcus and I both are wondering about that," he replied, running his hand through his hair. "That he's choosing to do nothing is what concerns me most. He's sadistic, Ruby. Whatever he's up to...it isn't good." He looked deeply thoughtful, staring away from me for the first time that evening. He really was concerned, which only amplified my own need to panic. He had said Sean was capable of anything. I didn't want to be on the receiving end of whatever "anything" implied.

I waited silently while Eric sorted some things out in his mind. He snapped his attention back to me, and upon seeing the distress on my face, softened his expression to a tight smile.

"I will do whatever I must to keep you safe. He will *not* hurt you. Not while I'm alive," he vowed. That part of me inside that I didn't fully understand rumbled at his words. I felt at peace knowing that he meant everything he said.

He would die for me.

I had to literally shake my head to regain my train of thought before I rubbed my palm lightly down the side of his face to show my belief in him. My fingertips lightly touched his lips and he kissed them softly.

"I trust you," I whispered, "but I need you to tell me how you know so much about this. If everything I've known to be true about Sean is a lie, I want to really know what you know."

He leaned in carefully and kissed my mouth, only once, before sitting back. His expression was pained, and I realized that whatever had happened between them had left him with an outcome that he didn't enjoy.

"Sean and I were friends, a long, long time ago. He was my mentor, my trainer, my big brother. My mother died when I was young. I never knew my father. When the brotherhood found me and realized who I was and that I belonged with them, Sean took me under his wing and never left my side."

I was pretty sure my jaw was sagging down somewhere around my navel. I thought the story was going to illustrate how awful Sean was and why he was a killer, but it started off like a Lifetime movie. That was the Sean I knew.

"At first I didn't understand who and what he was. I'd heard rumors, locker-room type talk of kills he'd made and things he'd done, but never confronted him about it. I'd assumed it just wasn't true. He was our leader...I *couldn't* believe it. Over the years, though, I witnessed more and more of his true nature. I realized that he not only enjoyed killing, he reveled in it. It drove him. He needed it like air to breathe."

I sat still and silent, filled with an unbridled anticipation and expectant horror. It was like knowing an accident was about to occur in front of me and being completely unable or unwilling to look away from it.

"The very last kill I saw unraveled my whole world. I went to the Elders, the ones who govern the brotherhood, to share my concerns about his behavior.

Someone needed to let them know that he was going too far, that he needed to be controlled. To my face, they agreed.

Later on, they must have told him what I'd done. For this, he punished me."

"Punished? Punished how? You were trying to protect everyone!" I protested, jumping to my feet.

"We were out patrolling a pack that was allegedly attacking the locals and creating a spectacle of themselves. A fight ensued, and I was left alone, surrounded by a dozen or more weres. Some of them were very old and very skilled. I was bitten and thus infected during the fight. When it was over, I looked up to see Sean watching from afar, smiling. He'd *allowed* it to happen. He intentionally didn't come to my aid."

"But why wouldn't he? I don't understand," I asked, trying to see where the punishment was in Sean's actions.

"Weres cannot be in the brotherhood, Ruby. Being infected had unofficially excommunicated me from the group. They wouldn't even have waited for the Change to occur," he said with a bitter tone. "Sean set me up. I was betrayed by my own family."

His last comment stung. My ability to both feel his pain and sympathize with it all at once was far too much for me. I ran across the room to find stability against the window frame. My head hung low as I tried to breathe slow and sure breaths. I didn't want to believe what he told me. Any of it. The Sean I knew, or believed I knew, was nothing like the man Eric described. Was it really all a lie?

"What happened then?" I asked.

"Shortly after my abandonment, I met Marcus. He led me to where I am now. He's my family now," he said, rising to join me. "So is his pack."

No wonder he'd been so upset when I commented about the party. I'd insulted the only people that really ever cared about him. My sensitivity skills were mind-blowing.

"And Sean?" I prompted.

His face darkened from across the room, and I would've sworn the temperature dropped about ten degrees.

"He got exactly what he wanted," he said coolly.

We stared at each other for what seemed like forever. Eric understood pain. It was a trait I appreciated immensely in him.

A blaring sound from the apartment downstairs broke our silence. Cell phone. Eric stirred on the other side of the room, recognizing the ring. He quickly walked towards the door.

"It's Marcus," he said, running for the stairs. "It's his ringtone. I have to take this, Ruby. I'll be right back."

I watched his form disappear from the room, but a heaviness remained. I stood frozen—a statue, a breathing, empty shell of who I used to be, or thought I was at least.

I heard Eric's voice echo through the stairwell, but didn't even try to discern what he was saying. It didn't matter. So little did. My life was filled with lies, deceit, and treachery, and not by my doing.

Eric suddenly appeared before me, speaking, though I didn't seem to hear what he was saying at all.

"Did you get that?" he asked, grabbing my shoulders. "I have to go. I'm so sorry to leave you. I wanted to bring you with me, but it's a pack matter...I can't," he said, looking pained by his situation.

I tried to smile.

"I'm sorry. I was thinking," I said. "Go. I'll be fine. I'll drive down in the morning. We can figure out what to do then."

"Marcus will know," he said, caressing the side of my face tenderly.

"I hope so," I replied with a wan smile. He kissed me softly, but pulled away before the heat built up between us.

"And what about Sean?" he asked, suddenly looking ferocious. "I can't leave you here, Ruby. He can't be trusted."

"There's no reason for me to see him, Eric. It'll be okay," I said, leaning my body into his. "If he calls, I'll just give him a lame excuse and tell him I'll see him tomorrow. He won't think anything of it. I do that all the time."

I forced a chuckle.

Eric grabbed my arms firmly, but not aggressively, in response.

"He is not to be toyed with, Ruby. Nor is he easy to lie to. If he calls, I want you to leave immediately. Just get in your car and drive. Call me. Marcus will find a way around Sean."

"You need clothes," I said absentmindedly as I looked down and realized what he still *wasn't* wearing.

"Only you, Ruby, would care about that at a time like this," he said, smiling, brushing away a loose strand of my hair. I shied away and ran downstairs to my room in search of anything that would fit him. A white V-neck men's undershirt and charcoal grey sweats from Old Navy were all I had for menswear. Sometimes I liked to wear extremely baggy clothes.

He threw them on quickly and grabbed his phone and keys.

"Remember," he said, taking my chin in his hands, "you get in your car and drive like a bat out of hell if he tries to see you."

"And call you immediately," I said with the faintest hint of mocking. He furrowed his brow. "I know, I know, he's not to be trifled with. I don't have a death wish," I said, hoping to placate his growing anxiety.

"You'd better not," he said, stealing a kiss before running

out the door. He was off to his home, his family. It made me long for mine.

I stood in the middle of the room, unmoving—I barely breathed. My life had just become surreal, impossible, and one enormous lie. I needed to go, to run somewhere, anywhere to beat back the reality that was rapidly closing in around me. The image of him was burned into my retina, flashing over and over again like a warning. He was trapped somewhere between human and decidedly not, and I realized that was my new reality.

I was too.

I wondered if my blackouts served as a kind way of saving my mind from the reality that I was indeed a monster. *I killed those men...that's how I got away...*

A knock on the door snapped me out of my pending meltdown. Every cell in my body froze—only one person would come over unannounced in the middle of the night. *Shit...I didn't lock the door again.* My lack of eye for detail was sure to get me killed one day. Maybe sooner than I thought.

Another knock echoed through my apartment more loudly and sharply than the last. He knew I was home. There was no escaping him. He would know if I went for the fire escape, and in the process I would lose the only advantage I had; he didn't know how much I knew. If I were able to put on the performance of a lifetime, it could save my ass. At least for the night.

His pounding vibrated the wall hangings. As if that weren't subtle enough, he hollered my name, demanding that I open the door or he'd do unfavorable things to it to remove it from his path. I pulled myself and my story together as quickly as possible.

I opened the door to see a vicious-looking Sean looming right over top of me.

"What's wrong?" he asked, his voice measured and controlled. He had no idea about the shit that had gone down, or if he did, he certainly didn't let on. I was suddenly terrified of him; he was my assassin. A fever flushed my cheeks in an instant despite my every effort to contain it. Once he knew the truth it would be the end of me. I needed to play the situation up well against he-who-was-not-to-be-trifled-with.

I snapped out of my inner plotting when two large hands encircled my biceps and started to shake me.

"RUBY!" he yelled. "What's wrong?"

I stood silently, trying to figure out the best plan of action. While I did, his face plunged dangerously near mine as he searched it for signs of something.

"I...I had a rough night, Sean. I'd really prefer it if you leave. I want to be alone," I whispered, trying to put on what I thought was my best wounded face.

"Rough night my ass," he scoffed. "What's going on with you? You look like you've seen a ghost."

My acting needed improvement ASAP. I knew his persistence was only beginning and it irritated the shit out of me.

"Really, Sean. I'm so not in the mood for this song and dance with you right now. Go, and I'll talk to you about it tomorrow," I demanded, hoping upon hope that he was buying what I was selling.

He took a quick inventory of the room. *Shit!* I'd forgotten what the scene must have looked like. Shredded clothes lay on the living room floor and furniture was askew. I hadn't noticed earlier; I was too busy trying not to die.

"Who was here?" he asked calmly.

I looked at the floor while rubbing the toes of my shoes together. I didn't know what the best move was, but I figured lying wasn't a good game plan, as I would have bet money on him knowing that little detail already. He only asked to maintain his charade.

"Eric," I muttered to the floor.

"Why was *he* here?"

I still couldn't bring my eyes up to his. "He was worried about me."

"Why are there ripped clothes on the floor?"

"Something happened," I whispered, head hung low.

"What did he do to you?" he asked with decidedly more heat in his voice.

I maintained my eye line, trying to find answers in the patterned grain of the hardwood floor.

"TELL ME WHAT HE DID!" he screamed.

I literally jumped, snapping my attention to the hate on his face. The animosity between the two men was more plain to see than ever. I continued to say nothing, hoping that divine inspiration would strike and help me lie my way out of the deteriorating situation, but God clearly had more pressing issues to attend to.

Sean's face softened slightly, seeing my fear. The killer's edge diminished, but his body was still coiled with rage.

"If he touched you, I'll kill him...tear him apart with my bare hands," he said, trailing off as he broke away from me to angrily investigate my apartment.

"Could you?" I asked under my breath, thinking he was out of earshot.

"*What* did you say?" he asked, crouched down next to the pile of tattered clothes. Assuming that he couldn't hear me proved to be a bad move on my part. If only I lacked the power of speech.

He stalked towards me as I frantically thought of things that could replace what I'd said. "Please do," "would you," and "me too" all came to mind, but none came out.

"What did you say?" he repeated, moving so near me that I could feel the heat radiating off of him.

Fuck it.

I figured that I couldn't wiggle my way out of the hole I'd dug, so I threw caution to the wind. If I was going to die, I was going down fighting, not cowering in a corner.

"Could you?" I asked, raising my fury-filled eyes to his. "Tear him apart, I mean?" I was baiting him and I knew it. Eric had warned me that Sean's temper was not to be trusted, but I was too far past rational thought to care. A fight was just what I wanted. "You'd have to be *pretty* strong to literally 'tear him apart'," I mocked.

"What's wrong with you?" he asked with a questioning tilt of his head.

"Wrong with me? Hmm...where do I start? Let's see. It could be that I just saw a man's flesh tear open and morph into a wolf, or that the reason I have blackouts isn't medical at all, but in fact it's that I have a little condition that makes me a monster when I'm scared, or that someone I trusted, my friend, is actually an assassin sent to kill me!" I yelled. My hysteria hit a crescendo before I paused to take a deep breath, hoping to regain some level of composure—calm people were far more scary. "But maybe it's just that I broke a nail...who really knows."

I could feel the anger in my face contorting and warming it while I waited for the shitstorm to hit. During my rant I watched his face slowly change from hurt and concerned to defensive and angry, then eerily calm and collected.

"So I guess your little friend has been busy spilling the beans, so to speak. I'm sorry I missed his little show, but I'll see him soon enough to discuss his performance."

"Performance? It wasn't a play, Sean; I nearly shit my pants!" I snarled. "And you knew. You knew all along!"

"You seem to be blowing this out of proportion," he said, cool as a cucumber. My temper flared.

"Are you not a killer, or did I blow that out of proportion as well?"

"No, Ruby, that's true enough," he said, his lips pressed tightly together.

I went pale at his nonchalance. He was a murderer; Eric was right. My stomach jumped at the thought that everything he'd told me was true.

"Then before we do this, you will clarify some things for me. You owe me that," I said, puffing my chest up towards his.

A half-smile twitched across his face.

"Before we do what exactly?" he asked, looking down at my aforementioned chest.

"Drop the act, Sean. I'm not going to be played any longer. If you're going to kill me, respect me enough not insult me first."

Everything changed in an instant. He looked confused, his posture softened, and he actually took an uncoordinated step backward as if I'd hit him.

Then it was my turn to look confused.

"You are here to kill me, right?" I asked, trailing off quietly.

"You think that's why I'm here? To kill you? What the fuck has he been telling you?" he asked, truly looking wounded by my comment.

Bullshit.

"You just admitted to being a killer like it was a regular career, Sean! Why wouldn't I think you were here to kill me? Eric was right about everything else," I cried.

He said nothing.

"You know what I am, don't you?" I shouted, unable to hold back the tears that were streaming down my face. "I know what I am, why I have all those blackouts when I'm scared. I also know why you've been following me around, trying to get close to me; Eric told me everything."

I was borderline hysterical, and that border was rapidly disappearing. I flailed my arms while I screamed all my newfound information at him. I hit him in the chest, the face, and anywhere else I could connect with, until he finally pinned my arms behind my back with one large hand encircling both wrists. I watched his eyes change color as they closed in on mine. They were darkening by the second.

His smile was long gone, replaced by hostility. Looking at him, I realized I'd never really *seen* him before.

"He lied to you," he said while I squirmed helplessly in his grasp. I took his squeezing as a sign that I should settle down and did so.

"No, no he didn't lie. He exposed you for what you really are and why you're *really* after me. You're not my friend at all," I choked out while the circulation faded in my hands. "You're a callous and vicious killer who exterminates my kind. I'd make you pay for it if I could."

"Are you quite finished," he asked, "because you're really starting to sound like a crazy person, and it's trying my patience." I started to say something else but a large hand clasped over my mouth, cutting me off. "It was a rhetorical question, Ruby. You *will* be quiet now, and you *will* hear my side of this. You owe *me* that."

He slowly removed his hand, waiting for me to pipe up again. He'd taken most of the fight out of me by then, leaving me mostly saddened and scared, awaiting my punishment for merely being.

"So you know everything now, eh? I highly doubt that. I'm going to tell you the *whole* story from the beginning. You will be quiet and you will listen," he said calmly. "I am an assassin Ruby, and I will not suffer your shit with a smile. Am I understood?"

I gulped in agreement and he continued.

"If you really want to know who I am, I'll tell you," he said, taking a breath to calm himself further. "I am a member of the Patronus Ceteri, which is loosely translated into English as the 'protectors of the others.' We have been around for millennia to mediate between the worlds of the natural and supernatural. We are born into this position and many die carrying out its laws," he said, allowing me to sit on the couch and get more comfortable. With the way he was preparing me, I knew I was in for a doozy of a story.

"I was sent to America in the early 1800's to be sure that the balance was kept in the New World as it continued to grow and populate. We hadn't planned well in advance and there were a few...*incidents*," he said matter-of-factly.

"Sorry, *when* did you come here? 1800's? Is this a joke?" I asked, completely baffled by what he was saying. Eric seemed to leave out the part about Sean being a gazillion years old, or him for that matter.

He frowned and glared at me.

"You're really trying my patience this evening, Ruby. Most people don't survive such an affront," he warned. *Point taken*. I quickly shut my mouth and listened to what became the most unbelievable story I'd ever heard.

"Like I said, in the 1800's, my personal job was to make sure that the worlds were balanced and separate in the New World. Weres could not take advantage of humans, and humans couldn't know about the existence of weres. It was a delicate situation and required constant attention and intervention on both sides. I was responsible for the extermination of rogue wolves, alphas with a penchant for destruction, and the Rouge et Blanc," he stated.

I opened my mouth to ask some clarifying questions and was met with a rough hand across my mouth to shut it. I got the message loud and clear, sighing loudly before he continued.

"Rogues are wolves who've not tolerated the Change well, or were derelict to begin with; the Change will not improve on such a thing. The Alphas are what you'd expect, the leaders of large packs. In the US we try to keep packs to the larger cities, allowing them to blend in. There are no packs in Portsmouth," he stated.

Boring. I didn't want a history lesson, I wanted answers.

"The Rouge et Blanc are an anomaly of the werewolf community. They were thought to be extinct, the Patronus Ceteri having systematically wiped out all the ones in existence as well as their line. They were typically killed as children immediately after their Change. They couldn't be controlled and their powers were too great to leave in the hands of children," he said. I raised my hand, a la grade school, in a desperate attempt to be allowed to speak. I was nothing short of amazed when he acknowledged me.

"Why are their powers so dangerous?" I asked, trying to sound casual, but truly dying to know. Perhaps he could add some specifics that Eric couldn't.

"Most wolves can be influenced by those around them, especially in a pack setting. Those that are prone to violence, for example, can be balanced by a more submissive mate or pack member. RBs cannot. All weres in wolf form are extremely strong, fast, and ruthless. Apply those characteristics to a child who's angry that they can't have ice cream for dinner. Instead of a pout and tantrum, they may go on a rampage through town and kill hundreds. For many reasons, this could not be allowed."

"How long has it been since there's been one?" I asked, knowing that I was pushing my luck.

"The last one recorded anywhere was in 1897 and it was here in New England," he said. "He was five years old."

"So you killed him?"

He nodded.

Terror and anger flowed through my veins. He'd killed my family, my line. He would kill me.

"Why are they called that?" I demanded.

He settled into the sofa across from me and took in a deep breath.

"Rouge et Blanc means red and white in French."

Duh.

"I'm aware of that. I've been through this once already this evening. What I want to know is how that figures into the equation."

"Which is exactly what I was going to tell you," he said as his eyes narrowed. "Do not interrupt me again if you wish to know anything."

He inhaled deeply before continuing.

"They originated in Switzerland in the late 1700's to the best of our knowledge. They stayed in that area until they became problematic. That's when the Patronus Ceteri had to step in and...take care of the situation. You have to keep in mind that once the Change takes place, all weres remain that age for the remainder of their existence. The RBs would never mature beyond the age they were and would remain a threat forever. Because of the nature of what brings about their Change, it tends to happen before the age of ten. Exposure to violence, emotional trauma, abuse, or extreme illness will all bring on the Change. You have to remember that in those times these conditions were commonplace."

"Never age?"

"No."

"So I'll be twenty-eight for the rest of my life?" *Or at least the next ten minutes...*

"Yes."

"How old was the oldest RB?" I asked.

"Nine. She Changed two years prior, but her powers were contained to keep her from destroying everyone and everything around her. It was brought to our attention finally, and the situation was rectified."

"Rectified? Do you believe this shit coming out of your mouth? You really can justify your behavior, can't you?" I sneered, hearing the disgust in my own voice. The direness of the situation had sunk in enough to cause unbridled rage. My filter was gone. Whatever I thought of him and his charade was coming out loud and messy. "They were children, Sean, kids! It wasn't their fault; they didn't want that kind of power. Did you ever try to help them or did you just mow them down?" I seethed through gritted teeth, fists balling up the couch fabric. He had no conscience. This was just work for him, a task to fulfill. He'd kill me without a glance, a hesitation, a tug at his moral fiber.

He was looking at me strangely, a cross between frustration, sorrow, and rage. It wasn't pretty.

"You have to understand sacrifice for the greater good. It's been over one hundred years since one existed. There was no knowledge of DNA and genetic coding until very recently. We'd pieced together over the years that it was somehow handed down by parents and we tried to isolate it as best we could. Through genetics we've been able to piece together that you have to have two parents with recessive genes for the disease to create an RB child," he said. "There are only two ways to become a were: genetics, and infection of the blood stream. To the best of our knowledge, all the carriers had been eliminated.

"The day I found you in the woods, I knew what you were immediately. Being a neowere, you didn't have much in the way of increased abilities. However, you still survived things that humans could not."

"So you've known this whole time? You've known why I've had the blackouts and never bothered to tell me it's because I'm not human? Thanks a lot, asshole!" I shouted. "I've been making myself *crazy* over this for months, and you just stood idly by, pretending to be supportive, when all the while you've been enjoying my pain and plotting my death," I said, staring him down. "I guess it'd make it pretty special, too, since it's been so long."

"I wouldn't *plot* anyone's death, so I don't..."

"CAN IT!" I shouted over him. "How *convenient* that you just happened to be in the woods that day. Or that you happen to live in the same town as me now. Did you set this up? Did the PC want me Changed?"

I tried desperately to keep my anger in front, and the tears welling up out of sight.

"Did they want to do a little experiment with Ruby the RB and sent you, the big, bad biology PhD, to carry it out?"

I had trusted him. He'd saved me. He was my friend, or so I thought. I wasn't sure I could survive this level of betrayal. How comforting that I wouldn't have to survive it for long.

I fell to my knees in despair. He flew at me from across the room, where he'd been pacing by the window, and yanked me up to stand nose-to-nose with him.

Time's up...

"You think I did that to you? You think I attacked you and killed your parents?" he growled as he breathed down my face. "It wasn't a coincidence that I was there that day at all. I was informed that we had an incident that needed to be cleaned up. You left pieces of those boys all over the clearing, Ruby. You didn't kill them; you destroyed them. The PC had *nothing* to do with anything that happened to you."

I'd had my eyes closed when he grabbed me. It was easier to revert back to the senses I had always counted on, and sight still seemed to confuse things for me. I wanted to die in the dark, as I'd lived. Sean was scaring me something fierce, and I couldn't stand to look into those ever-darkening eyes and see a person I didn't recognize as my final vision.

He did nothing, said nothing. I peeked an eye open enough to see a face that more closely resembled the one I knew. I opened the other eye. Still nothing. My nerves took over and I started to ramble.

"I did kill them...," I whimpered, unable to conceal the horror and regret I felt. "I remember...I remember now. The bodies. I see them. They're everywhere. Oh God! I...I...," Even though they attacked me and slaughtered my parents, I couldn't stand the thought of being a murderer.

"Why did you call yourself RB?" he asked, snapping me out of my descent into hysteria.

"You know," I said accusingly. "I *know* you know."

"What are you saying? You're not making sense. You need to sit down," he said, placing me back on the couch.

"I'm your enemy. You killed us, killed us all. All but me."

"Ruby, you're totally losing it. Why are you saying this?"

"Eric said his friend from the party the other night recognized me; said I looked just like someone he knew

149

from years past, and that she was RB," I muttered, staring blankly off into the distance. "And that I must..."

He shook me suddenly and violently.

"Snap out of it. RUBY! Pull it together," he shouted. My teeth were banging together from the jarring of my body. Though unpleasant, it seemed effective. I started to focus my eyes again, and there he was.

"You are *not* RB. Eric is a liar with no honor. He's always been this way and always will be, and I want you to stay the fuck away from him." He yelled at me so loudly that my vase on the table rattled.

I started to cry silent tears. One by one they fell softly down my face, leaving a trail behind them. I wanted this to be over. I couldn't understand his need for cruelty. Why couldn't he just admit his game and be done with me?

He visibly calmed himself before continuing.

"So you believe that I'm here to kill you because of what he said?"

"Yes."

"And you believe you're an RB because of what he told you?"

"Yes."

"And you've never considered that he could be wrong, or have his own agenda in this?"

"No," I answered before thinking. Then it dawned on me. Maybe Eric wasn't right about everything. Sean may be who Eric said he was, but he'd done nothing previously, or that night, that would have led me to believe he would kill or even harm me. I stood silently, ashamed that I never thought to give Sean the benefit of the doubt. Maybe Marcus was wrong.

"Sean, I don't understand what's going on here. I thought that..."

"You didn't think, Ruby. You rarely do," he retorted.

I averted my eyes and felt him snort a sound of disgust as he turned to leave. I looked to see him standing in the threshold with his hand white-knuckling the handle.

"I'm glad to know that you esteem me so highly that you would trust the word of a traitor over that of your self-professed 'friend'."

And with that he slammed the door behind him.

I assumed it was for the last time.

21

My eyes burned fiercely, yet no tears quenched them. I was beyond crying, falling straight into a sadness so penetrating that it numbed me. I remained where I lay, contemplating what had just occurred. The loss of a relationship, however strange it might have been, was gut-wrenching. I'd had so few in my life that I wasn't in a position to squander them.

I was homeschooled and did virtually nothing outside of that. My parents chaperoned everything I did and never really encouraged me to make friends. I would say that I'd always had acquaintances, but never really anyone who was closer than that. I never had sleepovers, went to the movies, stayed up all night on the phone talking about boys, or dated.

I lived with my parents while I was an undergrad at Dartmouth College. Aside from classroom interaction, I really didn't know anyone on campus or do any of the typical "college" things like get knock-down drunk only to do the walk of shame the next morning, eat pizza at four a.m. because you could, or saran wrap someone's toilet. It was always strange to me that they were willing to take me all over the world so that I could "see" every-thing, but at the same time wouldn't let me live a normal life while at home. I missed out on the things that helped a person to shape their sense of self and their place in the world. No amount of shopping in Paris could make up for that.

Dating was never a problem. My parents wouldn't allow it when I was in my teens, and quite frankly, it was a non-issue. There weren't exactly throngs of teenage boys hanging around my house waiting to ask me out. I didn't have much interest in the opposite sex until college. However, when I was there, it didn't seem like too many people were jumping at the chance to date the blind girl. It was hard to know how to fit in when so much about social interaction was based on the visual realm: how you dressed, what you looked like, your hair, your makeup, your affectations, and your expressions all silently spoke volumes about you. I had never known what my style was, though my mother would allegedly take me to all the right stores and have the cutest girl there dress me. I never knew what I looked like, though my parents would constantly assure me that I looked fine. They weren't especially helpful.

The first and only time I really took a shot at dating was during my sophomore year when I met a guy in my organic chemistry class. I was sitting in the back, trying desperately to make sense of the Fisher projections the professor was going on about, when the boy next to me leaned into my ear and said "Are you following this shit, because I'm starting to think that I need to change my major." I giggled but didn't reply, assuming it was rhetorical. He leaned in again to introduce himself. His name was Kevin.

I never lifted my hand from my Braille, but returned the introduction, and so began a two-month flirting extravaganza. We'd make snide remarks through class and he'd walk me to *calculus directly afterward. I learned that he was the captain of the soccer team, which was apparently impressive because of his sophomore status. He was from New Jersey and had a strange but endearing accent. He was sweet to me when nobody else was.*

One time while gathering up our books after class, he asked if I wanted to go "ta da bar," and I eagerly agreed. I'd heard girls in the hall talk about how gorgeous he was, that he had an incredible body and that they wanted to do some very interesting, not to mention anatomically questionable, things to him. I thought I was so lucky that he wanted to go out with me.

Apparently he thought that too.

After our date (which I thought was amazing), he was supposed to take me home. Apparently he had other plans in mind. He took me out to a parking lot next to a local hiking area. He informed me that no other guy would take someone like me out and that I owed him a favor for such an act of generosity. When I declined and demanded that he take me home, he didn't take it very well, to say the least. I ended up alone and frightened in a parking lot with a rapidly swelling cheekbone, listening to the gravel fly out from the wheels of his fleeing car.

It was hours before I was spotted by a passing police car. The officer was so kind and tried to take me home, but whenever his footsteps got close enough to me, I'd start screaming uncontrollably. He settled for calling my parents, who came and got me. Reports were later filed, and because of my parents' influence on campus, the soccer team was shortly thereafter looking for a new captain.

I never dated again.

I must have fallen asleep because I was dreaming of floating through the forest, looking up at the canopy of trees above. I played with the silver band on my hand as the light shone down through the slits between the leaves, warming my face. I slid it off and on repeatedly, watching as the sun's rays bounced off the metallic surface, catching in the well-worn grooves of the nearly faded engravings. My attention was distracted as I felt my body lowered slowly and nestled into a bed of grass.

A man appeared out of nowhere, hovering above me, his eyes a green so bright that cut emerald paled in comparison. He leaned in slowly, closing the distance between our faces as if to kiss me. He reached behind me and drew his hand slowly through my hair so gently that it tickled. He did it over and over, lulling me to sleep. Just as I reached the edge of slumber, he reached back one last time and grabbed a fistful of that hair and yanked it back so harshly that my head extended beyond its physiological limits. I screamed and struggled to look at my captor.

When his face slowly rounded my chin to come over me and reach my eyes, I was staring into two pools of forest-black and a face so feral I wasn't sure anything could contain him...

My eyes shot open to see those same dark eyes looking down at me. They were very, very real. Sean loomed over me, and I stiffened under his gaze. I wasn't sure how long it took before I felt the weight of his hand at my throat. *God, I can be so stupid. Eric had been right about everything else. Why did I fall for Sean's innocent and wounded routine earlier? If I hadn't, I could be far away from here by now. Eric would have protected me.*

My pulse quickened with his erratic breathing, his hand continually flexing over my throat tighter and tighter. I was going to die by those hands. The hands of someone I cared about.

Or thought I did.

I closed my eyes and prayed for death to come quickly, but instead it waited for me in the distance, never moving closer or farther away. I supposed that there was something sort of poetic about the situation, and that I should find comfort in the fact that I would soon see my parents again and be around the only ones who ever loved me.

Opening my eyes for what I presumed was the last time, I found his only inches from my face. I could feel the warmth of his breath on my neck and chin. It was rhythmic and soothing, though fear still predominated my state. I tried to let it lull me into my subconscious, hoping that it would lessen the pain of what was inevitably about to occur. Just as I let it take me away, he abruptly stopped.

"It's been so long," he said so softly that it was barely a whisper on the air. The way he said it with eyes closed and face soft, I started to wonder exactly what "it" was and exactly how long "it" had been. When he appeared to be coming out of whatever memory lane he'd been down, his eyes opened.

He quickly froze.

"Your eyes," he said, pulling away from me. "It's true."

His grip lessened for a fraction of a second, and I tried to sit up to see what in God's name he was talking about. I struggled my way up against his weight to see my reflection in the mirror across the room. Even with only the light of the moon shining through the windows, what I saw was undeniable. The face looking back at me was my own, except for the scarlet, blood-red eyes staring back at me.

Sean truly hadn't known.

Shit.

When I brought my focus back to Sean, he had regained his all-business face. I didn't take it as a good sign. I screamed as loudly as I could, but it was in vain; nobody lived in the surrounding buildings and passersby would never hear me through the street noise. His hand quickly found my throat again and tightened around it, slowly cutting off all sound.

Along with my air.

22

"Shut up," he whispered in my ear. I didn't have a lot of other options, given how his tightening fist was recalibrating my vocal cords. "I need to think."

Thinking was better than killing in my book, so I laid still and let him. He was breathing frantically while he extended his fingers to release some of the pressure on my neck. I didn't dare move. He looked so torn, fighting an internal battle that had nothing to do with the physical one in process. I closed my eyes and just concentrated on the sound of our breathing and the feel of his energy. I tried to emit the most calming force I could, willing it to be effective.

"I didn't want to believe it," he said through gritted teeth. "I had to be sure. I couldn't risk it." He paused for a moment, inhaling deeply, then slowly releasing it before he spoke again. "I have to tell them," he said, sounding pained and exhausted. "I have to tell the Elders."

He abruptly released me, standing up to leave. I scrambled inelegantly to my feet and followed after him as he reached for the door.

"You're going to tell them?" I asked, panic straining my

voice. "They'll want me dead. Why don't you kill me now and get it over with?" I asked, feigning bravery.

"I need to see how they want to proceed. This is unprecedented, Ruby. The normal protocol doesn't seem applicable. You haven't killed anyone since your Change...I need to see if there are options. See if it's possible to let you live," he said, appearing flustered.

He looked down at the floor for several seconds and said nothing. His silence was maddening. The entire situation was frying my brain, so I tried to backtrack my thoughts to make some sense of everything that had occurred in the last twenty-four hours. Before I got very far, a hand crashed through my plaster wall, snapping me out of my cerebral ramblings.

"DAMMIT!" he yelled, while blood rolled off his knuckles onto the hardwood floor. I reflexively moved towards him to try to help in some way. "Do not touch me" was the thanks I got for my effort.

"I don't want to kill you Ruby," he said, his voice strained, his words concise. "I need you to know that. There are things about me I haven't explained yet and it took everything I had just now not to finish you off," he whispered shamefully. His mannerisms, expression, and eyes were back to the Sean I knew; like a switch to another personality. "I need to leave. *Now*," he said softly as he walked out of the bedroom. "I have to get away from you."

I wanted to follow but glued my feet to the floor, honoring his earlier request to stay away.

"I know you're not a danger, Ruby...not if you can contain the wolf," he said, pausing in the hall. "I'll do what I can for you."

"Where are you going?" I asked, slowly moving to the bedroom door.

"The Elders are in Milano, Italy, near the border of Switzerland. I must go and speak to them in person," he replied with a look of distaste. Something about the word "Elders" sounded offensive when he said it. "I will be back with...instructions...in a few days."

He turned to look at me and gave me a ghost of a smile that faded quickly. I couldn't fight my need to comfort him, as ridiculous as that seemed in the moment, and I slowly approached him, hoping I wouldn't set him off again.

He said nothing as I moved closer, finally coming to rest with our toes nearly touching. I had no idea what to say, but I couldn't leave things the way they were even under the circumstances. I looked down at my feet, searching for words, feeling awkward and inappropriate. Telling him that I was still the same "person," the same girl he had saved, seemed a good place to start, but I mostly wanted to tell him "thank you."

I felt his right hand slide along my cheek, lifting my face up to his gaze. The green eyes I knew from a rescue long past stared kindly into mine. He drew tiny circles with his thumbs along my cheekbone, and I pressed the weight of my head into his hand, seeking comfort. His left hand came to the other cheek and picked up the same pattern of circular stroking. The coldness I'd felt deep in my bones since the fighting that night was slowly rubbed away, a warming sensation replacing it. I'd never known that human touch could feel so welcome.

He lowered his face down to my ear at a tentative pace. His thumbs stopped, and along with the rest of his hands, cupped my face. His breath was heavy on my ear, and the silence in the room was deafening. My nerve endings were alight with tingling, burning, and other foreign sensations, making me want to jump out of my skin and crawl back into it over and over again. He opened his mouth, lips brushing my earlobe, and a fire shot through me from top to bottom. My face flushed. My breathing quickened.

"Don't go anywhere," he whispered in my ear, pausing to rest his nose against my temple. My vocal function was lost amid the other nerve signals being processed by my brain, so the warning given didn't absorb immediately. I focused hard to push my words out, but, before I could, he walked briskly to the apartment door and slid out, closing it softly behind him, leaving me confused and alone.

Again.

23

I passed out from sheer exhaustion shortly after he left. Impending doom or not, I needed to sleep, and I didn't plan on waking for a long time. The blaring of my cell phone startled me out of my stress-induced slumber and scared the ever-loving shit out of me.

Eric.

He said he'd check in with me, that he planned to relocate me to keep me safe. *Talk about being right on the money.* He had no idea how right he was, or how imperative it was that he figured something out, and fast. Even though I believed Sean didn't want to kill me, I didn't doubt that he would or could. That fact outweighed his personal sentiment, and even though Eric was wrong about Sean's knowledge, he was right about everything else. I wasn't about to tempt fate a second time and stick around waiting for Sean to return to Portsmouth carrying my death warrant. I needed to bail and soon, so I placed my trust in Eric with the hope that we would successfully escape.

By the time I wrestled my phone out of the covers, it had gone to voicemail. Figuring this would send him into a state of overprotective meltdown, I immediately hit the return call button. He answered immediately.

"Ruby? Is everything okay?"

"Hmm...let's see: two arms, two legs, one head, still breathing. Yep, everything seems to be good," I joked, hoping to ease his tension. Something in his voice was off. Though I didn't know him well, I could read voices regardless of depth of relationship. He sounded stressed.

"I don't find that funny," he replied, sounding painfully honest.

"Sorry, I joke when I'm stressed," I returned.

"I see that," he replied flatly. "How was the rest of your evening? Uneventful, I hope."

"Um," I stuttered as I fought for a good way to bring up my impending doom.

"Um?" he asked, "I'm not sure what that means."

"I had company last night. He showed up right after you—"

"SEAN?" he shouted. "And why aren't you here? Are you stupid? He could have killed you...ruined everything."

"I'm fine, thanks for asking," I snarled back at him, cutting him off this time. "He came, I blustered. He threatened, I threatened back. He enlightened, I absorbed. Then he left, and then he came back, then he left again. For good, like left the country. He's off to Italy."

"Italy? He's gone to the PC. Good. That buys us time," he said, lowering his voice. "Maybe he needs permission to take you out, though that seems unlikely. I do like the thought of him on a tighter leash." Eric was silent on the line for a moment. "I'm glad he's gone, Ruby, but we still have to go. It's not safe. He'll come back soon enough. You can't be here when he does. Marcus has arranged for a safe house. I told him the whole story after our pack business was settled. He called a friend immediately after I explained the danger you were in. He wasn't aware of Sean's involvement before now. It complicates things, but doesn't change them. I will keep you away from him."

I relaxed at the sentiment, though I still wasn't sure where his earlier outburst of anger came from. He never struck me as the yell-at-someone-because-you-were-worried type. Clarification was necessary.

"Why did you freak out on me just now? Way to pull a Jekyll and Hyde," I said, keeping my tone level. "And what exactly could he have ruined?"

"I'm sorry, Ruby. It was a knee-jerk reflex. Sean brings out the worst in my personality," he apologized, sounding dutifully contrite. "You're not stupid at all, quite the opposite in fact, but a terrible judge of character."

I smiled at the phone. *That's a recurring theme...*

"And the ruined comment?"

"I just meant that he could've taken everything from me. Again," he whispered. "He's very good at that."

I felt saddened by his tone, and a twinge of anger flared deep in my core. An uncharacteristic flash of violence shot through my mind. *Sean will pay for this.*

I shook my head, surprised by what my mind was thinking, and disturbed by the unfamiliarity of it. "Ruby?"

"Yeah, sorry, I'm here. What's the plan?"

"You need to get down here as quickly as you can. Marcus has booked us tickets for this afternoon out of Logan. You're going to be gone for a long time, so be sure you pack accordingly."

"But how long? What about the store? I have to let Ronnie know I'm leaving and find someone who can..."

"NO!" he yelled, quickly interrupting me. "You can't let anyone know you're leaving or where you've gone. They'll be in danger. He'll use them to track you far too easily. Leave everything as it is; the pack will take care of everything else. I'm sorry about the shop...I know it means a lot to you."

I pondered what he said for a moment and then realized the sobering truth—nobody would really feel my absence. There was nobody to report me missing, nobody to send out a search party for me. I had isolated myself to the point that my existence didn't register on the map. Ronnie would notice, of course, but wouldn't think much of it. We didn't have the depth of relationship that would require me to announce an extended vacation. It'd likely pique her interest for a while and then be forgotten. It was a sad reality to face. Luckily, I had Eric; maybe I'd make some new friends where we were going. I promised myself right then that I would make a concerted effort to do so.

"Okay," I replied. "I'll be down in a couple of hours."

"Meet me outside Marcus's building. I'll be waiting," he said softly. "And Ruby...don't worry."

I started to say that I wasn't when it became clear that that was his sign-off for the conversation.

Guess he needs to go pack, too.

24

As I drove to Boston, I thought about how rapidly my life was changing and how I was so not in control of any of it. The past few days had been a roller coaster of revelations and experiences that amounted to more than most people would have in a lifetime. Next on the agenda was going into hiding with Eric; yet another adventure for sure, though I wasn't convinced it was necessarily positive. Somehow I got the sneaking suspicion that Sean would not be easily evaded if he had a duty to carry out, or his eyes fixed on a target. It made me wish I wasn't one.

I managed to snap myself out of a downward spiral by thinking of the state my apartment was in. My mother would never have tolerated such mayhem. Eric told me to bring a lot of stuff since we would be gone for an undetermined amount of time. He also told me to get my ass down to Boston ASAP.

Major packing in a short period of time could only lead to one thing: complete wardrobe explosion. There were panties hanging from the chandelier, boots in the sock drawer, and jewelry dotting a trail through the hall. I had also gone quickly through the bathroom, collecting products I would need in a not-so-organized fashion. The only casualty in the whole thing was a bottle of perfume that I adored dearly, its remains shattered across the tile floor. It was a limited edition too. I seemed to always break things that couldn't be replaced. I giggled to myself thinking of the virtual crime scene I'd be leaving behind.

I rolled up outside Marcus's place about an hour and a half after I spoke to Eric, having driven as fast as I'd packed. Eric was waiting on the steps of the building for me, alone. He met me at my car as I parked it, looking surprisingly unfazed.

"Did you do as I instructed?" he asked pleasantly, helping me out of the driver's seat. His touch sent energy prickling through my body.

"Yes. I'm packed and didn't mention my travels to anyone, if that's what you mean."

"Good," he replied. "This needs to be secretive."

I looked around for Marcus, knowing we needed to leave soon. Since he was taking us to the airport, I was curious as to his whereabouts.

"He's upstairs," Eric said coolly, having read my mind. "He's finalizing the agreement."

"Oh. I hope he didn't have to trouble himself too much."

I wasn't sure what there was to finalize, though I was admittedly new to this whole pack thing, and I figured they must have their own protocols for lending asylum to foreign wolves. At that moment Marcus appeared through the double doors, looking as dapper as I'd remembered him in a full three-piece suit that fit him beautifully. His energy still wasn't sitting well with me, but I just couldn't put my finger on why. I then remembered that Eric had said that Marcus was one of the "old ones." Maybe age created a certain aura or frequency that I just wasn't attuned to. It was irrelevant anyway, because he was willing to help me out of one hell of a jam. He thought nothing of lending a helping hand when I needed it, and regardless of my sixth-sense confusion about him, I owed him my gratitude, not my scrutiny.

He reached out his arms to embrace me as he approached. I went to him uncomfortably, silently repeating the mantra "I owe him my life, I owe him my life." I felt like a five-year-old who didn't want to give grandma a kiss.

"Ruby, my dear," he said affectionately as he held me. "I'm so sorry about all this nonsense. I had no idea that Sean was up to something."

"It's okay," I said as I tried to politely wriggle free of him. "You can't know everything about everybody. Besides, I'm not sure he knew, but I don't want to stick around and find out what the verdict is from Italy once *they* know."

"Smart girl," he said, releasing me from his embrace. "That's an attractive quality in a woman." He sneaked a glance at Eric and they both laughed out loud.

Before I got the chance to ask what the punch line was, Eric turned and addressed the issue.

"It certainly is," he said, his eyes swallowing me up. "High praise from Marcus is hard to come by, Ruby. He knows something valuable when he sees it."

"It's true. I've made a career that has spanned lifetimes out of seeing the worth of something that others couldn't. We all have gifts..." Marcus said, trailing off as he looked at me intently. "Now my dear, we must get you out of here."

He and Eric snatched up my bags and threw them into the empty trunk of the Mercedes. Eric motioned me over to the car and into the backseat while he and Marcus sat up front. It was a quick trip to Logan Airport, filled mainly with idle banter and trivial conversation. I had so many questions to ask about where we were going, what it'd be like, and how long we'd be staying, but I couldn't bring myself to ask. Maybe a leap of faith was exactly what I needed.

We pulled up to the Northwest terminal and parked curbside to unload. As Eric brought the bags out, Marcus came over to say goodbye.

"It's been such a pleasure," he said as he hugged me yet again.

It seemed an odd thing to say, but I was starting to realize that Marcus was an odd kind of guy, so strange things coming out of his mouth seemed more appropriate than not.

"You say that like you won't see me again." I chuckled nervously as he slowly released me from his grasp.

"Perhaps I will," he said, and nothing more.

"Time to head out," Eric called from behind me.

The two men shook hands, leaning in close. Marcus said something amusing, and a wide smile crossed Eric's face in response, but he said nothing in return.

Maybe werewolves don't hug...

Marcus turned and waved goodbye as he rounded the driver's side of his Mercedes and got in, leaving Eric and me to our luggage and our adventure. I looked ominously at the monstrous pile of bags, wondering exactly how we were going to manage to get them all inside at once. It had taken me three trips to load my car. I rifled through the stack, looking for things that could easily be slung over my shoulder before picking up things that actually had to be carried by hand. I would have killed for some bags with wheels at that moment. While I wrestled to sling a duffel on, Eric asked if I was ready yet. I looked up to see him stocked up with two other duffels, holding a suitcase in each hand. All the bags were mine.

"Are you ready or what? The plane doesn't leave from the parking lot." He was looking at me with feigned annoyance.

"Where is all your stuff?" I asked, thoroughly confused as to why I'd packed like Paris Hilton and he'd brought nothing.

"My things aren't necessary there. You'll see," he said as if that made all the sense in the world. Why he didn't need a stitch of clothing, while I needed a wardrobe to dress a movie set, was beyond me. Pack life was something that was going to take some getting used to—a lot.

We went through the usual rituals to get on the plane, and after we were seated in a row all our own, I finally got to ask what the plan was.

"It's not that exciting, Ruby. We're going out to Utah to stay with the Provo pack. They're amazingly self-contained; the perfect place to go if you never want to be found," he said reassuringly as he reached over and grabbed my hand. I melted instantly.

"How long will I be there?" I asked.

"Indefinitely," he said as he raised my hand up to his lips and kissed it. "It's important that we know what's going on with the PC before we do anything. Marcus has people abroad working for him to find out the ruling regarding your life. When we know this, we can plan better. Until then, you will stay put in Utah."

"So Marcus will be in contact with you while we're there?"

"He'll be sure that I know Sean's status."

"OK," I muttered quietly. After a long pause I meekly asked, "Do you think I'll like it there?"

A crooked smile stretched across his face.

"I think you'll learn to love it."

I smiled and nestled into my seat. The flight was direct into Salt Lake City and promised to be a long one; a nap was in order. As I drifted off to sleep, my head resting on Eric's shoulder, I felt at ease. The situation was harrowing, attempting to avoid my death and all, but there was comfort in knowing that Eric would be with me, keeping me safe as he promised.

Though he seemed a bit out of sorts, not quite himself all morning, I realized that this was an intense situation for him, too. There would be retribution, surely, for those who helped me if I were caught. He was also now in charge, and going to be away from his mentor and pack. I was selfish to not acknowledge that this was equally stressful for him.

I smiled as I dozed off. Regardless of what Sean had said, Eric did have honor. The fact that he was willing to risk his life to keep me safe proved that in my eyes. Perhaps it really was true that duress could forge the strongest bonds and bring two people together. It appeared to be working in our case.

I slept peacefully at the thought.

25

I stared at the sizable crowd that crammed together on the front lawn. *That's a lot of friends.* I couldn't fathom how Eric knew all those people or why they'd all gotten together. It couldn't have been him coming to visit.

Weres.

It was the only thing that made any sense. They lived as a pack and this 'house' we were visiting was more like a compound than anything else, stretching over acres and acres of land. I wondered if maybe he had been somehow affiliated with them before and wanted to show me off to them. I smiled to myself at that thought. Perhaps that was another reason why he had been so off on the trip out—he was nervous about me being accepted by his friends.

It was the only thing that made any sense. They lived as a pack and this 'house' we were visiting was more like a compound than anything else, stretching over acres and acres of land. I wondered if maybe he had been somehow affiliated with them before and wanted to show me off to them. I smiled to myself at that thought. Perhaps that was another reason why he had been so off on the trip out—he was nervous about me being accepted by his friends.

He came around to the side of the car and opened the door for me. I had been so consumed by the grandeur of both the building and the crowd that I had forgotten to get out of the car. He half-smiled at me, then cast his eyes over to a man emerging from the group. Eric took my hand and led the way over to him.

They shook hands like business associates rather than old chums. I was surprised by the gesture, but I figured that, like with Marcus, maybe male weres weren't big huggers. Maybe it took the testosterone level down too far for their liking. I stood behind them a few feet, still engrossed with the surroundings and the crowd that was slowly closing in around us.

I never really paid attention to what was being talked about between Eric and his mystery friend, but rather focused on the faces of those around us. They were painfully hard to read, but I became more aware of one thing as they neared us—they were *not* friendly. The energy I was picking up on was lust, peppered with malice.

The lust made sense. Eric had said that male wolves could smell an unmated female and it made them crazy. The malice, however, made no sense at all. *Maybe he didn't leave on the best of terms with these guys...*

"And here she is," Eric was saying. It snapped me back to attention as I turned and smiled at my new acquaintance. I reached my hand forward to shake his and was met with a strange expression as he turned to look at Eric with incredulity. I wasn't sure if I had offended him somehow. Maybe I had violated some rule I was unaware of. Surely Eric would have told them that this was all new to me and some concessions would have been made.

A smile slowly crossed his face as he shook lightly at first, slowly working himself into a low-rolling laugh that spread eerily through the hundreds on the lawn.

Left in the dark yet again...

"She doesn't know why she's here?" he asked Eric, looking painfully amused. Eric was laughing now too, wearing a matching expression.

"Not a clue. I knew she was naïve, but this is way beyond that."

I tried to join in with the laughter to cover up my confusion and not feel like the odd man out, but it was unsuccessful. I tried desperately to see what I was missing, what my naivety had left me ignorant of.

"I'm not sure she's going to be pleased with you when she finds out," he said, still carrying a note of mocking. I started to not care for him very much.

"No," Eric replied, stepping closer to me. "I'm not sure she will be."

The laughter died down and the tone became increasingly serious. As the two of them bantered enigmatically back and forth, I heard someone approaching from behind me. I turned to see a black-haired, twenty-something male directly behind me. He did nothing and appeared to be awaiting acknowledgment from the man in charge.

I saw the leader nod in his direction, and before I knew what was happening, my hands were shackled behind my back. At that point I was aware that something was wrong. Very, very wrong. I felt my fight-or-flight response go into overdrive and I looked to Eric for assistance. I was met with a cold, complacent expression.

"Oh, that's just darling, Eric. She thinks you'll save her," said Eric's strange companion as he stepped closer to me.

He gently took my face in his hands and bent down to put his directly in mine. "There's no helping you now, dear."

I tried to tear my head from his hands, but his grip tightened violently and squeezed until I thought my facial bones would break like glass.

"I've waited centuries for one of you. You will give me the power to change all of this mess, and your offspring will be invaluable to the cause."

Hatred coursed through my veins. He was evil incarnate, a cocktail of Satan, Hitler, and Bin Laden all rolled up into one. I was his, and I was terrified. My shaking became uncontrollable and I wasn't sure if it was driven more by anger or fear—perhaps a healthy dose of both.

"Would you like a moment to say goodbye to her properly?" he asked Eric.

Fuck that!

"Yes. I think I'd enjoy that."

With that, the man I presumed to be the Alpha turned to the group and ordered them all inside. He backed away, leaving Eric and me to our privacy that I was so not interested in at that moment. The only privacy I wanted with Eric was in a torture chamber with him on the receiving end.

He stood in front of me and had the gall to look me directly in the eyes.

"Ruby, Ruby, Ruby...what can I say?" he asked, shrugging his shoulders for effect. "I thought you and I would work out, but I guess you could say I got a better offer." I could think of nothing to say, so I spat in his face instead. He scoffed to himself as he wiped the phlegm off with his shirt sleeve. "Oh, Ruby, you're taking this so personally, but it's business, babe. Just good business."

"For you," I shouted at him, kicking him square in the

kneecap, driving his leg backwards. He stumbled for a moment then slowly returned to his position.

"I take it that means you haven't forgiven me yet?" he asked condescendingly.

"You're a dead man."

"Ahhh...and how will you accomplish that, my dear?" he asked, stroking his index finger down my cheek. "You'll be locked up here with no chance of escape, and nobody knows where you are. Not even your precious Sean. You made sure of that."

The truth of that statement abruptly took any wind I had left in my sails out. He was right. I was alone, completely without aid. Seeing this realization flash over my face, Eric moved in closer to me. He reached around my back to where my hands were shackled and wiggled my ring off. He then held it up in front of my face.

"You won't be needing this any more, and, frankly, I'd love to have a token to remind me of you in your absence. I really am going to miss our time together, Ruby. It's regrettable that we didn't have a little more."

I felt a single tear spring from my eye and roll slowly down my face.

"Oh, don't worry, Ruby. I'll miss you too, but I'm sure one of the fine young gentlemen here will suit you just as well. They're *very* eager to make your acquaintance," he said as a self-satisfied grin crossed his face. "I'm done with her now. You can take her away," he shouted to the dark-haired man, all the while never taking his eyes off of mine. Another male emerged from the house to aid with my removal. They both grabbed me around the biceps and hauled me away like a criminal. A prisoner. I guess that's what I was about to be.

I looked back to see Eric and the Alpha shaking hands as they exchanged a large metal briefcase.

"The hood, you idiots. I told you to hood her," the Alpha shouted to my escorts. We stopped briefly, just long enough for one to pull a black bag out of his pocket and roughly pull it down over my head. Our journey then continued.

Just as I was dragged up the front steps I heard two loud clicks followed by a high pitched whistle that trailed off in both volume and pitch.

"So it's all here?" Eric asked.

"It is," the Alpha replied. "Tell Marcus it's been a pleasure doing business with him."

26

The darkness was strangely calming and familiar amid the chaos. I took solace in it while I was ushered into a building, bound at the wrists, surrounded by a frantic crowd. My captors wound me through the corridors for a minute or so, and my sense of direction by that point was completely lost. We ground to a halt suddenly and I was wedged into position between my two delightful escorts. I could tell little about my surroundings other than that the room was vast and lofty; it echoed with the slightest sound. As the pack closed in around us, the noise boomed through the air, obscuring my hearing. The only senses I had left at my disposal were taste and smell, which seemed to be the worst hand I could possibly have been dealt—they were useless for defense or escape.

My head pounded from the mob's cacophony, my body completely overwhelmed by the energies around me. My mind couldn't process them all. I could only assume that the group was moving about based on the sheer number of emotions swirling around me, assaulting me unknowingly. I tried to reassure myself that at least I had that one trick up my sleeve. Eric hadn't known about my gift, so therefore the clowns who abducted me didn't know either. The downside was that there was little advantage in that for me.

The crowd started to settle down, unprompted by any audible cues. When it was quiet enough to hear a pin drop, a lone set of footsteps could be heard approaching me. *Alpha*. As he neared, I knew I was right. Evil has a very distinct feel.

"My gift to you has arrived," he declared. The crowd instantly roared its approval, then settled without prompting. "My plan can now be put into motion. I've made promises to you for decades, and now, my children, we will make them realities."

The crowd exploded.

"Once she is bound to the pack, we will have the power we need. An unstoppable power that will change the way things are and have always been."

I shifted in my stance unknowingly, trying to understand his cryptic speech. I drew attention to myself in the process, which proved to be an unwelcome move. The Alpha grabbed me violently by the back of the neck, lifting me up onto my tiptoes.

"It starts tonight," he screamed. "You will make her one of us!"

The males of the pack, which seemed to be the overwhelming population, went crazy. That did not bode well for me. I sensed their energies pressing closer, until I physically felt people brushing up against me, sniffing me, sizing me up like a steak for dinner. I tried to find a happy place in my mind. I knew there was no physical escape for me right then, but they couldn't imprison my mind. I thought of home. I saw myself dancing to music I loved, blocking out everything else around me. Dance could always do that.

I heard the Alpha's voice in my ear as I was released from his grip.

"Now the fun begins, my dear. You have no idea what you're in for; they've been waiting for you for a long, long time."

On the creepy scale, I gave that speech a nine out of ten.

Why can't any of these assholes actually get to the point and say what they mean?

Without a chance to ask that question out loud, I was on the move again, although this time I was carried. I could only assume they wanted to further skew my sense of direction. The irony was that I had a horrible one to start with, so they were going to great lengths to accomplish something that could have been done with a couple of quick turns in place. I laughed to myself inside.

My transporters took me through various halls again, though this time those halls were silent except for their conversational chatter. I gave up on paying attention to my surroundings and focused all my energy on what they were saying, hoping to get some idea of what was going on.

"Where are you in the order?" the one asked.

"I don't have the seniority you do, but I'm somewhere in the top fifty, I think," the other replied.

"You don't stand a chance then," number one snickered, "it'll never make it that far. She'll never make it past me."

"Oh yeah, Bryan, she's totally losing her shit for you. Look at her; she's champing at the bit to get to you."

"Fuck you, Aaron. You're not exactly having an effect yourself. Besides, he said it didn't work like that."

I assumed that "he" was the infamous Alpha yet again.

Doesn't this psycho have a name?

"How do *you* know how it works?" Aaron asked.

"The Alpha pulled a few of us aside one day and

explained it all. He said that once we were placed together, there would be an inexplicable connection. Once truly mated, you could never be parted. Only by death."

This. Is. So. Not. Happening.

"So we're just gonna walk in the room and see if sparks fly? That's so lame."

"Oh, I never said we were just going to be in the room together," Bryan said, chuckling to himself.

"Oooh," Aaron replied, joining in with the laughter.

Not wanting to acknowledge where this conversation was going, I started to think about what the Alpha had been telling them. How could he know how this worked? Eric and I were bonded from across a room in a crowded club, and we certainly weren't mated; and he sure as hell parted with me pretty easily. No, the Alpha was wrong, though I doubted those two chuckleheads would be interested in that little tidbit. I was about to be subjected to what I assumed would best be described as speed-dating from hell, and for nothing.

"So what's the big plan after my mating?" I asked casually.

"Ah, ah, ah. No pillow talk until after, girlie," Bryan chided.

"Why all the secrecy? It's not like I'm going anywhere," I said, hoping upon hope that they'd buy my act and fill me in. I hadn't given up on escaping, but I wanted to know everything I could while these guys were in the talking mood.

"Let's just say that he wants to shake up the division a bit," Aaron replied.

"The division?" I asked.

"Between our world and the human one."

"Enough," Bryan commanded. He seemed irritated with

what Aaron had told me, which was amusing since it made precious little sense. "We're almost there. No more questions from you, bitch. You can ask all the questions you want when I see you later tonight. Unfortunately for you, I'll be too busy to answer them."

The anxiety that I'd been trying so hard to stifle was edging upwards. I hadn't reached the point of blacking out, but I was starting to near that line. The shaking started as my pulse raced without end.

A hand reached up into my hood and stroked my face.

"Shhhhh, it'll be over soon," Bryan said. "We're here."

He put me on my feet and pushed me through a doorway. My hood was removed, as were some other clothing items I'd rather have kept on. It did nothing to control my shaking.

I could see his face now and realized that Bryan was the black-haired guy who had shackled me outside in the yard. He grabbed me by my hair and yanked me towards his face.

"Like I said, this will all be over soon. I'll be back for you in an hour," Bryan said as a smile danced across his face. "I get second dibs."

I could only assume that meant the Alpha was going to be visiting me shortly, and I choked on a whimper that threatened to escape at the thought.

The two of them slammed the door to my cell and left me alone in a dark, cold, musty room, nearly naked, and completely terrified. There would be no white knight coming to save me. There certainly would be no saving myself.

The proverbial shit had hit the fan, and I was neck-deep in it.

27

Time passed slowly, and the process was starting to break me. I was deprived of virtually all sensations, and the few I was granted were not the sort I would have chosen. The darkness was so complete that I had no concept of night or day, date or time. I could have been there three weeks or three months for all I knew; it was all the same to me. I tried to count my meals to gauge how much time had passed, but that was based on the premise that they were feeding me three squares a day, and judging by how skeletal my naked body felt, that was a terrible assumption.

I was cold to the core in a way that I could not be certain I would ever warm up again. Then there was the coldness that wasn't temperature related at all. Sometimes cold evolved from an evil so pure, so thorough, that it could permeate the soul of even the most God-fearing individual. I had that, and it scared me to death.

The smell of must and dankness had coated my mucosa so thoroughly that I couldn't escape it. If it hadn't been for my ability to hear and feel the footsteps coming, I'd have never known when they were approaching. Normally, when alone, I was surrounded by thick, heavy silence. It was inescapable. Only those brief visits by the others broke that silence. Those were the only times I wished it back.

As I sat on the damp, packed-dirt floor, I tried to keep the images of what I'd endured pushed way down deep in my mind. Just when I felt my sanity slipping, my attention was snapped back to the more pressing issue of unwelcome footsteps echoing through the corridor to my cell. The sound started faint and distant, gaining strength and vibration to become deeper in tone and more rapid in pace, as though the approacher couldn't wait to see what was behind the door and rushed with anticipation.

My body rushed with adrenaline.

My heart quickened, blood racing to extremities that begged to either run or fight. I was unable to comply with either, still bound in iron shackles to the wall. Apparently my not-so-good behavior had done little to impress my captors and even less to gain their trust.

I sprang to my feet as always, making me look less like a victim, even if only to myself. I waited for the door to open. Whoever was out there appeared to be hovering by the door, a very unexpected behavior, as everyone else had all but taken it off the hinges to get in. I didn't enjoy his theatrics, knowing that he was either taking his time in an effort to frighten me further—which really wasn't possible—or contemplating how best to impress me with his entrance.

Awesome. I so need one with a flair for the dramatic!

My skin itched and crawled, a final plea from my nervous system to react. Though I couldn't do what it wanted, I tried to release some of the energy I was amassing by the second. I screamed as loudly as I could.

The door came crashing in, and, in an instant, a tall, lean but muscular man came flying through it straight towards me. I backed up as quickly as possible, completely unprepared for his attack. I needed room to figure out some way to defend myself, to find anything to gain leverage with. I was almost frantic when he stopped just short of me. He did nothing but look.

I realized in our proximity that he wasn't as threatening as the others had been. With that victory, I slowly released myself from my defensive posture and looked right back at him. We stared at each other for what seemed like a lifetime; apparently he was in no hurry to get down to business.

"You were screaming," he said, eyeing me closely. "Are you hurt?"

I was completely puzzled. Days and days of treatment so vile the UN would've been writing sanctions for years, and he asked if I was hurt.

Ah...now they send Captain Perceptive. I knew there had to be a MENSA candidate in this bunch.

"No, I'm fucking peachy, and you?" I snarled at him and his mock sympathy. He looked sheepish after my response, running his hand through his golden curls as he let out a deep breath. It appeared as though he had been holding it for quite some time.

"I don't want to be here," he said quietly. I cocked my head to the side and gave him my very best "and I fucking do?" look. He seemed to catch my drift. "I'm not here to hurt you. I don't want a part of...this...any of it," he said while making a dismissive wave of his hands around the room, at my restraints, and at me.

"Really? This isn't your dating scene? Seems to work for everyone else in your little group," I said with venom on my tongue. "But hey, if you're so morally opposed to this, why don't you get me the hell out of here?"

"That was my plan," he said as his voice drifted off quietly. "To get us *both* out of here." I stared blankly at him, completely mute. Usually my mouth served to get me into a lot of trouble, especially when cornered.

Imagine my surprise.

"Us?" I asked gently, as though I was afraid in that fraction of a moment the answer had changed.

"Yes, Ruby. *Us.*"

I slid down the wall I was backed up against, landing inelegantly on the floor. I pulled my knees tight to my chest and rested my head atop them. Somehow modesty, in light of my new situation, became a top priority.

I couldn't look at him. Embarrassed, drained, and emotionally scarred, I tried to hide my relief from the only ally I now had. I didn't realize I was crying until I felt his fingertip brush across my cheek. I snapped my head up to see him kneeling in front of me, our faces so close I could feel his breath on my face. The silence was back, and I couldn't tolerate it one second longer, my panic starting to rise.

"Why?" I asked, if for no other reason than to hear something echo through my cell.

"Because I never wanted to be here. You never wanted to be here. You're not safe here, and you never will be. I've heard the Alpha speak of his plans for you." He broke eye contact with me after his last sentence, looking down at the ground, taking a sudden interest in the nothingness there. "No one should live like that and I want no part in it. The only part I'll play is the one that sees you free and safe."

It was in that moment I knew he wouldn't harm me. He was so earnest. His chivalrous nature was from another era, one where people died over principles, over right and wrong. I reached down and grabbed his hand, careful not to move from my carefully chosen position. I pulled him in close to me so that he could hear my whisper.

"What do we need to do?"

28

"First we need to remove your bindings, don't you think?" he asked with a mischievous grin. Without any pomp and circumstance, he removed what I could only assume was the key from his jeans pocket. He held it up and turned up the wattage of his smile. "Sometimes it's good to go unnoticed. For once my unimportance served me well." There was a bite to his statement, and as curious as I was to know why, I was learning that my feet best served me when they were nowhere near the vicinity of my mouth.

I reached my arms out towards him with my wrists pressed together like a prisoner in a bad cop movie, anticipating my freedom. He took one wrist in his hand and winked at me as he fit the key into the lock and gracefully sprung the shackle open. He repeated this on the other side, sans wink.

The inside of the shackles gleamed in the fraction of light that spilled in through the tiny opening in the door. The silvery metal was in great contrast to the iron exterior

I'd been looking at for God knew how long. I rubbed my wrists gingerly as they'd been worn raw from my fruitless attempts at escaping the shackles, and the others' overzealous attempts to win my "affection."

He quickly eyed my nearly naked state and mumbled something as he removed his shirt. He leaned closer to me and drew it around my shoulders, letting it drape delicately before he slowly stood up and backed away a few paces. He then turned both his eyes and body away from me.

"It'll be too big for you. I didn't know you had nothing else. I'm sorry I didn't plan that better," he said remorsefully. I slid my arms in and buttoned the front as quickly as my frozen hands would let me. The sleeves were much too long, so I rolled them to the elbow just to be sure they wouldn't get in the way while we made our escape. I stood up tall to ensure the length of the shirt was sufficient. The white, collared oxford fell to just short of mid-thigh, which was a vast improvement in my eyes. I cleared my throat to get his attention, and he turned to see if his offering would do the trick for now. He looked very pleased with himself.

"So where to now?" I asked. His smile quickly faded.

"Unfortunately, this was the easy part. Nobody will be suspicious of me being in here; it was my scheduled turn. However, we have many other things working against us," he observed solemnly. Things working against me was beginning to be a theme. I made a mental note to find the perfect theme song to go with that when I got home. If I got home.

"Eventually someone is going to notice the key is missing, and lucky for us, those someones are the most lethal in the pack." *Stellar.* "Even luckier still, we have to get through the secured area housing a couple of armed guards, because apparently being a werewolf isn't weapon enough around here, and then waltz out the back door of the compound."

"So when are you going to get to the bad news?" I asked with every ounce of sarcasm I had left in me. He just smiled.

"I thought you'd never ask. The best part of all this is that, if we live to breathe the outside air again, we then have to run through woods that are peppered with Watchers, those that keep the property under surveillance. They're in constant communication with the Alpha. We'll never see them. If, or perhaps better stated, *when* they see us, they'll send for reinforcements. You're probably too weak to Change and I can't fight them all alone. We'll be no match for them."

I gulped back the bile that surged into my mouth.

"What will happen if they catch us?" I asked meekly.

"*You* will be returned to your current accommodations. *I* will be dealt with, so to speak."

I knew instantly what was on the line for both of us. Both my freedom and his life depended on this plan going exceptionally well. That was the understatement of the century.

"How far?" I asked.

"What?"

"You never said how far we had to go to be...well...wherever it is we're going."

"Twelve miles. We have to run through twelve miles of guarded woods, cross a river, and then be exposed through one large clearing before we're in town."

I thought I was going to choke. *Twelve miles?* I felt defeated before we even started our little suicide mission. The logistics were grim to say the least. I was weak, hungry, and dehydrated. I would slow us terribly. He was one wolf against an entire pack, the cavalry. Though I didn't doubt his abilities or strength, the math just wasn't working out in our favor.

He could see me working through the scenario in my head, my face clearly displaying my anxieties. His expression softened as he straightened his posture and squared his shoulders.

"I've made arrangements, Ruby. If we can get there in one piece, the rest will seem like shooting fish in a barrel." Though I was completely unfamiliar with the saying, I took it to mean that the remainder of our plan was relatively simple if we lived to see it. *What is it with men and fishing?*

I scrounged up what scraps of courage I could find. If I was going to follow through with this plan, I knew I had two potential outcomes: freedom or death. I would not return to that subterranean hell. That was not living.

No more cages.

"So, partner, when does the tour begin?" I asked, trying to look as enthusiastic as possible given the scenario.

"Cooper. My name is Cooper," he said, grinning from ear to ear. Apparently we shared the same need to find shreds of humor in the most dire situations.

"Okay, Cooper," I said, returning his smile. "When does the tour begin?"

A man of more action than words, he grabbed my hand and led me to the only door in the cell. It was still slightly ajar from when he came in, shedding the faintest but most welcome light into the room. When he stood in the sliver of illumination, I saw how truly beautiful he was. His face had delicate but manly features and his skin was sun-kissed. The wavy hair I had seen was the most golden blond. His eyes were a strange mix of hazel and green and were painfully honest, with pale eyelashes to frame them.

His build was deceiving. I had first thought him to be

thin, but with the light highlighting his definition, he looked like a yoga instructor or surfer: lean, but powerful and defined. His unassuming, laid-back posture and demeanor were misleading, and I could see why people underestimated him.

I would not.

Realizing that I was completely staring at his naked torso, my gaze shot to his face, only to find that he was assessing me too, probably trying to figure out what all the fuss was about. I wondered that a lot myself. I knew I wasn't looking my personal best, having lived virtually naked on a dirt floor and not showering for God only knew how long. I was sure it did amazing things for my general appearance.

"I can see it," he said. His eyebrow perked up ever so slightly.

See what?

Completely at a loss as to what he was talking about, I raised my hands in a questioning gesture and gave him my very best "what the crap" face. He laughed—*really* laughed.

"Why they wanted you so badly. You've got a caged beast in you somewhere. You just don't know how to let it out yet."

"Yet?" I asked, looking past him to the hallway I wanted to sprint down.

"Hmm. So pretty, but so ignorant. You really have no idea what you are or what you can do, do you?" I thought that was relatively obvious by that point, but I played along.

"Nope. 'Parently not. Please feel free to learn me somethin' new then," I said with my best southern, backwoods accent.

"So much protective sarcasm. Someone really did a number on you, didn't they?" he observed, his eyes sympathetic. "Your defenses are always up."

The truth really hurt, especially when I was slapped in

the face with it by a complete stranger who had figured me out in about five minutes flat. That stung even worse.

"Then enlighten me," I demanded quietly.

"Now isn't the time," he said, grabbing my hand. "We've gotta move. Now."

With that, we burst into the hallway.

29

I welcomed the light in the corridor at first, though my eyes burned for a few moments, having not been exposed to it for a long time. Cooper waited patiently while I adapted. When my squinting lessened, he seemed satisfied and led the way down the hall. There was stone everywhere: above, below, beside, around. It was like being in a secret underground passageway from castles of old, or at least how Hollywood portrayed them. The tunnel of limestone seemed to go on forever and was completely monotonous. There were no doors, no hallways, no electricity, just stone and torches. The ceiling clearance was maybe six feet, which made Cooper taller than that. His shoulders were slouched and head angled forward to avoid scraping.

We were silent while we walked, though it made little difference. If someone had been up ahead, they would have heard the echo of our footsteps coming long before we arrived. A stealth mission it was not. I was becoming increasingly annoyed with our lack of conversation as time passed, even though we must have been walking for at least fifteen minutes without a break in scenery or direction.

"Where are we exactly?" I inquired.

"We're under the lawn of the compound. The cells are kept away from the main house for numerous reasons, the primary being that it's easy to forget about things that you can't see or hear," he said matter-of-factly.

"How long before we get to the guards, or anybody else for that matter?"

"It'll be another mile at least," he replied, still moving forward.

"Can you please tell me about what I am? Please? I know I'm some aberration, or abomination depending on who you ask, but I don't know anything else," I pleaded, grabbing his elbow.

He stopped and turned to see the pain on my face. I'd never had a strong sense of self. Gaining vision had complicated that at first, but was starting to help in the long run—that is, until I found out about my not-so-human status. I was desperate to understand even the smallest thing about my new identity: what it meant, what I could do, how to control it. I needed just a tiny thread to hold on to while everything else around me unraveled.

"I'll tell you what I know, but it isn't much. Before you came, there were rumors of your existence and our potential acquisition of you. I kept my ears open and my head down. I also went into the archives to dig up what little had been recorded in the past, though it was all legend and conjecture," he said, looking professorial. "Exactly what do you know?"

"I know I'm Rouge et Blanc. I know that we were thought to be extinct. I know that we were the most ruthless killers among our kind and were taken out after our first Change to protect both humans and weres alike," I admitted. "I also know the PC has been told about me; they'll have to kill me. I can never go home."

He looked at me with pity in his eyes, but also understanding. He could never go home again either. We were kindred spirits in so many ways. He beckoned me forward and started to pick up the pace. I hurried to keep up with his long strides.

"Okay, so that's what I know. Time for you to fill in some blanks, Coop," I said.

"I don't know too much more than you. The pack was speculating about mating. They seemed to believe that there was the possibility of carriers in the pack. They believed that if you were put into close contact with them that your wolf would recognize the RB genes and bond with that male."

"So they wanted to *breed* me?" I asked, furious with the idea.

"Yes, but that's not all they wanted. They knew that, if the rumors and stories were true, you'd be the greatest weapon the pack could ever have. It's been said that the RB could take out entire villages without being seen or stopped. Nobody knows exactly how your powers work; they were just banking on you having them."

"But that's the thing. I don't know how to use my powers either. I don't think I have any. The only times I've Changed have been out of sheer terror. I black out and come to later without any recollection of what happened."

He looked at me curiously before a laugh broke free. After a moment or two, it was all I could do to get him to stop. He nearly fell down to the pavers in a heap, convulsing from his hysterics.

The first kick didn't seem to do much, but the second appeared to snap him out of his comedic breakdown.

"What the hell is so funny?" I yelled.

"What's funny is the irony. You've had the answer the whole time and didn't know it. You *can* control your Change, Ruby," he said. "And you kick like a girl."

"Care to share the big secret then?" I asked in annoyance, ignoring his last remark.

"To force your Change, you must dull your surroundings, block out all sensory stimulation. Your blackouts have been blocking things out, out of necessity. Had you learned to "black out" the things around you before and focus, you'd have been in control a long time ago. You never would have ended up here," he said softly.

Never would have ended up here? The fact that that was even potentially true burned me to the core. *If only I'd known, none of this would have happened.*

I sat in silence for a moment and stewed about my newfound information. I needed to blame someone, anyone. And Cooper would do.

Just as I readied myself for an epic screaming match, we heard a sound from deep in the corridor, right where we were headed. Cooper's hand shot to my mouth and covered it, or smothered it, however you cared to look at it. He didn't seem to think my breathing was necessary at that point in time. I was starting to question it myself.

Another sound, louder than the first, echoed through the hall. Then another, and another. All were gaining in strength and volume. *Footsteps.*

I pinched Cooper hard to get him to release my face. I really was in no hurry to draw any more attention to us than he was, so there was no need for my muzzle. We looked at each other, desperately seeking knowledge of what to do in the other one's face. We needed a game plan and we were both coming up short. I looked down the hall to see if there was some other way out, or to get a glimpse of what was coming for us. I could see neither, just an ever-darkening void as the approaching body blocked out the light behind it. Our circumstances were not encouraging.

When the darkness was only a few yards away, a voice came from it. A low, evil, don't-want-to meet-you-in-a-back-alley (or corridor) kind of voice.

"Thinking of taking the prize for yourself, are you, Cooper?" the voice said. "I don't sense an unbreakable bond, or that there's even been a mating. I'm curious, my friend, as to what exactly you think you're doing?"

Cooper became instantly rigid. I was slammed with a tsunami of fear coming straight from him, which did little to boost my morale. I surmised that the new guy was one of the few who knew where the key was, "the most lethal in the pack," Cooper had called them. *Not good. So not good.*

"And you, my little Ruby, leaving so soon? We haven't all had our chance to play yet. I haven't had my chance to play yet." His tone went from civil to lustful. It was so not an improvement.

"I think I'm all done with play time for now," I said shakily. "I never was big on it."

From out of the shadows stepped a man as big as an oak tree, both in height and girth. All of my false bravado washed away as my own little wave of fear crashed through the hall.

He laughed.

"Maybe you weren't playing with big enough toys."

I'd so like a do-over right now. Now, now, now, now.

As my fear worsened by the second, Cooper seemed to gain some sort of testicular second wind. He stepped in front of me, shielding me from the oak-man's view.

"What do you want, Nicholas?" Cooper demanded in an authoritative tone I didn't know he was capable of.

"What we all want, Cooper. The Rouge," he said nonchalantly. "It's my turn, though I'm now curious as to why you've let her out of her cage. You wouldn't be trying to free our new pet, would you?"

"I'm nobody's fuck—"

I was violently shoved before I knew what had happened. Apparently my limbs didn't know what was occurring and were ill-prepared to stop my body from being smashed to the ground. I cracked my head hard on the wall and must have been knocked out. When I came to, Cooper stood above me, covered in blood. The barely recognizable remnants of Nicholas were lying at our feet.

I looked up again at Cooper and saw wildness in his eyes as he stared into mine. I slowly tried to get up and reached for his hand to gain some leverage; he backed away from me slowly, never unlocking his gaze from mine. I assumed he was a little shell-shocked from what had happened while I was in la-la land, so I tried to pull myself up on the wall. My hand instantly slipped and I wound up plastered to the ground again. When I looked at myself, I realized that I too was covered in blood.

Far more than Cooper.

It wasn't until I saw the bits of flesh and questionable matter clinging to my arms and under my fingernails that I began screaming. Since Cooper still seemed a bit gun-shy around me, it went on for a good couple of minutes. He must have been getting concerned about the potential for alarming the guards—or his auditory health—because he finally came over to snap me out of it with a backhand across the face. It was painful, but highly effective. I stopped immediately. The wildness in his eyes was gone and the warmth had returned.

"I'm sorry," he said, wincing at his actions. "I had to do it."

"It's okay...I'm sorry. I don't know...I didn't expect to...what the hell happened?"

He quickly relayed the events as they had occurred, though I was certain he'd done some Hollywood editing to make the story more "PG-13" than "R.' Apparently in my attempt to verbally attack the tree-named-Nicholas, the tree became unamused with the entire situation. He lunged at me and Cooper threw me, literally, out of the way. I did hit my head and it did stun me, but I wasn't knocked out. Nicholas was distracted enough by Cooper to take the bait for a while.

"You just sat there, slumped against the wall, looking at me while he was choking me. His back was to you. You must have known on some level what was happening, because the rage that crossed your face was unlike anything I've ever seen before, and that's when it happened. I don't know if your concussed state was the perfect amount of forced blackout or what, but you Changed right then," he said, looking distant. "I've never seen anything like it. It was beautiful and horrifying at the same time. And the speed with which you Change...it's unnatural."

"Isn't the fact that I do it at all unnatural?" I joked, trying to again make light of something decidedly not. It wasn't well received in that instant. He was really freaked out.

"My humor isn't only a defense mechanism, Coop. It's handy when I'm scared or about to lose my shit."

At that he smiled.

"My sense of humor has never abandoned me before

now," he replied. Silence hung between us for the briefest of moments.

"What happened after I Changed?"

"You tore through Nicholas like a sword through paper. I just stood there while you made minced meat out of him in about five seconds. Maybe six."

"So I did *that*?" I said, dubiously pointing at the pile of Nicholas on the floor.

"Yup."

"Huh. And you didn't help at all?"

"I was too busy trying to stay out of the way. Smart people don't jump in front of freight trains."

A wave of nausea surged through me with the most horrific thought.

"I didn't eat him, did I?"

"No," he said, choking on a laugh. "Just diced him up, walked over to where you are now, and laid down like you were going to take a nap. A couple of minutes later you morphed back into human form and woke up instantly."

"So I never went after you?" I asked.

"I don't think you even knew I was there. You were on a mission with a one-track mind: kill Nicky."

"Where did all your blood come from then?"

"Are you kidding me? That attack was as messy as turning on a blender without the lid on. CSI techs would have a field day with this mess."

A huge smile slowly spread across my face.

"Ahhh, and the humor returns."

30

I learned a valuable lesson that day: you can trick your mind into believing, or not believing, just about anything, so long as you don't really have to face it. I knew what I was, and what I had done in the woods to my attackers the night of my Change. What I didn't realize, *really* realize, was that I was a cold-blooded killer—efficient and effective. Apparently, lying covered in a man's blood corrected that erroneous neural pathway. I couldn't rationalize, lie, or evade my way out of that, nor could I spin it in my imagination to be anything other than what it was. My shirt was a shredded, blood-spattered reminder. I had to get it off. Immediately.

I started to take it off when Cooper grabbed my hands and held them tightly.

"You can't take it off, Ruby. We can find something else for you upstairs, but this will mask your scent even further. No one here will bat an eyelash at the smell of someone's blood," he told me. "Violence is part and parcel of the compound experience. We're not really a warm fuzzy, feel-good kind of family."

His words were so thick with grief and sadness that they pulled me from the depths of my self-pity. He too had been lying to himself, and for a lot longer than I cared to imagine.

"Okay," I conceded, grabbing his hand to pull myself up.

"We're going to have to do this with a little less stealth and a lot more speed now," he said while snapping me upright. "The guards are less than a mile away now. We're going to have to kill them. There's no way around that," he said solemnly.

"That seems to be my current MO," I quipped. "I'll have to be human, though. I can't lie down to sleep even for a couple of minutes afterward. We don't have the time."

"What is your strength like in human form?"

"I'm strong, but nothing special. I'll be of no use in a fist-fight if that's what you're hoping for."

"Hmm. Perhaps you'll just have to be a distraction then. The two guards that are on duty are strong, but maybe not the sharpest. I can easily dispose of one before the other knows what's happening."

"When you say distraction, I'm assuming you don't want me to do my best rendition of 'All That Jazz,' right?"

"No, but I would *love* to see that sometime," he said, his eyes bright. "Can you really sing and dance?"

I wasn't sure which part was more disturbing—that he was again laughing during a non-humorous event, or that he really seemed intrigued by my potential ability to do both of those activities.

"Hey Chuckles, could we focus here?" I groused. Maybe he needed a slap across the face to snap *him* back into the here and now. "The guards? What exactly do you want me to do? And you'd better keep it clean, smartass."

Just as he had earlier, he managed to get himself together and refocus on the task at hand. He looked pensive for a moment—even scratched and rubbed at his chin, though I was completely convinced that was solely for effect.

"You're going to have to go in alone. Your current state, combined with the fact that you're loose, will be more than enough cause for immediate alarm and action of their part. They'll assume you've killed both Nick and myself, so they won't be focused on anything but you. If you can draw them back, effectively cornering yourself, I can get them close enough together to make fast work of them. Neither will have a chance to react."

It sounded like a solid enough plan, but he was leaving one small detail out.

"Didn't you say they were armed?" I asked with a heavy dose of skepticism.

"What?"

"Armed...you know, guns with real bullets—the kind that can kill. *That* armed." He looked confounded for a moment before blowing off my concerns.

"Yeah, there's that. That won't be a problem. They won't shoot you, and they won't see me coming. They'll be dead before they draw."

His ambivalence was awe-inspiring and wicked annoying. *Yeah, no biggie. Nothing could possibly go wrong with that plan.*

We jogged the rest of the way down through the stone tunnel. I was too weak to both run and talk, so Cooper mainly just babbled beside me about everything and nothing. The light started to dim as we neared what I assumed to be the end. Cooper was silent for the last fifty or so yards, but what he failed to mention in his silence was that the door was rapidly approaching and that perhaps it would be a good idea to slow down. No such good luck for me; I ran full speed right into it. Staggering back away from it, I gave myself a full view of the solid oak door that stood before me, ominous and foreboding.

So much for the element of surprise.

Now instead of getting a chance to quietly rehash the plan with Coop, I was being thrust through that door into a large foyer of sorts by my unhappy companion.

It was much brighter in there and it took me a moment to get my bearings. The room was circular in shape with four egresses, each equally spaced out along the wall. The ceiling was at least four times the height of what I'd just traveled down, with an enormous lantern-esque light fixture hanging like a chandelier in the center. The walls were still stone, but much more inviting in that amount of light.

What wasn't that inviting were the two meat-heads directly across the room from me about twenty-five feet away. They seemed to be as startled by my appearance as I was by my surroundings. I completely panicked and forgot the game plan. *Was there a game plan?*

I ran at them with as much wildness and craziness as my energy stores could provide. They took the bait and lunged towards me, coming at me from each side. I ducked to the right, hoping the door there might be unlocked, but no such good luck. Seeing that I had nowhere to go, they slowed their pace to an intimidating walk, each with his own pleased look on his face.

Where the hell is Cooper?

The taller one on my right got to me first. He said nothing, but slid the back of his hand down the side of my face, and then slowly brushed it back up again. His buddy stayed a couple of feet back from him, just out of his periphery. He appeared to be watching the taller one's behavior, studying it as if he were his mentor.

Up and down, up and down, the hand caressed the side of my face. He didn't say a word.

WHERE THE FUCK ARE YOU, COOPER?

There are many different types of scary. This guy was serial-killer-scary. The kind of psychopath who would take his time gutting you, then sit across from you at the dining room table and tell you about his day while you slowly bled to death. He would enjoy his meal, too.

Has Cooper chickened out? How could he leave me here with this sociopath?

Tears were starting to sting the back of my eyes. Cooper said these guys wouldn't kill me, but I was getting concerned about how closely they might like to push the envelope. I wasn't really in the mood for permanent damage. As those thoughts went through my mind, I felt the darkness coming. *Oh shit, oh shit, oh shit...*

As my vision tunneled, I saw a flash of movement cross the room, but I was unable to focus. My Change was coming and there was nothing I could do. Though I knew it wasn't the worst thing that could happen, I was afraid my lanky caresser would be forced to shoot me, and that *would* be the worst thing.

Again I saw a something blur through my periphery, but much closer this time. I heard a loud crunch, a faint grunt from one of the men, and then something loud fall on the floor. The hand immediately left my face.

I could see the fight more clearly now, but it was gray and fuzzy and pixelated-looking. Cooper was in a knock-down, drag-out fight with Lanky. It was hard to watch with this unfamiliar vision. Everything appeared less defined, with a lack of clarity to their movement. It almost nauseated me to watch. I started to wonder if stress affected my eyesight as well; it would have been par for the course.

Suddenly I saw a flash of metal. I knew they were fighting over the gun, the gun-that-wouldn't-have-time-to-be-drawn in Cooper's plan. I had no idea what to do. They seemed evenly matched, but that gun was trump, and I had no clue as to who had the better handle on it. I knew I couldn't just mold myself to the wall and hope for the best, maybe cheer Cooper on. No, I had to help somehow.

I watched for a bit longer, waiting for Lanky to turn his back to me. Cooper may not have known my plan, but right on cue, he twirled his attacker a few steps sideways, giving me exactly what I wanted. I surged towards him, mouth open, hands ready. I sprang up and latched on with my nails dug into his shoulders and feet pressed into the small of his back. Before I knew what I was doing, I had my mouth buried in his carotid region and was tearing at his throat with all my resolve. He screamed like a rabbit caught in a trap. It was a bloodcurdling sound that made my insides squirm with delight. I released him, expecting to come crashing to the ground, but instead I landed elegantly.

On four feet.

I had Changed and not even known. I felt nothing but the raw emotions that had fueled it in the first place. There was no pain, nothing like I had seen Eric experience with his.

When I looked back up at Lanky, I saw that the fight hadn't fully left him while he struggled with Cooper for control of the gun. The floor was rapidly puddling with blood due to the arterial spray that rained around us, making it a balance hazard for the two fighting in it. Cooper went down hard and fast, bringing his opponent down on top of him. He was securely pinned under the other were-wolf with the gun still up for grabs.

I locked my mouth back around Lanky's neck to rip him

off. That's when I heard the shot. By heard, I mean my eardrums virtually exploded from the volume and vibration of it. It rang through the foyer for an eternity, making the nightmare that was unfolding in front of me seem never-ending.

It was the only sound.

Both men lay still. Nobody moved, nobody spoke, nobody breathed. Not even me.

And the blood was everywhere.

31

I stood frozen, staring at the pile of bodies. In that moment I was convinced that not seeing Cooper dead would make him less so. He died trying to get me out, someone he didn't even know.

The color was returning to my vision, and I looked away. Not seeing the red of blood somehow made it less real; however, the ever-increasing mass of liquid surrounding them could only be denied for so long. I looked down to see my naked body, human and fully intact. I had shifted back without passing out and, again, without any pain. I wondered if being RB made many things different for me.

Though I wanted to contemplate the wonders of my Change, my attention quickly returned to the issue at hand. I looked down at the two men lying motionless, both coated in blood. The thought of Cooper lying dead under that animal sickened me into action. I prowled over to him and pulled the guard off of Cooper and onto his back. He looked up into the ceiling, his face contorted with pain and fear. I couldn't bear the sight of him and turned to see Cooper, lying still with his eyes closed, curled on his right side into a semi-fetal position. My stomach jumped into my throat. Just below his sternum was a circular, thick, black smudge, with a stream flowing down his trunk to the floor.

Instinctively I reached for him, slipping in the blood, landing sprawled out on top of him. Finding my voice, I hysterically called his name while trying violently to shake the life back into him.

"COOPER! Don't you fucking die on me," I screamed over and over again until my throat burned of rawness and my eyes stung with tears flowing so uncontrollably they streamed off of my chin, pooling on his face. I carried this on until my voice threatened to give out. Tiring from my efforts and emotionally exhausted, I fell back onto his chest and laid my head gently on his shoulder.

"Please...Cooper. Please don't leave me," I whispered to no one but myself. I closed my eyes and gave into my emotions further, allowing myself this one and only good cry.

After a few minutes my shaking lessened, though it was still intense enough to almost hide the fraction of movement under my chest that was out of sync with my own breathing. I stopped immediately. Again, a faint rise and fall occurred below me. I pressed into a plank position above him to take my weight off and to see his face. His eyelids fluttered rapidly, and his respiration slowly increased in speed. I could actually hear the rush of air in and out of his nose.

"Cooper? Can you hear me?" I asked softly, afraid to disturb his recovery. I looked down at his chest to see where to apply pressure to stop the bleeding, now that he was alive, only to find a perfect torso with not so much as a scar or scratch on it, only a lot of blood. *Not possible...so not possible.*

I stared open-mouthed in utter disbelief. The wound I

thought I had seen earlier was gone. No bleeding. No gaping hole. No nothing.

I slowly scanned his body for an injury I might have missed earlier in my distress. Still nothing. I thought I was going crazy, that this was the result of little food, lots of stress, and entirely too much trauma. I squeezed my eyes shut, counted to ten, and snapped them open to see Cooper's face, staring up at mine.

My rational mind was not able to easily accept what I was seeing. Dead people didn't breathe. Dead people didn't blink. Dead people didn't smile at you like nothing in the world was wrong.

Screw my rational mind.

I dropped myself back down on to him and threw my arms violently around his neck. I hugged him so hard that he was in jeopardy of losing his newfound ability to breathe. He coughed a bit in my ear, and then I felt his arms slowly slide around the small of my back, hugging me back.

"Any chance of you letting me up? This floor isn't exactly downy soft on my back, you know?" he said with a smile in his voice. "How long was I out for?"

"Out for? Cooper, you were *dead*!" True to form, he found me amusing when I *so* wasn't trying to be.

"I wasn't dead, crazy girl. I was healing. Gunshot wounds aren't exactly a walk in the park you know. Thank God it wasn't silver, or we wouldn't be having this conversation at all right now," he said soberly. "Glad to see that the Alpha hasn't taken things to that level yet."

So many questions ran through my mind that it was like an Amtrak on a runaway course. *How is this possible? Why can't I do that? Is he completely back to normal? Why couldn't he hear me? Can silver really kill you? Can it kill me too? What do you mean the Alpha hasn't taken it to that level? Is this guy completely...*

"Earth to Ruby...," he said, waving a hand in my face and smiling. His smile faded a bit, unearthing a much more serious expression. "I'm fine, I promise. I'll explain it later and answer the questions I can see running through your mind, but we have to go now. This is getting more complicated by the moment."

"About ten minutes maybe...I'm not sure exactly. It all happened so fast," I replied.

"What? Oh! Ten minutes? Are you sure?" he asked seriously. "That can't be right."

"Listen, I didn't bust out a stopwatch and time your death for you. That's my best guess, ten minutes."

He looked at me disbelievingly for a minute, then appeared to blow it off entirely like it was never of consequence.

"Doesn't matter. It's time to go."

Captain Serious was back again. I wanted so badly to know what he was hiding from me that I could barely put one foot in front of the other. I was so frustrated by my lack of info, as well as those who insisted upon withholding said useful information from me. My inner five-year-old wanted to fight fire with fire. The unfortunate part was that I didn't have any information of my own to withhold. I felt like I was always showing up to a gunfight without any ammo. It was beginning to be the story of my life.

We cleaned as much blood as we could off of ourselves, using the other dead guard's shirt and socks. Cooper took the man's pants, trading them for his blood-soaked ones, and I was left with the same tattered shreds of shirt that I had before. We looked disastrous, but I didn't think a shower was factored into our escape plan. I hoped for a stream or something to dunk myself in if we ever made it to the woods.

I begrudgingly followed him through the formerly guarded door. As soon as we stepped through we nearly tripped on a stairway that went straight up for God only knew how long. Funny how I didn't remember any mention of an Alpine climb on our trip. He was a good twelve steps ahead of me when I let go of a huge, melodramatic sigh and started to make my way up the stairway-not-to-heaven.

"Your huffing and puffing won't make this go any more smoothly, dear," he said.

"No, I don't suppose it will, but it gives me such satisfaction, especially if it's annoying you," I retorted. If he wanted to be an information-hoarding pain in my ass, I'd do everything I could to return the favor. Bitterness and grudge-holding were two of my finer qualities.

"So tell me something, Ruby. Why were you so upset by my death?" He was totally baiting me with that question and I knew it, but embarrassment and anger got the better of me and I walked right into his little interrogation. By the tone of his voice, he was already enjoying it.

"I wasn't upset that you died, you arrogant ass. I was freaking out because my ticket out of here checked out, leaving me totally bent over, so to speak," I responded as calmly as I was capable of, which sadly wasn't nearly as impressive as I'd have liked it to be. He laughed. I was really starting to hate that response to my bullshit.

"Ruby, honey, you can go sell that shit somewhere else because I'm not buying it. What was the *real* reason you were so upset?"

I was getting horribly embarrassed at that point. At an early age I learned that excessive emotions were totally inappropriate and that crying was simply unproductive and a complete waste of time. The fact that I had allowed myself the indulgence of a breakdown was gnawing at my pride, but to have someone witness it was far more unforgivable.

My parents never liked me having Nibbles in the first place, but it was one of the few concessions they made in my life. Just before my eighth birthday I begged, pleaded, threatened and blackmailed my parents into buying me an albino rabbit. My parents thought it was a hideous rodent, but I loved her dearly. She was my best friend. She was so soft, and loved to be cuddled; I slept with her in my bed every night, unbeknownst to my parents. She'd sit in my lap while I did my schoolwork. I always felt like she knew I was different, that I needed more attention. We were completely inseparable, much to my parents' chagrin.

Three years later, I woke up one morning to find that Nibbles was not in bed with me. I searched the house on hands and knees, frantically patting everything in my path to find her. When I started hysterically calling for her, my father came to me from the living room. He informed me that they had given her away because my mother was developing an allergy to her. I sat where I was and started to cry so hard I was certain I'd pass out from lack of oxygen. My father yelled at me, trying to get me to stop, but it was impossible. My mother stepped in by giving me a firm, open-handed smack to the face. When she seemed satisfied that she had my hysterics under control, she proceeded to tell me that crying over anything, especially a pet, was stupid and embarrassing. My father chimed in to inform me that he was disappointed in my weakness and never wanted to see it again, that the Dees were not emotionally unstable pansies, and I needed to learn to deal with the harshness of life and move on.

From that day forward I never really cried. Occasionally I teared up, maybe even shed a few, but never really cried.

Not even when I buried my parents.

"Why do you even care?" I screamed. I knew my anger

was inappropriately directed, but that knowledge did nothing to cage the rage inside of me. "You think I care about you? Let me explain something to you so you understand clearly. I've cared about two people in my life and they're dead. What makes you think you're so fucking special?"

I'd said it just to hurt him and I knew it. It wasn't even true—close, but not really. I'd cared for four people in my life, to be exact: two were dead, one betrayed me, and one was going to have to kill me. Relationships 4, Ruby 0.

Cooper stopped and turned to look at me with genuinely wounded eyes. He'd pushed me too far without knowing it, and I'd lashed back so painfully that he felt the full brunt of it. I was instantly ashamed of myself for being so ruthless but was too prideful to apologize. I stared back defiantly, remorselessly.

He finally dropped his head and turned, picking up his pace. I figured he couldn't wait to get away from me.

I couldn't wait to get away from me either.

32

As we neared what appeared to be the end of the unending staircase, I saw another ominous door. I was getting really tired of finding out the hard way what was behind door number two. Cooper stopped before opening it and bent over slowly to whisper in my ear.

"This is the main house. This is where the poo could really start to hit the fan."

Against every shred of will in my body, a smile squeezed out onto my face. *The poo? Who says poo?* He mirrored my response with a grin that even the most devilish of children would have envied. I took this to mean that things were cautiously comfortable between us for the time being, making up for the ten minutes of unaltered silence we had just shared.

With our uneasy bond renewed, I felt much more ready to face what lay behind the massive oak barrier. He explained briefly the immediate layout of the room we'd enter. Absorbing great verbal detail had never been my forte, and doing so under duress rendered me basically useless. I nodded when appropriate and crossed my fingers for luck. The main thing I'd gotten from his instruction was which way *not* to run in case of emergency. That one stuck out soundly and I was determined not to screw that up if need be.

The plan was to get inside undetected, sneak through the major common areas undetected, and then out the main back door undetected. It was a lot of *undetecteds* for my liking. It was like standing on a brightly lit stage in the middle of Times Square hoping to go unnoticed—not promising by any means. We had no disguise for me, so anyone who saw me would know who I was in a flash and would alert the entire pack, which at Cooper's best guess tallied five hundred or more. I was never a gambler, but I knew shitty odds when I saw them.

Without time to ponder our imminent demise further, he opened the door and peeked around the corner.

"Ah...feeding time. Good thing for us the kitchen isn't on the tour," he said soberly. *Feeding time. What in the hell is that?*

"So...it's lunch time?" I asked, trying to get a feel for what time of day it was.

"Nope. Smells like midnight snack to me."

"What exactly is midnight snack?" I queried, not sure that I wanted to know the answer. He looked around, not acknowledging my question at all. I was once again pissed off with his lack of compliance and info hoarding, until I heard it too.

Footsteps.

My inner "oh shit" alarm was screaming and my sympathetic nervous system was starting to have its way with me. Coop looked worried too, and was calmly trying to figure a way out of our impending doom. There was a door to what appeared to be a TV den of some sort open in front of us. He dragged me in there so fast, I wasn't sure all of me made the transition. In hindsight, making it into the room was the easy part. Where to hide was the complication. Closets were not an option because we'd be sniffed out for sure. The rest of the room was vast, open space, with couches and chairs all turned to face the enormous projection screen hanging from the near wall. I thought that maybe if we crouched down behind a sofa and were super quiet, they would just continue on past our room, no big deal.

My panic increased with the proximity of the footsteps, and I knew my fear was only making things worse. Cooper was kind enough to point that fact out to me. Just when I thought our collective goose was cooked, Cooper made his move. He didn't bother to take the time to fill me in on what he was doing; he just grabbed me. He seemed to think ad-libbing was the way to go in that situation.

Before I knew it, I was on my back lying across the couch that sat roughly in the center of the room. My first reaction was that hiding in plain sight probably wasn't such a stellar plan with a house full of werewolves. Then I saw the blanket come flying over the back of the sofa to cover us. It didn't seem to be much of an improvement, but it was a camouflage of sorts, so I went with it. At that point I was willing to take whatever cover I could get, or so I thought initially. When Cooper started climbing on top of me with the blanket draped over him, I rethought that idea.

I didn't dare speak because the potential whistle blower was almost upon us, but I sure as hell wanted to know what his plan was. If he was hoping to go out with a bang, literally, he had another think coming.

When he finished draping the blanket so it covered everything but our feet and ankles, he whispered oh-so-quietly in my ear.

"Just play along. It's our best chance," he said, as I lay perfectly still below him. "And make it believable." Though I was uncomfortable with losing that much control, I didn't see any other way. I nodded hesitantly.

I'd no sooner rested my head back down before his lips were all over mine. And they were busy. When I realized what the rest of him was doing, or at least pretending to do, things started to sort of click into place. If only we'd had a "do not disturb" sign. I was furious and horribly uncomfortable, but even in my hostile state, I had to admit that it was the best idea he could have come up with.

While we moved awkwardly under the blanket, low moaning sounds rumbled through his throat and brought attention to the fact that I wasn't playing along very well. The irony was that I didn't know *how* to play along well. The only people I'd been with had not exactly been invited. Thank God for trashy TV and movies on demand. I wiggled around a bit and tried to channel my inner Angelina Jolie. If she wasn't a role model for sexy, I didn't know who was.

In my concerted effort to do the right things and make the right sounds, I'd become oblivious to the fact that there was someone breathing heavily in the doorway. I fought my urge to freeze. Cooper pulled me closer to him, pressing his body against mine so tightly that breathing became laborious. Lack of oxygen, however, was not enough to distract me from exactly *what* was pressing against me.

"Well, well, well, what have we here?" the stranger asked mockingly, like he really needed the obvious pointed out to him.

"Fuck off, Jeran!" Cooper shouted.

"Cooper? Are you trying to keep a snack from the rest of us?" he asked. I could hear the finger-wagging in his tone.

"You know how the Alpha feels about playing with our food."

Cooper's heart was racing, and I was crazy to think that it was because of what was going on under the blanket. He stuck his head out, being careful to keep me covered.

"This one is *not* for sharing."

"Ooooooh, you found yourself a keeper, did you? Lemme see it."

I heard him approaching and my skin started to itch all over. Cooper growled a warning like a cornered dog.

"She is here neither for your approval, nor your entertainment. Get out before I get tired of this shit," Cooper warned in a tone that made me think he was possessed by someone of extreme and ultimate power. I was awestruck.

There were a couple of tense minutes where I wasn't sure how the standoff was going to end.

There was no further conversation. Cooper's anxiety was palpable to me, and my empathic powers were nearly overwhelmed. I couldn't feel Jeran's because I was totally occupied by Cooper's. My assumption was that they were sizing each other up; Cooper to intimidate Jeran, and Jeran to see if it was worth his while to fight Cooper to get to me. If only he knew. Had he known it was me under the blanket, I was certain that would have clouded his judgment.

I felt the floor vibrate as he took one more step closer. Cooper snarled and his body coiled, preparing to fight.

"All right, all right. Fuck, where did your sense of humor go? You're becoming a real prick, you know that?" he said with distaste. Cooper gave no response.

The silence was broken by the sound of Jeran's retreat into the hallway. We waited motionless for a couple of minutes to be very certain he was gone. Cooper turned to look down into my eyes, making me painfully aware that he was still mounting me. I shoved him aside and sprang from the couch.

"Get me out of here, now," I whispered angrily, contorting my face into all sorts of emphatic angles. He smiled on cue, as I knew only he could.

"My pleasure, miss."

33

The rest of our journey through the house was completely uneventful. Really. We didn't run into anything that elicited so much as a suction of breath. Of course I kept waiting for the other shoe to drop because if things kept up with the modus operandi du jour, something deadly *had* to be waiting around the next corner. With a chainsaw. And some dynamite. In a grenade launcher, fully equipped with a heat-seeking feature. And my name on it.

Things went so well that Cooper and I were even able to procure some new clothing as we sneaked through the laundry room and out the back door. We didn't have time to be picky, so we snatched what was on top of the pile and did a quick size check. There were no pants in the basket, so I wound up with a cleaner version of what I already had on, white and all. Cooper scored a graphic t-shirt from Ed Hardy that fit like it was painted on him, and I wasn't complaining. Staring at him without a shirt on was becoming a challenge, even in life-threatening situations. He was eye candy for sure.

Once outside, my attention snapped back to the fact that we had a long way to go before we were home free. He'd said we had twelve miles before we reached the clearing, and that our getaway car was just beyond that. My feet were going to be in horrible shape by the end of the journey, but anything was better than the alternative, and I chose to focus on that. We made a quick dash across the short span of open backyard and broke through the tree line.

As we ran in single file, Cooper continually flashed hand signals at me. I was sure they were a desperate attempt to communicate things of great importance, but I wasn't sure exactly what. I couldn't tell if he was attempting to warn me, direct me, or tell me I should swing at the next fastball. His random flailing did nothing to help me know what was going on. In my growing frustration I poured on some speed to put me at his side while we hurtled through the unbroken underbrush.

"I'm sure that your gestures are supposed to have some deep and purposeful meaning, but I'm at a complete loss. Care to share?" I asked between gasps of breath.

"Keep your voice down. The Watchers are everywhere. Try to let us get some ground between the pack and us before you come up on their radar," he whispered just loudly enough for me to hear.

"Sorry," I replied, trying to keep my voice low. "What do you want?"

"I was *trying* to tell you to keep pace with me and fan out to the right a bit, but it's apparent that you didn't grow up in a military family."

"Not exactly," I said, stifling an inappropriate laugh. "They had some militant qualities, does that count?" His bitter laugh made me think that it did not.

"No, it doesn't."

I wasn't anxious to keep up that line of conversation, so I tried to refocus on the task at hand.

"So how long will this take?"

"We're running about a six-minute mile. Do the math."

Um, seventy-two? It was hard to do math in my head while dodging branches in the dark.

"So it's a bit over an hour to freedom. What's the plan when we get to the car?"

He audibly sighed, sounding a heavy combination of exhausted and frustrated.

"I have no idea. I was hoping maybe you'd have an idea. Is it safe to go back to your place?"

It was my turn to smile inappropriately, if only to myself. He couldn't be serious. With Marcus and Eric sure to find out that their little sale went a bit south, and Sean likely to return with my death warrant in hand from the PC powers-that-be any time, I thought my place was a close second in the you'll-be-sure-to-meet-your-maker contest. The situation we were in, of course, came in first.

"No, it's not," I responded, thinking that simplicity seemed the way to go, and besides, maybe I needed to hoard a little info myself. He didn't need to know everything that I was running from. I didn't ask for his life story.

After that brief dialog, neither of us said anything for an eternity. We ran in silence, with only the sound of the branches and leaves crunching under our feet. There was no sign of any Watcher, but from what I understood, that meant precious little to our safety.

"So what is a Watcher exactly?" I asked, unable to stand my forced silence any longer. Without skipping a beat, he shot back an answer I found impossible to swallow, which was ironic given that I was running from a pack of morally reprehensible werewolves who wanted to make me their secret weapon. That, however, was clearly digestible.

"They're the ghosts of the woods. The eyes of the forest. They're..." he responded, but I interrupted him with a bout of hysterical laughter. "No laughing matter," he said, finishing his thought. I could hear the annoyance in his voice, but I couldn't help it. The church giggles were in full effect and there was no stopping them. The more serious his tone, the more intense my laughter became.

"Sweet Jesus, how did I get stuck with you? Is this penance for past wrongs?" he asked rhetorically. I snorted a few times as I tried to pull it together.

"I'm sorry, it's just a little tough to swallow. There are ghosts patrolling the woods for your Alpha? Did you get drunk one night and somebody fed you that shit? They must have nearly peed their pants watching your face as you soaked it up."

"Believe it or not. It's of little consequence to me. You don't have to believe in the Boogeyman for him to be real."

My stress level was oddly lessened. I felt for once that something hanging over my head was removed and I could breathe a little easier, except for the running of course.

"Okay, so we're just going to have to agree to disagree on your woodland specter theory for now. I'll keep my voice down though, just to be sure I don't send your blood pressure through the roof."

"Such a big concession from such a small mind." He was by far the biggest button-pusher I'd ever met. Luckily for me, I was so elated by the lack of threat in the woods that I just wasn't going to let him get to me. I let the comment hang in the air a bit before changing the tone of the conversation. I thought I'd go on a fishing expedition and try to extract a little background info on this character that I'd been so dubiously bound to.

"So your parents were in the military?"

"My father was a scout sniper in the Marines. He believed in three things: order, obedience, and omission."

"Omission?"

"He was a big fan of only telling what needed to be told. I'm quite certain I never heard an entire story from him in my whole life," he recounted in a distant and disappointed voice. "Of course, I never knew this growing up. I thought he was the epitome of what a father should be: role model, provider, disciplinarian, coach, and, on rare occasions, a buddy. What I didn't know, what none of us knew, was that he was such a great family man that he decided to have two of them. I found him out when I was nineteen. I went to visit a friend two towns over and we ran into him and his *other* family leaving the movie theater as we were going in. It took me two weeks to break the news to my mother. I think I was secretly hoping that he would man up and tell her himself, but the arrogant bastard figured I'd never have the balls to tell her. It's probably the only time in his life that he underestimated his enemy."

I paused before speaking, trying to choose my words very carefully. I was stunned by the historical bomb he'd just dropped and wanted to be sensitive with my further inquisitions.

"Your poor mother. How badly did she take it?"

"She didn't take it at all," he said, sounding dejected. "She refused to believe what I told her. She told me that she didn't harbor liars in her house, then kicked me out." My heart instantly dropped.

"Betrayal is something that cuts you in places that

cannot be healed," I said, knowing that fact all too well. "But to be cut there by your own mother..."

"I appreciate your sentiments, but it's done. I don't think about it much," he stated in an attempt to console me. I was not the one in need of consoling.

"Not thinking about it much is not proof of healing, nor is the ability to speak about your painful event indifferently. The absence of one or presence of the other proves nothing."

"Thanks for that, Dr. Drew. Your insight is both useless and unappreciated, as usual," he retorted, with what I perceived was real anger. Anger with the bite of unresolved daddy issues. Those could really leave a mark.

"You don't have to be totally douchetastic about it. I was just making a point."

"As am I. Drop it," he stated with true finality in his voice. The man who had saved our asses back in the den of the compound was back, and I got the feeling I didn't really want to poke that bear with a short stick.

"It's dropped, but do me a favor? If you have nasty scars, don't flash them around and then get pissed off when people stare at them."

"Duly noted. A mistake I won't repeat again," he snarled.

Note to self: daddy is off limits.

34

To distract myself from my traveling companion's mood, I shifted my attention to the woods surrounding me. I hadn't noticed much about my "haunted" surroundings while running for my life, but there was a beauty there that couldn't be denied once I bothered to notice it. It was a forest, so all of the usual suspects were there: trees, underbrush, scrubby looking bushes, fallen branches and leaves, but there was something glorious about the way the stars and moon cast light onto the trees. They appeared to be covered in the thinnest layer of melting ice, a sheen of silver just grazing the surface. I was fascinated by it, having never seen anything like it before. I tried to look up at the canopy above to take in as much as I could while staying upright and keeping pace. I was rewarded with stars that were bigger and brighter than anything I had seen in New Hampshire. They had far more celestial magic in Utah.

While appreciating said celestial magic, I inelegantly caught my foot on a downed tree and took a digger into a random collection of rocks. Cooper, being the saint he was, came over to help me up and force me along. When I looked at his face, it reminded me of one of the first paintings I'd ever seen. It was by an unknown artist from a century ago, and the image he painted was the face of God. What had always struck me about it was the play of light—half of his face was highlighted incandescently while the other lay hidden in darkness and shadow. It must have been a metaphor for something, but art had never been my thing. They didn't make a Braille version of it.

I stared open-mouthed at him for a moment, his beauty remarkable. The light danced across his exposed features flaunting perfect curves and angles. The painting's metaphor may not have been clear, but this one was. The surface was angelic and pure, but there was a darker, hidden side. One that, if I were smart, I would not go exploring. Not without suffering the consequences.

"Are dancers always this clumsy, or are you just gifted?"

I scowled quickly.

"We're all grace on a stage or in a studio, but follow us through the day-to-day and we're hot messes," I responded truthfully.

"I'm not sure what that is exactly, but I'll assume I don't want to be one," he said, grunting for effect while he heaved me up onto my feet.

"That's safe to say."

"If you're quite done living up to your reputation, I'd like to get this last mile over with. I haven't heard the approach of anyone yet. I'd like to try to keep it that way."

I smiled at him because I couldn't help it. We had but one mile before freedom was ours. I suppressed the laughter that was rolling inside only because, once unleashed, I wasn't sure I could regain control. I took off at a total sprint, juiced up on adrenaline and anticipation of our completed escape. Cooper was quickly at my side, and together we tore through the remainder of woods like our pants were on fire, hurdling fallen branches and dodging trees, all while maintaining a cat burglar's stealth.

We encountered a small brook as our final destination approached, and he suggested taking a second to clean up so we wouldn't look quite as ghastly driving cross-country covered in filth and blood. He stripped off his shirt and dunked his entire upper body in the water, wiping off what he could by hand. I wasn't excited by the thought of getting naked in front of him again, but I really needed to wash a little more thoroughly than he did, so off my shirt came. I sat down, chest deep in the cool running water, scrubbing my skin violently with leaves. I dunked my head a few times, thinking my hair would not likely improve much with the effort. When I couldn't take the temperature any longer, I got out and tried to whisk the droplets from my skin with my hands.

Cooper was dressed and ready to go, his back to me, scanning the forest for dangers. Once my shirt was on, I made my way over to him and we resumed our journey. I knew we had only minutes to go before freedom was ours.

I could see the brightness slowly widening, growing larger before us as we ran. *The clearing.* Seconds later we broke through the last of prickly underbrush to land soundly on the edge of a vast open field. It was different than I had pictured it. I had thought it would be some overgrown field with waist-high grass that spanned a square mile or so. I wasn't expecting a space that was approximately the size of two football fields. I also didn't expect it to be about as manicured as one either. It looked man-made and well maintained, though for what purpose I couldn't imagine. Cooper had said we were miles from town and that nobody lived out here.

Does the compound use this for something?

Cooper rattled me out of my postulation by grabbing my hand and nearly dragging me across the field. We were halfway across when I regained my appendage. I shot him a look of complete and utter belligerence. When I opened my mouth to ask what this "clearing" really was, no sound came out. That was because I had been abruptly stopped by an outstretched arm to my abdomen.

While doubled over in pain, I tried to see why Cooper had stopped, and furthermore, why he'd stopped me. Stopping wasn't part of the plan. All I could see were his bare feet covered in healing cuts and dried blood, and his torn pant legs. He was facing in the direction we were headed, and he was utterly still. My stomach hurt too much to stand up straight, but I had just enough wind in me to interrogate.

"What are you..."

"Shhhh," he whispered.

"Doing?" I asked.

"Don't. Move," he ordered, telling me to follow his example.

My heart instantly relocated to my stomach. We had made it too far to be brought down in our final stretch. I slowly raised my head with a sick need to see what fate had in store for us.

Throughout my lifetime, I had often pondered my death, as I assumed many people did. I would think of all the equally pleasant and horrible ways to go: dying quietly in my sleep, surrounded by those that loved me, or conversely burning in a house fire, or drowning in a car I couldn't escape that had plunged off of a bridge. After staring my fate in the eyes, I moved the latter two options to the "pleasant" list by comparison. I didn't know what I'd done to piss fate off, but I made a mental note to send flowers. We had to get on better terms.

Cooper and I remained frozen. Neither of us moved, nor spoke, nor had a fucking clue how to get out of our predicament, probably because there wasn't going to be a way out. Not unless death was considered an option, in which case we were definitely getting out. I felt like a deer in headlights, frozen, frightened, and without viable options. I looked up at Cooper and then back into those eyes that seemed to be moving closer to us. I was mesmerized by death. I nearly jumped out of my skin when he spoke.

"*Ruby.*"

It's never a good thing when death knows you by name.

35

Cooper grabbed my wrist and squeezed to get my attention.

He knows who you are, Ruby," he whispered without moving his mouth.

No shit.

I hadn't a clue what to do or say. I was mute. I desperately scrounged for a way to negotiate a way out of this one, but deep down I knew I was done for. My mouth continually opened and closed unproductively, like a fish out of water gasping for air, trying to physically project words out. I stared into his deep, green eyes and was paralyzed, internally begging for someone to save me from my verbal breakdown.

He gave me a good look-over from head to toe, then obliged.

"Are you hurt?" Sean asked, feigning concern.

Why? Will it ruin the pleasure for you if I'm already wounded?

"I'm fine," I whispered. "It's only surface scratches. They bleed more than you'd expect."

He looked completely unsatisfied by my answer and I had no idea why. I wondered if not being at the top of my game was taking the sport out of it for him, leaving him greatly displeased. I was pretty certain that angering him further was a bad idea.

"I came back for you," he said.

Funny, I've been running from you.

His words chilled me to the bone. Any remote possibility of this being a social call or rescue attempt was thrown out the window in an instant. He really had betrayed me. The only person who seemed to understand me. The only person besides my parents who I'd really cared for, even if he didn't know it.

Despair took over, quickly sucking away the last bit of will to live that I had. My body slumped, shoulders rounding as my head rejected his gaze to look at the ground at his feet.

"Where are you going?" he asked patiently.

I didn't answer. Cooper tried.

"We were trying to escape..."

"Ruby," he snarled, snapping my attention back to his face in a hurry. I assumed that was the response he was looking for. "Where. Are. You. Going?" he asked, pointedly over-enunciating each word as though English was a foreign language to me.

I looked up at Cooper, who stood fidgeting slightly beside me, then sighed.

"We were escaping the compound. Cooper has a car waiting for us up ahead."

"Ah, yes. The Jeep Wrangler, I assume. Excellent choice for the off-roading portion of your journey," he said, still staring us down from a few feet away. "I'm still left wondering exactly where that journey would be to. You wouldn't be evading my question, would you?"

"We don't know," I answered softly. "Somewhere far away from here though."

"No plans to return home?" he asked with an upward inflection in his voice. "I wondered where you had gone. I stopped by to pay you a visit when I got back. I was worried when I found your business abandoned and your residence trashed. You really should have somebody attend to your mail if you're going out of town, you know," he said, carefully masking his expression as one of casual indifference. I knew better than to buy that. I was getting frustrated with our petty banter and wanted to get the whole thing over with.

But I wanted answers first.

"How did you find me?" I asked while I puffed myself up with some bravado, not all of which was false.

"I have something for you," he said in his annoyingly complacent voice.

"ANSWER ME!" I shouted, lunging towards him while Cooper not-so-delicately restrained me. I was enraged by the entire situation. The fact that he was shamelessly toying with me was more shit than I would suffer.

He slowly reached into the front pocket of his pants and produced a closed fist to me. He uncurled his fingers to show me my ring, just as he'd done before in my store months ago.

How quickly things changed.

His expression softened as he extended his hand and the ring towards me further, silently coaxing me to take it. I couldn't do it. Eric had taken my ring from me when he sold me to the Alpha. He'd told me that I'd no longer be needing it. Sean had clearly been to pay him a visit, but why? Did he know why I was here? Did he kill Eric to get the info he wanted?

The implications were not good. He obviously went to great lengths to track me down and wasn't afraid to take a few bodies down in the process. I had to admit that part of me was glad to know that Eric was dead. That fucker deserved it in an epic way. However, knowing that information only further cemented my not-so-distant future. Sean would kill me.

Cooper moved quickly beside me, turning towards the haunted woods. I searched his face for a sign of what was going on, but I didn't dare take my eyes off of Sean for more than a moment. I could sense Coop's increasing anxiety. It was different than it had been originally when he saw Sean. It was less alarm, but equal concern. I could only assume one thing—the pack had found us.

"It's over, Ruby. There's no way out of this now," Cooper reported to me with dejection and resignation in his tone. I wondered what had taken him so long to get there.

Sean was getting impatient with me. He inched forward with his arm outstretched, still offering my ring. It was in that moment that I realized Cooper was wrong. He was so wrong. There was a way out. Its outcome may have ultimately been the same, but I wouldn't be a victim, nor would I wait for death on someone else's terms.

With my newfound realization releasing the tension from my body, creating an eerie calm, I turned and winked at Cooper. He looked distraught, as though he had an inkling of what I was about to do. I then shifted my full gaze to Sean and smiled.

He gave me a confused smile in return.

I didn't know for certain, but I was pretty sure that smile faded quickly when I turned and ran full-speed towards the pack, which was spilling out into the clearing. Their "weapon" was about to take as many of them down as she could, and it was the most comforting thought I'd had in years.

With that, the calm enveloped me, and I Changed.

36

I heard the shouting as I ran, but it came across like voices do when you're underwater—you know what they are but have no idea what they're saying. That's when I realized that I was fully aware and cognizant of what was going on around me while in wolf form. Pleased with my apparent gain in control, I smiled a very strange and unfamiliar smile as I bulldozed into the pack.

It was an odd feeling to be inside a body you weren't at all familiar with, like trying someone else on for size. Literally. Though I felt perfectly coordinated, something about my movement was awkward. My senses were heightened, yet foreign. It reminded me of when I first gained my vision. I decided to not think, but just act, and take a back seat to my instincts.

I ran like a bull charging the red cape, the cape being the Alpha that I had a bone to pick with. *That arrogant son of a bitch is gonna bleed.* I took out anything that moved around me. Pack members were desperate to get in between us, to save their master. *Cannon fodder.* I don't even remember breaking stride while tearing them limb from limb. It was like chewing gum and walking; it couldn't have been simpler. I saw no faces, knew no names, and had no remorse. I was nothing like the human me; somebody else was at the helm.

My fur felt matted and heavy, congealing with blood and other unmentionables, and still I broke through the pack like a shark through a school of fish, only they weren't scattering intentionally. I took the liberty of doing that for them.

I could discern screaming, even as a wolf. It was crystal clear and drove my bloodlust further. It thrilled me when it should have horrified. There were cries of sheer terror, then pain. Most were very short-lived.

There was also distinct howling. I was aware that some of my victims were fighting as wolves, the ones who lived long enough to Change. It seemed to have little effect, though. Nothing could stop me or my reign of terror, and I was starting to think that my plan wasn't such a kamikaze move after all. I enjoyed every moment.

My vision was tunneled in an inhuman way. All I could see was the target ahead of me, and I was homing in on it. I heard the shouting again, getting nearer. The clarity improved with the closing distance, but it was still unintelligible. The voice, however, was familiar. It got louder and louder as I neared the Alpha. His followers seemed to have abandoned him to his fate.

Smart little doggies.

I pinned him back against a rocky outcropping at the edge of the forest. His face burned with rage and his body coiled with the will to fight, but he knew there was no point, and I could smell it. Defeat stung my nostrils, a glorious odor when it came from someone else. I growled and stalked towards him, drawing it out as long as I could will myself to, wanting him to suffer as I had suffered.

The voice was upon me again. He said something into my ear, and I turned to see a man reaching a hand toward me. With cat-like reflexes he lunged, and I saw the flash of light reflect off of the object in his hand. I didn't have time to react.

Everything went dark.

37

I slowly awoke to a light and low thrumming sound. My eyelids felt impossibly heavy and my throat was perilously dry, with a strange metallic taste in my mouth. My body was slightly reclined with something restraining me, holding me to the seat I was in. A strong pine scent permeated the air with a hint of something I recognized. *Cooper.* I tried to call his name, but instead an incoherent grumble came out. I tried to sit up but I felt so heavy, weighed down by something I could neither see nor feel.

I struggled again with my eyelids, trying to will them open to take in my surroundings. Just as they started to make some progress, a cool hand rested across them, accompanied by a light hushing sound.

"Rest, Ruby. I need you to rest," he whispered so faintly, like he was speaking to an infant. His sensitivity was reassuring at first, but quickly became disconcerting. I didn't know why he sounded so concerned. Why did I need rest so badly? I fought against my restraint with eyes closed, furiously tugging and thrashing around.

It took about a minute before I realized that this was familiar; I knew the shape and texture of the strap holding me down. I fumbled with my left hand by my waist until I found what I was looking for: the release mechanism. I was in a car. It clicked open and I inelegantly sat up.

"Water" I rasped. "I need some water." A plastic bottle was placed firmly in my hands and I drank the entire thing. "More."

I heard the crackle of plastic then the snapping sound of a twist-off cap. Again a bottle was placed in my hands, though I drank only part of it. I had plans for the rest. In my more alert state, I realized that my eyes were actually caked shut with something, making it difficult for them to open. I poured water into my left hand and cupped it to my lids in an attempt to flush it out. I repeated it over and over again on both sides. Finally the crust let go, and I was able to carefully but painfully open my eyes. The dash lights flooded in and my retinas burned. I snapped them shut immediately. It was as if they'd never been exposed to light before, as though my rods and cones had no idea how to process such a stress. It took a few minutes of gradually peeking them open and closed to make it tolerable to expose them to the dim lighting of the car.

I did a quick survey of the interior. I was engulfed by a sea of tan: all plastic, no frills, with heavily tinted windows. There was a CD player that lay dormant in the dash, and a narrow backseat. There was also a very conflicted driver staring at me with a look of both relief and concern. He was assessing something, seeking something from me.

"What?" I squeaked. My voice was coming back, but it wasn't a pretty process.

"I'm checking to make sure you're okay. I've been really worried. What the fuck was that stunt you pulled back there?" he asked, trying to stare at me and watch the road simultaneously.

The decibel level was increasing with his soliloquy. He really had been freaked out by something.

"I decided that if I was going down, I would kill those who hurt me in the process. It seemed the most rational and effective plan."

Ever the pragmatist.

I very conveniently left out the part about not being able to stand the thought of Sean betraying me, and that my death would be at his hands. That thought reminded me of something.

"How did I get out of there alive? Wait, scratch that. First, how long have I been out?" I asked, trying to wiggle myself into a more comfortable position. My body ached and I was glad the light wasn't brighter to show me why.

"You haven't woken up for twenty-four hours, Ruby. I was starting to worry. He said it shouldn't take more than twelve."

"Are you shitting me? Why? Why couldn't I wake up? What the hell is going on here?" I tried to shout, with gravel in my voice. "You said it only took a couple of minutes for me to come out of it when I Changed!"

I was getting concerned too.

"Sean said that you should...," Cooper started.

"*Sean* said? What do you mean Sean said?" I yelled, grabbing his arm to get his attention back on me.

He sighed.

"Sean said that bringing you out of it would alter your normal recovery time. He tried to factor in some healing time too. You took a few bad hits, Rubes," he said, getting that concerned, furrowed brow again. I was normally pretty quick on the uptake, but at that moment, I was seriously lost. I was trying to keep track of all the things I needed clarification on and in what order I wanted them.

Why is there never pen and paper when you need it?

"Wait, wait...waaaait. You're telling me that you and Sean had a little tête-à-tête while I was...well, whatever I was doing?" I asked with a great deal of disbelief shining through.

He sighed again.

"Let me start from the beginning, or, well, more like the end for you, at least as far as your cognition goes."

"Fine, but I'm interrupting at will," I informed him, letting go of his sleeve. "There's a lot of stuff not making a whole lot of sense to me right now, and it had better start to *soon*," I threatened.

"Fine," he returned. "But don't think you're getting off scot-free here, missy. You've got some 'splainin to do," he said with the faintest of a smile curling the corner of his mouth.

"Fine. Start," I demanded.

He took a long, dramatic pause before he started in.

"When you turned and winked at me, I saw two things that frightened me: hopelessness and acceptance. There was a little crazy sprinkled in there too. I knew what you were about to do, but had no way to stop you. Sean could have, but he didn't seem to realize what you were up to. Quite frankly, he looked downright dumbfounded when you busted out a sprint in the opposite direction."

A smile of satisfaction slowly spread over his face as he said his last statement.

"You were halfway through the pack, amassing a body count when we figured out a plan. The rest of the PC joined us from the woods and decided they were going to distribute some justice of their own to take some of the burden off of you. I was to join them. Sean was to deal with you."

"What do you mean exactly when you say 'deal with'?" I asked.

"I had to clarify that myself before I'd let him go. I wasn't sure why he was there in the first place and I wasn't just going to hand you over to him on a platter. He swore on the brotherhood that he would not harm you in his effort to get you to stop. I believed him."

"You believed a man whose sole purpose in life is to eradicate those like me? Wow, little lack of judgment there, don't you think? Were you running low on blood sugar?" I asked, laying on the sarcasm.

He pressed his lips together firmly, making them turn white around the edges.

"You're alive, aren't you? My judgment can't possibly be that poor," he snipped.

"About that, how did we manage that?"

"We? *We* didn't do anything. Sean and I saved your ass. You may be the most lethal thing I've ever seen on four legs, Rubes, but I've got a little news flash for you...you're not invincible. I've seen less damage in a ten car pile-up!" he recounted very snidely.

"I couldn't have been that hurt. I don't heal like you do in human form. I'd be dead!"

"Ah, again why you have Sean and me to thank. I don't know exactly what he did, but he must've worked some voodoo on you after he turned you back because your flesh started reknitting as I ran you out of there in my arms."

It was a lot to take in at once—the proverbial mind-fuck.

"Why didn't Sean just kill me and get it over with? Why go to all the trouble of finding me only to let me go with you? Is there supposed to be some ceremony to killing the RB?"

He scoffed, which quickly became laughter. It was good to know that I could amuse him with so little effort.

"God, you're thick. You still don't get it, do you? You really don't know why he was there?"

"No, Coop, my list of ideas is pretty short. Care to share what you've got on yours?" He just hung his head and shook it slowly back and forth in an act of pure frustration. When he raised it up, his neutral expression had returned.

"The Alpha is dead," he told me, risking a look across the center console.

"How?" I asked, forgetting the importance of my previous question.

"Let's just say that his justice was neither swift, nor painless."

"Were you there?" I asked.

"Yes."

My voice lowered and softened with every question asked.

"Did you do it?"

"Yes."

"Why?"

His brow furrowed again, and I realized that, in the short time I'd known him, he seemed to do that frequently.

"Some things are better left alone, Rubes. Just know that I had my reasons," he said.

Even I knew to take that cue. He was on terra firma as far as that was concerned. The truth was that his manner of death wasn't really important to me, just the outcome.

A long silence stretched out slowly, seemingly with no end in sight. I craved conversation, anything human at that moment, and went for a change of subject entirely.

"Where are the PC now?" I asked conversationally.

"They're doing what they do best, cleaning up the mess."

"Do you mean that figuratively or literally?" I asked, knowing that the answer was likely both. He turned his head and answered with a half-smile that said "silly girl, you don't need me to answer that for you." *Point taken.*

"So what do we do now?"

"We go home," he said matter-of-factly.

Hmm. Unless he knew something that I didn't, he didn't have a home because we just annihilated it, and mine was about as safe to go to as a minefield.

"And where would that be?" I asked.

"If you don't remember where you live, dear, I think this trip is about to get more complicated than I expected," he said with a laugh. "It figures. Why do women always have to complicate things?" Cooper asked, finally regaining some much-needed focus on the road ahead.

Well that was a weighted statement if I've ever heard one.

I smiled my saccharin-sweet smile his way to show my vast appreciation for his last statement. He laughed harder. At least I wasn't predictable.

"That's my girl."

"So how much farther do we have to go?" I asked, still not knowing where we were.

"About ten more hours, but we're going to stop and eat first, and get you cleaned up and into some fresh clothes. I love ya girlie, but you're really starting to funk up the car. The pine tree can only do so much," he kidded.

Touché.

Logic like that couldn't be argued with.

38

We made a quick stop in Erie, Pennsylvania to pee, eat, and procure some new threads, or, in my case, any threads. I'd once again been given Coop's shirt to cover myself up with. A sudden flash of me being carried by Cooper across the clearing wearing only my birthday suit made me turn scarlet. I was beginning to think he'd seen me naked more than dressed. Somehow, I didn't think he minded.

He'd purchased some baby wipes in the convenience store and I scrubbed myself up as best I could before making a mad dash to the bathroom around the back. I scrubbed out my hair and put on the clothes, hoping that nobody saw my state and called the cops. I looked like an extra in a horror film.

Having not run into any problems, we continued on our way. We managed to make it all the way to Worcester, Massachusetts with only idle chat or silence, and random sing-alongs to Neil Diamond's Greatest Hits, which neither of us would ever have admitted to if confronted. Our similarities in childhood torture were never-ending.

With only two hours left in the car together, I wanted to get a few basics ironed out before we arrived.

"So where do you plan on staying?" I asked casually, as if not invested in the answer at all. That couldn't have been further from the truth.

"With you, roomie," he replied in a sing-song voice. "Where else could I stay? Besides, I'm under strict orders." His carefree demeanor sobered with his last statement. Judging by the immediate grimace on his face, he wasn't supposed to let that last part slip. It sounded like he was ordered to hold me under some kind of house arrest. I assumed that applied only until Sean showed up. There wouldn't be any need for it after that.

"Excellent! A chaperone in my own home. Christmas really can come twice in one year," I said with sarcasm dripping from every word. "I must have been extra good." My witty comeback was met with a faint shaking of his head, his face dressed with a frown.

"No comment," was his weak response.

"No, seriously. What if I don't want you living with me?"

"It appears that you have no choice," he replied.

Fuck that!

"I don't have a choice? Are you shitting me right now? Do you really want to take it there, Coop? I've got choices coming out of unmentionable orifices at a rate that rivals the speed of sound."

"Such as...?" he inquired condescendingly.

"Stay or leave? Surrender or fight? Live or die? You know, the really simple things in life to answer."

"None of those are choices you have to make, Rubes. You're *choosing* to make them and your reasoning is ill-advised. You still know nothing about what you speak of."

"I'm about five seconds away from putting your head

through the window if you don't start spilling the shit you know and stop speaking in riddles, Dr. Seuss."

"But I'm not supposed to say anything..."

"SPILL IT NOW!" I screamed, punching the dash for effect.

He got my point loud and clear, and sang like a songbird. His sudden compliance wasn't really all that surprising given that he had recently seen me take out virtually an entire pack single-handedly. I wouldn't want that coming down on me either.

"Do you want the full thing or just the nuts and bolts of it?" he asked, sighing heavily.

"I want the whole kit and kaboodle."

"Sean finished up doing whatever it was he was doing to you about the same time as I was, well, wrapping things up with the Alpha," he explained. "And before you ask, *no*, I don't know what he was doing to you, and no, he didn't feel it necessary to tell me after the fact."

He was right to clarify that last point. I was about to interrupt him when he did.

"The PC had the few survivors occupied at the time, and Sean gestured me over to him. I wasn't entirely sure if doing what he asked was a good idea since he and his brothers were in the process of taking out my whole clan, but I complied."

"So you *can* follow directions. Duly noted," I said dryly. He didn't bother with a retort.

"Anyway, he gave me explicit orders that I was to follow to the letter as my continued respiration depended on it. I was to do three things, well, four things really: be sure you had your ring, drive you to Portsmouth without stopping for anything more than gas and food, and wait for him there when we arrived."

"That's only three. What was the fourth?" I asked, confused.

He swallowed audibly.

"Keep you alive."

And there went my stomach again, launching directly into my airway, which technically wasn't anatomically feasible, yet continued to occur.

"Did he say why?"

"Oh yes, Ruby, he explained himself at length. He was extremely compliant and forthcoming. He gave me his life story while he was at it, if you're interested in a recap of that as well."

"Fine. Did he say anything else?" I asked.

"Yes, but it wasn't said for or about you," he said, gripping the wheel tighter.

"Soooo? What was it?" I prodded.

He pursed his lips so tightly that they disappeared from his profile entirely.

"You could say that he made it very clear that you were his and that he wasn't especially fond or trusting of me."

"*Why* would he say that? Do you two have history or something?" I asked, searching his face for an answer.

"Not exactly, Rubes, but he's legendary. All weres know and fear him; his presence is never a good sign. He keeps the line between the mortal world and the not-so-mortal world intact, and if he pays you a visit, it's because you've done something to endanger that and will be disposed of accordingly. All the brothers do this. I've never heard of so many of them being in one place at the same time. It's totally unprecedented! Talk about the shit hitting the fan."

My chest tightened a bit, and since my stomach hadn't returned to its place of origin, breathing was out of the question. Sean had the PC on a hunt for me, the last of the RB, the most lethal of all weres. Sometimes setting records is not such a favorable thing.

I realized then what Sean's message had meant. He would finish cleaning up the mess in Utah, then come back with his boys to where I was effectively being held hostage by the numbnuts driving the car, and then kill me. Easy as pie.

While all these horrible images of my death swam through my mind, a random question popped in and then flew out of my mouth without time for me to filter it.

"Why did he tell you to make sure my ring was on?"

Cooper turned to look at me slowly, which I *really* hated because we were surrounded by Massachusetts drivers who were not known for their prowess behind the wheel. His look smacked of frustration from trying to figure that very thing out himself.

"I haven't a clue."

39

I spent the last hour of the trip battling my anxiety while it increased with every rotation of the odometer. I needed answers, but more than that, I needed a way out. Maybe I was way out of line about Sean and his plan to kill me, but I just couldn't see any other explanation. As much as I liked Cooper, I was not going to sit around and play good little hostage for him while I waited for Sean and whatever fate he had in store for me. However, I liked Cooper enough not to hand his ass over to Sean on a silver platter. I needed a way to escape that would get me long gone, and Cooper off the hook for never having been able to see my escape coming. At best I figured we had maybe a four-hour lead on them, so I wasn't working with a whole lot of wiggle room. Luckily for me, Cooper seemed oblivious to the fact that escaping was even on the menu for me. I found that extremely ironic.

Since Sean was working under the assumption that I knew nothing of his plan to return, he would be caught off guard by my breakout. In hindsight, he would realize that

Cooper was many things, but tight-lipped was not one of them. It would so work in my favor.

So with Cooper clueless and Sean ignorant, all I needed to do was invent a window of opportunity or diversion to occupy Cooper long enough for me to duck out and be long gone before he even noticed. I racked my brain for innocuous events that could lead to opportunity. For at least thirty minutes I came up with nothing, but then it hit me. We hadn't eaten since Erie and we were both clearly starving; the gurgling noises coming from both of our bellies were testament to that.

I realized that pizza delivery would be my deliverance. It was so simple it was genius. I would let Cooper order so he knew it was legit, lulling him into the perfect sense of false security, then I would run down to the main door to pay. Cooper would be in a lack-of-food haze, so his judgment would be impaired enough to let me go down there unescorted. From there I could sprint to the Audi, having already stashed the key in my pocket when we first arrived at the apartment.

Like taking candy from a baby.

I smiled outwardly while going over and over the logistics of my plan until I realized I had an audience and quickly wiped it from my face.

"Inside joke? Care to share?" he asked, mocking my favorite interrogation phrase.

"I'm an only child, Coop. I don't do sharing," I retorted.

"If I'd had one like you first, it'd be an only child too."

"You're an ass."

"You're a grump."

The way we bickered back and forth made me start to wonder if he wasn't auditioning to fill the absent sibling position himself.

WE PULLED up to my building around five p.m. that evening, after what I was told was a thirty-eight hour road trip with breaks included. Coop thought it best, given our appearances, to not break the speed limit at any point in time, though I was more convinced that it was because his getaway car wasn't exactly rented per se, but more "acquired" in the most dubious sense of the word. However, I was so glad to be home that I couldn't have cared less how we got there, and that included the legalities of our transportation.

I saw the window of my shop and got teary-eyed. I missed my home. I had no idea how long I'd been gone; yet another question off of the long list that had no answer to date. I had to remind myself that it wasn't back to business as usual, anyway. I wasn't staying long.

He handed me my keys, which Sean had procured from his little trip to Boston, no doubt. I unlocked the main door to the upstairs apartments, let Cooper in, and then followed him up.

Always good to keep them where you can see them...

"Which floor?" he asked.

"Second. Third floor is my dance studio."

"You own the whole building?" he asked, sounding surprised.

"Yes. I didn't want tenants, so I converted it over when I first moved in. It suits me just fine."

He shrugged in the way that means everything and nothing, and continued up to the door. I unlocked that as well and pushed it open with ease, but hesitated to enter, afraid of the normalcy it implied. Life had been so crazy for what seemed to be so long—I wasn't sure that I was ready for the mundane, however short a stop it may be.

Cooper, seeming to sense my unease, stepped in first and flipped on the wall switch, lighting the living room. He did the proverbial three-sixty turn to take the place in, which seemed comical given that it wasn't really all that big.

"This is going to be perfect, roomie. Where's my room?" he asked with a smile in his voice.

"Do your delusions impair *all* aspects of your life, or just the socially related ones?" I quipped, hoping the sting would take some of his enjoyment of our circumstances away. As was typical, it didn't.

"Not at all, my dear; in fact they greatly enhance it."

I really was beginning to hate him sometimes.

"The *guest* room is down the hall to your left, second door on the right. Hope you like pink," I chided.

"I make pink look *gooood*," he said as he passed me, sticking his face directly in mine.

Of course you do.

I was ready to put my plan into action, but I needed to get a few things accomplished first. I had to get some basics together for the trip and somehow hide them outside the apartment door to grab on the way down. I managed to pocket my keys without him being any the wiser, so that was one less thing to deal with.

"I'm going to grab a quick shower," I announced. An immediate smile crossed his face with that shit-eating-grin quality to it.

"Need some help?"

"Definitely not."

Again he shrugged and threw in a head tilt for good measure.

"Actually, yes."

With that his disappointed look transformed into one of pure, unadulterated interest.

"You can order pizza while I clean up. There should be a menu on the fridge. Get whatever, I've got cash in my room."

Before he could rebut, I scrambled down the hallway to my room and slammed the door, locking it behind me. I dove under my bed to find a duffel bag covered in dust. I shoved things into it frantically—a packer I was not. I kept reciting "the basics" song over and over in my head: undies, tees, jeans and bras...undies, tees, jeans and bras. In a sheer moment of clarity, I grabbed socks and a hoodie. I really did need to work them into the song somehow.

Everything else that was necessary was in the bathroom. I covered my bag with a towel and my clean clothes for camouflage. I breezed past Coop's door to the bathroom without so much as a peep out of him. Just like with toddlers, Cooper was at his most dangerous when quiet. It raised a lot of concern, but I had no time to worry. I shot into the bathroom and locked it, turned on the water immediately along with my iPod and began packing everything else I needed.

I did actually shower, but didn't make an all-day event out of it, just a quick wash and cleaned my face. There was no time to thoroughly wash my mop, so I rinsed and conditioned it as quickly as possible, knowing that I'd have to tie it back to keep it under control as it dried. A hat would likely be involved as well.

Once I was dressed and looking somewhat more myself in my favorite Seven brand jeans and a vintage tunic, I flashed down the hall again to stash my duffel under my bed. When I came out of my room, Coop was leaning against the guest room door frame. I had a sudden rush of panic, fearing he'd seen my dirty little secret and was gearing up to play with me about it before he crushed my escape plan.

"Got any clean towels?" he asked, still draped in the doorway.

I nodded a little too enthusiastically.

"In the linen closet, top shelf," I said. I walked past him, opened the closet door, and grabbed a towel. He accepted it when I passed it to him, but as I turned to head for the kitchen, he gently grabbed my arm.

"You're going to have to come with me," he said with a serious edge.

"Hell isn't freezing anytime soon, Cooper, nor am I going in that bathroom with you."

He moved closer to me. Too close. He looked down his perfect nose at me and repeated himself, reminding me that I was not to leave his sight.

"It's not like I can't sneak out of the room once you're actually in the shower. Besides, how far am I going to get before you hear me making a break for it?" I pleaded, trying desperately to get out of this one.

He slowly shook his head.

"Get in there," he said, shoving me towards the entrance.

"May I remind you that I'm a killing machine…"

"NOW!" he hollered.

Shit!

"Fine," I muttered under my breath as I made my way into the bathroom with Cooper hot on my heels.

He closed the door behind him and locked it. After starting the water up, he assessed the towel I had given him. *Apparently he's a connoisseur of terry cloth.*

When he started to undress, I snapped my eyes shut, squinting as hard as I could. I was pretty sure that he laughed as he entered the shower. Settling myself down on the toilet seat, I heard the screeching of the curtain rings as they passed along the rod, signaling that the coast was clear. At least it should have been.

I opened my eyes to the lightly tanned perfection that was Cooper's body. Apparently, in all his genius, he thought it best to only partially close the curtain, allowing him to cleanse and babysit all at the same time. I'd never met a man who could multitask before.

My brain was screaming at my eyes to close and my head to turn, but a coup had started inside my nervous system and neither was happening. By that time, he was very aware of my staring. He enjoyed it immensely. Though his face was playful, there was a heat in his eyes that I had not seen before. I was mesmerized. At least it kept my eyes above his neck.

"I had to keep you in sight. You understand, don't you?" he asked, running the soap up and down his chest. I watched the trail of suds wash down his stomach then slammed my eyes shut, shaking my head slightly. I nodded in response.

When I opened my eyes, I looked away from him, turning my body towards the door. He chuckled to himself and started whistling some tune I didn't know. I listened to the water bounce off of his body as he soaped and rinsed. He repeated the process so many times I lost count. He was taking forever. My knees bounced uncontrollably and I sat on my hands to keep me from biting my nails down to stubs. The pizza guy needed to show up sooner than later, or I was really going to lose my shit.

40

Cooper eventually emerged from the shower cleaner than a Michelin Star kitchen. I had managed to regain composure during his last five minutes in there, so I looked calm, cool, and collected. Unfortunately for me, I wasn't. The pizza guy was thus far a no-show, and I was starting to stress that somehow my great escape plan was foiled before it even got off the ground.

"So when's the pizza getting here?" I asked casually. "Did they say how long it'd be?"

He toweled himself off casually while I studied the cracks in the plaster ceiling, realizing that, if I tried hard enough, I really could see Jesus in just about anything.

"He said it'd be about forty-five minutes. Why?"

"Because I'm dying to find out his opinion on global warming," I said, hoping that sarcasm would maintain my facade of normalcy. "I'm starving, aren't you?" He stepped in front of my ceiling view and frowned down at me. I took that to mean he was hungry as well. "Okay then, I'll go round up some money. What's the total?"

"One hundred and thirty-five bucks," he responded.

"What the shit, Coop? Did you order *all* their pizza?" I cried, totally caught off guard. Werewolves were expensive to feed.

"You said to get 'whatever', did you not? I got what I wanted, and one pie for you." *How thoughtful. I'd only need a loan to pay for it.*

I took a deep breath and let it out oh-so-dramatically while I walked to my room to get the cash, feigning frustration about the whole thing. Everything was back on track, and I couldn't have been more pleased with myself, but I kept that smile to myself as I crossed the threshold to my room.

That was when everything went completely south, in a death-spin, crash-and-burn kind of way.

The doorbell rang, and I was nowhere near the apartment door. I panicked when I heard Cooper making his way towards it. I knew he couldn't go down to the outside entrance without the money, so he'd have to wait for me. But he wouldn't let me go down there alone if he was already in the hallway, and he'd know something was up if I insisted upon doing it. Worst of all, my bag wasn't stashed yet.

In all my smoothness, I sprinted for the living room as casually as one could and tried to calmly tell him I'd get it, but I could see his perfect profile completely ignoring me, turning the knob to enter the stairway.

It took a few seconds to register the gunshots after they went off.

Cooper stumbled back to the couch and collapsed half on it, half on the floor. I froze in the hall by the kitchen. I neither heard nor saw anyone, but I knew who it was, who it had to be. To think that this was how he thanked Cooper for his assistance was unfathomable, and I felt as though I'd never known him. Again. A true mercenary to the core.

My gaze snapped back and forth from the empty apartment doorway to where Cooper lay bleeding, nearly unconscious on the floor. I was giving myself whiplash while contemplating my next move. My autonomics were working on overdrive, and I couldn't understand how I was controlling a Change, thinking this would be the one time I'd really welcome it. I tried to focus as hard as I could on blocking everything out when I saw Coop lift his gaze to meet mine briefly.

"Run!" he whispered before losing consciousness or dying; I just couldn't tell.

"There's nowhere that little doggy can run that I can't find her," said a voice I knew, right before it burst into laughter so evil I was certain my crucifixes were melting off the wall.

Then he walked through the door.

41

E ric's entrance was followed quickly by about six others whom I recognized from the party at Marcus's flat. They strategically blocked my exit and had also conveniently moved to obscure my view of Cooper. I felt as though my heart was beating so fast that it was almost still.

"Ruby, Ruby, Ruby, whatever am I going to do with you?" he asked as he slowly stepped nearer to me with an eerie calm. His face was complacent, but his eyes anything but. They were a golden, flaming amber; he was enraged.

I stood my ground for no other reason than to salvage any shred of dignity I had left. That dignity was met with a backhand so hard it knocked me into the wall, leaving a hole where my elbow went through it. As I indelicately regained my balance, he pinned me against the wall with his body. He ran his thumb softly across my lip where it had split and was beginning to bleed. He stroked back and forth slowly, coating it in the blood he'd shed. He then brought it oh-so-slowly up to his mouth and sucked it off like a delicacy of the highest order.

"Mmmm," he hummed as his eyes rolled back in his head. "Some things really are too good to be true."

He grabbed me sharply by the chin and licked my lip, catching it in his mouth and sucking on it until it throbbed even harder than it originally had. I struggled against him to no avail. I needed to Change to win that fight, but nothing was happening.

He held me tightly against the wall with his pelvis ground into mine. It was in that moment I became startlingly aware of something: I felt nothing but hatred for him. There was no heated reaction I couldn't explain, no bad behavior I could excuse, and no magnetic draw I couldn't escape. Our bond was broken. I guess my wolf, who had been so drawn to his, didn't take too kindly to being sold for breeding rights and having her friend shot and bleeding in the other room.

Cooper.

I tried desperately to get a look at him, but Eric held my gaze by force and wasn't relenting one bit. I shut my eyes, trying to connect back to the days of old and tune into my other senses. I heard no movement in Cooper's direction. There was breathing, but it was too ordinary to be his. He'd taken three slugs to the chest from a sawed-off shotgun, which tended to make breathing laborious, and I heard nothing that sounded erratic and rushed. My pulse quickened as I assumed the worst. Cooper had once again landed in the line of fire to save my ass, and this time didn't make it safely to the other side. I tasted the salt of my tears as they streamed past my mouth. It mixed with the pungent metallic taste of my blood.

"I don't think you should worry about your friend anymore," Eric said with mock sympathy. "Silver has such a nasty way of poisoning the system quickly. He cannot undo what's been done. Neither can you."

"You fucker...you make me sick, you son of a bitch..."

"Shhh," he soothed, with a finger pressed so tightly to my lips that I could neither move nor feel the circulation in them. "Your friend is a pawn in this game, both useless and expendable. You, on the other hand, are beyond valuable, which leads me to discuss my current predicament."

I tried to yell profanities at him, but it came out as nothing more than mumbled gibberish, which really didn't have quite the sting I was looking for at the time.

"You see, Ruby, I'm in a bit of a pickle because of you. My investors are *scathingly* angry that you've not only escaped captivity, which we'll talk about in a moment, but also managed to kill an entire pack, including their CEO. I've done my best to assure them that this little misunderstanding can be taken care of, but they seem less than convinced. They're under the impression that you're a bit of a...hm...what was it they said? Ah, yes, 'a loose cannon'," he said conversationally. His breath was poison on my skin and it burned with his every exhale.

He removed his hand from my mouth, flipping it about to help emphasize his soliloquy with gestures. "I tried to remind them that if it hadn't been for a little help on the inside, you never would have been able to pull off this little stunt. An error that will certainly not occur again. All potential sympathizers have been identified and eradicated."

"So you're sending me back?" I whispered, realizing that death really wasn't the worst fate I faced.

He scoffed at the innocence in my voice.

"Well not back there, you've made that impossible. But there are others who would have you for similar reasons. You'll go to the highest bidder," he said, thrusting his body up against mine again. "What would you have me do? I'm a businessman, Ruby. It's nothing personal. Never was. I'd hoped to win you for myself given the bond our wolves had, but a better offer presented itself and I took it. Now that offer hangs in the balance, so I have to right it, whatever the cost may be."

"This is what he meant. You're nothing more than a lowlife sellout. Everything he said about you was true," I said with a sense of awe and regret hanging in the air with my words. Sean had said that Eric was only interested in himself and that he'd known from personal experience. "So what was it with you two? You owe me that!"

He seemed to consider my demand for a minute before he offered anything up.

"We know more about each other than you could ever possibly understand, but I'll tell you what you want to know anyway. We *were* once brothers. I was PC. For decades I served beside him and the others, maintaining the balance between worlds. One day I met Marcus, and he made me a better offer," he explained, pausing slightly. "Like I said, I'm a businessman. He Changed me that day and has been my mentor ever since." His expression changed from indifferent to anger in the blink of an eye, and my anxiety spiked instantly. "His death will be avenged. Your little wolf cub over there hardly counts as restitution on that front."

With that, he grabbed me by the arm and started to lead me to the door. Apparently our moment of sharing was over. I'd hit a nerve, and it zapped him right back into business mode. He was taking me down for transport to wherever my new "home" would be, and once again, nobody would know where I'd gone. That little theme in my life really needed to change; it was really getting old.

"Wait!" I yelled, trying to startle him into stopping. I had no plan, so stalling was the default in hopes that Sean was closer than I thought. "How did you get in here in the first place?" I asked, realizing how weak that sounded even as I said it. He laughed at me, looking all too aware of what I was trying to do. He surprised me when he actually answered.

"Simple. You left the door unlocked. Not a very smart move for a single woman living in town."

SHIT! I really have to stop doing that.

"And the pizza guy? What did you do with him?"

I had noticed the smell of pizza in the apartment and realized that they must have shanghai-ed the poor sap when he came to the door.

"Ruby, I'm not a mindless killer. I paid the man and told him I was heading up to the party," he said, looking truly affronted. "Really, six pies? You're going to lose your girlish figure at that rate," he said condescendingly.

After a moment he dropped the façade of concern and started marching me out the door. I assumed his humor had run out for the evening. Funny, so did my luck.

I threw subtlety out the window and went for obvious attempts at Changing. I panicked and tried to drive myself into a fear-based state that had worked so well in the past. I flailed, screamed, and tried to think of every awful thing that had happened to me over the last few months, but nothing worked. The group of them laughed and clutched their stomachs at my juvenile attempts to gain the upper hand. The one nearest to Cooper fell at his feet in comedic agony, wiping the tears from his face. I glanced at Cooper and nearly collapsed—his eyes were open.

He mouthed something to me, but I had no idea how to read lips. He tried to lift his right hand, but he hadn't the strength or nervous input to carry out the act. He winced with pain. I made a desperate move and dove for him, past the man on the floor. My landing wasn't pretty, but it put my face right up against his. With one last breath of strength he whispered the words "take...ring...off" directly into my ear.

I hadn't a clue why that was important, but, without time to analyze his wish, I did what he asked. I slid it off just as two arms went around my waist, yanking me to my feet. My ring flew through the air to land on Cooper's chest.

I felt a sudden surge of power, like a dam had been opened within me, hitting me with all that pent up fear and anxiety at once. It wasn't overwhelming, but empowering. An uncontrollable smile spread slowly across my lips as I broke free of the hold Eric had on me and turned to look at him.

As the blood drained not only from his face, but also from the faces behind him, I got a glimpse of what they were seeing, what had so quickly turned the tide. In the mirror, over the shoulder of the last of the men, were two glowing red eyes. My Change was going to occur, and they all knew it. Death was coming for them.

And she was some pissed off.

42

There was nothing but a carnage obstacle course to get to Eric, who had maneuvered himself conveniently behind his minions. It was no matter; an RB couldn't be stopped. It took little effort for me to cut through his not-so-human bodyguards, the rampage taking just under a minute. It was surprisingly unsatisfying and unchallenging. Anticlimactic even.

The shock and horror appeared to have frozen Eric in a state of half-Change. His stature was that of a human, but his eyes, teeth, and hands were in a blended state. Claws protruded from his fingertips, and sharp canines made his mouth shut awkwardly, though it was agape at the time. His eyes glowed an inhuman yellow and they read fear. He was afraid of me.

I quickly became aware that it wasn't really me that had him petrified, but more so the crazy person who was at the helm of my body. It was as if I was somewhere in the back seat of a careening sports car and couldn't reach the brake. The driver was reckless, impulsive and a little crazy. I envied her immensely.

She waded through intestines and questionable matter slowly and with a catwalk swagger. She smoothed down the tunic that was understandably disheveled and slipped off her hat. After meticulously untying the braid that bound the still-wet curls, she ran a delicate hand through my hair.

Our hair.

Eric clung to the wall as if it were his lifeline, plastered against it like a starfish. He still hadn't closed his mouth. She would do this for him. Upon reaching his body, she slowly crouched at his feet and, with snakelike grace, uncoiled herself, sliding along the length of his body in a sexual way until she was virtually nose-to-nose with him. She remained pressed against him until she felt him unwillingly press back against her, at least part of him anyway. She laughed an unfamiliar laugh that was far deeper and huskier than my own.

Stevie Nicks with a two pack a day smoking habit...

She then sucked his bottom lip into a kiss that was more rough than sensual and ended with that lip caught between her teeth, being pulled to the point of pain. He winced, then moaned, leaning away from her. I was starting to get pissed off. *Was she not present in that dungeon with me? Did she not endure what I did, or did she actually enjoy it?* I ran these questions through my mind over and over. Then I realized that she'd stopped toying with him, unless holding him off the ground by the throat was foreplay I'd not seen yet. And I'd seen a lot in Utah.

He gargled something incoherent and she dropped him to the floor in response, seemingly amused with her own antics. He coughed violently for a moment, and then, in a very hoarse voice, repeated himself.

"You don't want to do this. I can help you." I'm guessing that the reply she gave him broke at least four to five ribs on his right side. When he regained his breath, he started again. "I can help you escape the PC," he said as he braced himself for another blow. Instead, she cocked her head to the side, as if intrigued with a painting she couldn't quite figure out.

"Help me how?" she rasped.

"You forget that I was one. I know their methods of tracking, how they attack, operate, whom they answer to. You'll never escape them on your own. Nobody ever has," he said, gaining both strength of voice and will as he spoke. "You. Need. Me."

Ever the businessman, he was hoping to negotiate his way out of this, and to my horror, it appeared that she was listening. *No, no, no, no. Cooper, look at Cooper. Look at what he did to my friend, our friend! Eric is slime, the scum of the earth, and he'll sell us out at the first chance he gets. He doesn't care about us, he cares about what we can do to his bottom line. SNAP OUT OF IT!*

I screamed those messages repeatedly inside my head to try and break her out of his hold yet again. I thought it was working when she pinned him against the wall with her forearm to his throat, but he was still able to talk, and that seemed to have a hold on her. I needed something else, something more tangible for her to grab onto.

She released him as he told her his plan of immediate escape. He seemed to have put together that the PC would be coming for us sooner than later. While he walked around her, he caused her gaze to land upon Cooper's body sprawled lifelessly on the rug.

I seized my opportunity.

HE DID THAT! HE KILLED COOPER, THE ONLY PERSON WILLING TO HELP US WHEN NOBODY ELSE WOULD! KILL HIM!

Message received.

A guttural noise sprang from deep within her chest as she dove at Eric. He screamed for the briefest of moments until his vocal cords were strewn about the room, along with every other major organ contained within his body. She hovered over the tiny remains and shreds of clothing in front of her, allowing me a chance to take it all in. When I professed my satisfaction, she breathed deeply. A howl burst forth from her mouth, signaling the kill.

It went unanswered.

Cooper!

She scurried across the slippery floor to his side and tried to pick his head up. *So much blood,* we thought in unison. She spotted the ring, still perched delicately on his chest, and reached for it, hesitating to put it on, knowing that last time the switch knocked us out for a few minutes. Cooper would be dead for sure by then, and we would most likely be as well. She took a breath and stared at the innocuous circle of platinum.

Thank you, I whispered to her in our mind.

"No, thank you," she whispered back before sliding the ring onto my right hand.

43

I awoke on my side, staring at a wall so red that, for a moment, I really questioned if I had redecorated before I left. Then reality smacked me. I shot up onto my hands and knees and looked around until I found his body. Cooper still lay motionless.

I shuffled over until I straddled him, hovering over to get an aerial view of the damage. His chest looked like mincemeat and showed no signs of healing. I stood quickly and ran toward the bathroom for towels, antiseptic, and gauze, anything that could be helpful, or at least make me feel as though I was.

Stepping on something that resembled a spleen, I came crashing to the floor. Maybe it had been a kidney, but I just couldn't tell with my footprint embedded in it. Once on my feet again, I sprinted down the arterial-sprayed hall and dodged into the bathroom. I threw everything of inconvenience out of my way and collected my mission items, quickly turning and running back down the hall, hurdling any random flesh to avoid further incidents.

I didn't have a clear plan when I got back to his body,

but I had to do something. I plastered towels across his chest to stop the bleeding and wrapped an Ace bandage tightly around them to keep them on, just in case he decided to spring from his position and inform me that he was only kidding. I tried to examine him further, but my vision was blurred with tears I hadn't realized I was shedding. I was hysterical, and hysterically crying. Sobbing would have been a more accurate description. I tried to hear if he was breathing, but the only sounds I heard were the throbbing in my ears and wails escaping my mouth.

Déjà vu filled my mind as I dropped onto the towel-covered body, carrying on as though the world was ending. Perhaps it was.

I cried so hard that I could no longer breathe through my nose and was dangerously close to hyperventilating or passing out. I cried with an abandon unlike anything I'd ever experienced. Nothing else mattered in that moment—not Eric, not Sean, not Utah—only Cooper.

Again, I found myself begging him, incoherently, not to leave me. Over and over again I pleaded, bargaining anything I could think of with God so long as he let me have Cooper back. Then silently, I prayed.

I neither heard nor saw Sean come in. His voice broke through my prayers. Maybe he would answer them, I thought, or maybe he would send me to be with Cooper. I didn't seem to care either way.

He called to me again, and I wondered how long he'd been standing there doing that, unsuccessfully trying to get my attention. Just as I slowly lifted my head to see him, he perched down beside me, gently lifting me up off of Cooper's body. His eyes were kind, but his posture was still all business.

"It's silver. They shot him. He didn't do anything and they shot him," I babbled.

I sounded oddly removed from the situation, as if it suddenly became too much to bear. Sean tried to direct my attention by asking questions, but I just kept repeating myself while I looked back down at Cooper's body, my eyes glazed and unfocused.

"Ruby," he said, shaking me just a little. "What happened?" I stared at him mutely. "Ruby. I need you to pull it together," he said calmly. "Tell me what happened."

"Eric. He brought others," I said faintly.

Sean growled at the mere mention of Eric's name. It was echoed by others, who until that point, I hadn't noticed were even there.

"He was here?" he asked, scanning the apartment.

"He still is," I said meekly.

They all sprang to attention with fighting stances, looking around as if concerned about ambush.

"Where?" he asked, jumping to his feet.

"You're standing on him," I replied.

They looked around confused for a moment, then realization set in; the carnage had a name. Several names.

Sean leaned in closely to me, whispering in my ear.

"You did this?"

I nodded.

He leaned closer, brushing my ear with his lips.

"Good," he replied.

I looked at him with surprise.

"Are you going to kill me now?" I mouthed with barely a sound.

He looked at me with genuine surprise.

"No," he said without pause.

It was my turn to look surprised.

"Why did you come for me in Utah, then?" I whispered, narrowing the distance between us further.

A ghost of a smile flashed across his face, then quickly disappeared.

"I made you a promise once. I keep my promises, Ruby," he explained. "No more cages."

44

My heart burned, but in a good way for once. I'd forgotten all about that talk we'd had and how my upbringing had struck a chord with him. *He came back to save me.* Cooper's offhanded comments became so clear. No wonder he'd thought I was so thick. I had misread every action Sean ever took, interpreting it all as aggressive and malice-laden.

Cooper.

I looked at Sean with the pleading eyes of child, again shedding tears, though at a more subtle pace.

"Can you help him?" I asked, fearing the answer.

He pressed his lips together tightly as a foreign rumbling sound rattled his chest.

"No. I can't," was his reply. With that, the tears fell far more rapidly and I threw myself onto the body again, clutching the bloody mess to me like a teddy bear after a scary dream. Maybe that's what it was.

"Ruby. I said that *I* can't," Sean continued, his business voice returning. "But I know someone who can."

He seemed reluctant to share that information, as

though he wasn't looking forward to what it entailed. There was a collective rustling of movement behind him; the brothers were stirring about, cleaning up the mess I'd made. Sean grabbed one of them and started barking orders.

"Call her. Let her know we're on our way and that it's going to be a messy one. She'll want to put the tarp down."

His brother nodded and whipped out a cell phone. He was talking to someone as he left the apartment, but I was pretty sure it wasn't English and had no idea what was being said.

"Is he dead?" I asked innocently.

Sean furrowed his brow and then rubbed his forehead with his thumb and index finger.

"Sort of. It's complicated. He doesn't have much time, though."

I sprang to my feet like a springbok.

"Well, let's go then. We don't have much time. He can't die, Sean," I rambled as I ran about the room collecting things I thought we needed. When I witnessed Sean's inaction, I found myself grabbing him by the coat lapels and screaming into his face.

"HE CAN'T DIE, SEAN!"

There was a hush of silence from the group of rubber-neckers who were supposed to be cleaning. I scanned their faces to see utter shock and disbelief. I took this to mean that Sean was not only their leader, but someone who was never, ever, to be challenged or reprimanded in any way. I took the hint, slowly releasing his collar and smoothing it out, all the while apologizing for my tone.

"I can't lose him," I said, eyes downcast, posture submissive.

Sean said nothing in response, but scooped Cooper's body up and started down the stairs with him. I quickly followed, being literally pushed out by a room full of hostility and anger, all of which was apparently aimed at me. I didn't think his brothers liked me very much. I guess I was their sworn enemy, so it was hard to hold that against them.

The two of us ran out to the SUV he had driven and placed Coop in the back. When I went to get into the passenger seat, a hand grabbed me abruptly and swung me around.

"You can't go with me," Sean said.

"What do you mean? He's not going without me!" I said, fighting against his hold. "This is bullshit, Sean. He's like this because of me."

"Fine, but you have to take your own car," he conceded, seeing that I wasn't going to let it go. "You can't stay there."

I couldn't understand the expression on his face. It smacked of embarrassment and anger, with a hint of something I just couldn't quite place.

"I'll take the TT. Just drive fast," I told him, before realizing that our two cars weren't going to hold all the men in my apartment. "What about the guys?"

"They know where to go. They'll be there as soon as they're finished with your place. You gave them quite a job to do," he said while turning to walk away. For the briefest second I was sure that a smile of pride flashed across his face.

We drove through Portsmouth at a blistering pace, which was a challenge given the road layout. New England wasn't exactly built on a grid system. We ended up about fifteen minutes out of town in a slightly more rural area with large properties and plenty of trees covering them. We wound down the driveway to arrive at an unassuming blue cape with black shutters. A woman was waiting for us on the front step. An amazingly beautiful woman with a body that didn't quit. I got a good look at most of it, as she seemed to subscribe to the less-is-more school of dressing. I wasn't aware until then that it was socially acceptable to call a bra a top. I learned so much when I least expected to.

I followed Sean up the walkway, watching Cooper's head and legs dangle beyond his outline. The light of the moon cast an eerie glow on Cooper's face, making him look oh-so pale. My breath caught in my throat and I fought back tears with violent tenacity.

The strange woman greeted Sean (and I mean *greeted* him), then turned and led the way in without so much as a glance in my general direction. *Bitch.*

I bit my tongue to keep from saying something I was sure to regret later.

The house was sparsely furnished and plain inside. Nothing adorned the walls and there were few amenities overall. I spotted a couch, and without being offered, plopped myself down on it. That won me an unfriendly glance from the supermodel. Ruby, 1. Bitch, 0.

The two of them muttered something nonsensical to each other in the adjacent hallway. It seemed boring until the volume picked up. It wasn't English, but it didn't take a rocket scientist to pick up on pissed off in any language.

"She stays!" Sean yelled, then stormed into the room. He was beet red and breathing heavily.

"Don't move!" he commanded.

I was in no position to argue and did as I was told. The Bitch didn't return, and Sean left to join her.

I fiddled with the hem of my shirt for a while, then tried to clean the dried blood from under my fingernails; it was going to require soap and a brush, for sure. I giggled to myself, finding the thought comical. The sound of the front door opening snapped me out of that. In poured the brothers, all of them, and goody for me, they'd remembered to pack their hostility for the trip. I was met by dozens of angry stares, but, fortunately, nobody saw me fit to speak to, and that suited me just fine. They did, however, find it necessary to pin me into the center of the couch, surrounding me on both sides with walls of muscle and attitude.

Find a happy place, find a happy place...

The screaming started from the back room shortly after their arrival. It was like nothing I'd ever heard or would care to hear again. The first image in my head was of someone being burnt and skinned alive at the same time. There was horror and desperation in that scream and it pained me to hear it, especially when I realized that it belonged to Cooper.

I shot off the couch, aiming for the room the sound came from, but I didn't make it far. I was taken down by a brother standing just off to the side of the sofa. He pinned me to the floor with such hatred that I knew I'd be bruised for weeks after. I yelped at the pain and he laughed, continuing to say nothing. The silence from those guys was really starting to creep me out.

Sean's voice boomed through the room.

"Let her go!" he commanded to the man holding me down. When he didn't move quickly enough, Sean lunged at him. "NOW!"

Like a puppet on a string, the brother did exactly what he was told, but looked none too happy about it.

"What are you doing to Cooper? I want to see him!" I demanded.

"It's...messy," he replied, looking somewhat contrite. "You can't."

Another scream came from that room and I bolted for it,

only to be unsuccessful a second time. Sean held me tight to him.

"Ruby, you can't. It's for the best that you don't see what's going on."

I started crying in my mounting frustration.

"I need to see him. I can help him...I can speed his healing," I argued.

"You don't, and you can't. Everything that can be done is being done."

"But you don't understand, I *can* speed his healing. I did it when we..."

"ENOUGH!" he yelled, cutting me off, his eyes turning forest green before me. "You will sit and do as you're told. You will not meddle in this. I think you've done quite enough tonight."

Ouch. That was way harsh.

I sat where I'd stood, on the floor near the hallway. The brothers went back to diligently hating me, yet ignoring me at the same time. Sean returned to the room, where no subsequent sounds escaped.

It had to have been about forty-five minutes before anyone appeared. The Bitch strode down the hall, past the opening towards the far end. She was covered—better yet shellacked—with blood. Not a spot on her was untouched. The coating was thick and heavy and clung to her. I heard what must have been a bathroom door close and water start running. *I'd want to clean that off ASAP too.* Then I realized that I probably wasn't looking much better myself.

Sean emerged, looking fatigued. I'd never seen him like that before.

"He's going to be okay, but there's some possible permanent damage. We're unsure of how well he'll be once he's up and around."

"I want to see him," I pleaded.

"I will *not* get into this again. It's out of the question, Ruby. Leave him be for now. You will see him later."

"But he needs me," I whispered off into the distance.

"He needed *me*," a disembodied voice called from the hall. "Not you."

I looked up to see the Bitch draped all over Sean, again wearing precious little. Her silk mini robe was V-necked down to her navel, and her hem was flirting with peep-show length. She ran her hand in circles across his chest while she spoke.

"I think, little doggy, that it's time for you to go home. Run away now...shoo," she said with a heavy accent that I couldn't quite place—possibly Slavic or Mediterranean.

My blood was boiling. She had me all shades of pissed off, and I wanted to fight in a way that I should have been ashamed of. Too bad I wasn't.

I could hear a faint voice in the back of my head telling me to take off the ring. I think my wolf wanted a shot at her too, but it wasn't necessary. I'd make her proud on my own. If the Bitch wanted a fight, I was happy to oblige, verbally.

"Desperation is such a stinky cologne. Perhaps you should go back to the shower and try washing it off."

Her sickening, pleased-with-herself smile dissipated in no time flat. Ruby 2, Bitch 0. She repositioned herself in front of Sean, all the while never losing contact with him. I wanted to tear her face off.

"Get. Out," she spat.

I laughed. *That wasn't much of a comeback.*

"With. Pleasure."

I stormed to the front door, focused on nothing but leaving. I turned to slam it behind me and caught a glimpse of her all over Sean while he stood impassively looking at me. I hated him instantly.

I'm not exactly sure how I got home, given that I wasn't paying attention to how we got there in the first place, but somehow I arrived. I opened the main door, being sure to lock it behind me this time, seeing as how it seemed that whenever I didn't double-check, random people showed up in my place. I begrudgingly climbed the stairs and schlepped myself into the apartment. I turned on the lamp on the entryway table, too tired for full illumination.

I gasped when I looked up. The apartment was spotless, beyond white-glove clean. I would never have known that a bloodbath had taken place only hours earlier. I threw myself wearily into a living room chair, unable to go anywhere near the couch. I stared blankly at it for an eternity, thinking of nothing.

Eventually my eyelids sagged and began to slowly black out my vision entirely. I laid my head back against the chair and allowed myself to sleep. The mental and emotional stress of the last few days still resonated through my mind like an aftershock I couldn't escape. I tried to push past it, to let it go, to deal with it another day. It must have worked because I didn't remember anything after that until I was awoken by an unfamiliar voice a couple of hours later.

The words didn't register at first, so I forced my eyes to obey me and open. They were met by the most beautiful hazel pair.

"Sorry, roomie," he said with a wink. "You were snoring."

45

"Cooper!" I screamed, hurling my body at him, clinging to him like a koala. I buried my face in his neck and squeezed for dear life. I was met with a groan, then a chuckle.

"Easy, girlie," he groaned. His voice was scratchy and muted in a way that made laryngitis seem like a vast improvement. "I'm not up to snuff just yet."

I eased my head back off of his shoulder just enough to see his face. He was just as amazing as I'd remembered, and his smile warmed my insides. He reached his face towards me, and gently kissed my forehead. The tenderness of his action forced tears from my eyes.

"I'm so sorry, Coop. I'm so, so sorry," I squeaked. He squeezed me tighter in response. "I thought you were dead," I whispered.

"I know you did," he replied, stroking my hair.

I slowly climbed down off of him in total confusion.

"What do you mean by that?"

"It's complicated..."

"Why does everyone say that? Am I a halfwit? Are you worried I can't keep up?"

"Hey, Anger Management, you just got done telling me how sorry you were. Bitching at me doesn't give me the warm fuzzies, ya know?"

I reflected quickly on what he'd said and realized that my anger was horribly misdirected.

"I'm sorry," I said, feeling sheepish. "Will you tell me what you can?"

"I will, but then you need to tell me what happened while I was out. I only remember pieces of the evening and I'd appreciate having them put together," he requested.

"Fair enough."

He rubbed at his throat for a moment, then walked into the kitchen to get water. After two enormous glasses, he attempted to tell his tale. His voice was very weak and his throat presumably very sore. He decided it best to write down what he could, only hitting the high points.

While he wrote, I frantically dodged around over his shoulders, trying desperately to read it. I barked out random questions as they popped into my head with the hopes that he'd answer them if he could. He seemed completely unfazed.

A few minutes later I was given a bullet-form outline of the goings-on. He didn't go into great detail, but I hoped that I could draw more out of him where necessary.

NEVER SAW THE SHOT COMING.
Couldn't move after, effect of the silver...will explain later.
In and out while you and Eric "talked."
Went dark after you took off the ring.
Remember being healed...crazy shit.

Heard you and Sean talking.
Heard you and Sophie fighting.
Heard you didn't want to leave without me.
You left.
Sean told me he had to leave, not sure when back if at all.
Asked me to tell you goodbye...Sorry!

I DROPPED the paper to the floor. What a week it had been, and what a kick-in-the-nuts way to end it. I found out that I had a borderline-psycho who happened to live in my head, Cooper nearly died from silver poisoning only to be healed by a half-naked whore, and Sean, who really didn't want to kill me, who actually came back to save me, was now leaving forever (and didn't have the balls to tell me himself). It was a real shitter.

Cooper had just finished his third or fourth glass of water,and waved his hand to get my attention. He was preparing to speak when I cut him off.

"Tell me about the bit—" I started, cutting myself off. "The healer."

He gently cleared his throat in an act of determination to speak.

"It was some freaky shit," he whispered. "I can't be positive, but it felt like she was *inside* of me, literally pulling out the silver fragments and putting me back together."

I looked at him incredulously for a moment and then remembered what I had seen when she walked down the hallway at her house. She looked as if she'd been birthed, coated in blood and slime, and I realized that maybe he wasn't talking so crazy after all. My only concern had been her saving him, and she did just that. Her methods were inconsequential.

"I heard them fighting...about you," he continued.

"Who?" I asked, trying to determine who out of that crowd would have had something to say about me. "Who was fighting?"

"At first it was Sophie and Sean, but then some of the PC chimed in to share their not-so-flattering opinions of you."

"I don't care about the PC. They're a bunch of spineless dicks. What did the bitch...*Sophie* say?"

Cooper looked reserved for a moment and it was clear that he didn't want to answer my question. He rubbed his hand through his hair and sighed.

"She told him that he had to let his plaything go. That his fascination with you was only that, and it could never lead anywhere. That they were chosen for each other. 'That's the way it's always been,' she told him."

I looked at Cooper for a moment, unsure of what I'd been told. *Plaything? Fascination? Where did she get that shit from?* It wasn't like that, and never had been.

"What did he say?" I asked, curious to hear his response to the nonsense the Bitch had spewed.

"He agreed," was his only response.

A long silence stretched out between us.

"Shut the front door! Are you saying he actually thinks what she said is true? That's how he sees me?" I cried in total disbelief. "And now he's going off to be with her?" I rambled rhetorical questions off one after the other until I realized how hysterical I sounded.

Then it hit me.

So much started to make sense. I replayed every moment I'd spent with him from first to last, looking at it with a totally different set of eyes—his. I felt a wave of elation and horror travel through me. It was true. It was all true.

I had spent months misinterpreting everything he did and lying to myself about my own feelings. Once they were realized, they mattered not; he was to be with Sophie and he knew it, admitted it. The bond between them was obvious from the start. They clearly had a history.

And a future.

True to form, my emotions must have been plastered all over my face. Cooper scooted carefully towards me, slipping an arm around the back of my shoulders, pulling me into his chest and walking us towards the sofa. We both paused before it. He sighed and made the first move to sit, dragging me closely beside him onto it. He nestled himself into the corner with his head perched on the sofa arm and snuggled me into him in a half-on-half-off position. He pressed my head gently to his chest and held me. Neither of us said a thing.

For someone who'd known me for such a short time, I felt like he understood me better than anyone else ever had. I wasn't sure what the future held for him, but I was glad for that moment that he was there with me. My roomie.

We lay there silent for ten minutes or so, but I knew both of our minds were racing. It was usually the only time either of us was quiet, and I couldn't take it any longer. I needed to get some emotion out, and I was disgusted by the thought of crying any more. I was starting another "no cry" policy and strictly adhering to it. Maybe my parents really were onto something with that in the first place.

I told Coop I had to go upstairs for a bit to work some things out, and I'd be back in an hour or so. He said nothing in response, only smiled faintly. He knew exactly what I was going to do, but didn't want to rub my face in it. For all his faults, he really was turning out to be one hell of a friend.

I walked down the hall to my room and changed quickly

into a white V-neck T-shirt and some black boy shorts, my standard dance attire. I headed back out towards the living room and, on my way out the door, glanced back to see Cooper asleep on the couch. I smiled to myself and walked over, pulling a blanket off of a nearby chair on the way. I wrapped him in it and smoothed his hair away from his face. I turned off the lamp on my way out the door and closed it gently behind me.

I took the stairs two at a time and walked into the third floor studio. There, my therapy would begin. With so many emotions coursing through me, I wasn't sure what I was in the mood for. Before I turned on the elaborate sound system, I took a broom to the floor, removing the broken mirror that had shattered during Eric's last visit. The PC didn't get to that room to clean, apparently.

So as not to wake Cooper, I set the volume low and decided to put the iPod on shuffle and work with the first song that came on. I once again realized that the universe could have a perverse sense of humor. "Gravity" by Sara Bareilles was first on the list.

Gravity: A force between two objects that accelerates them towards one another that is affected by the objects' proximity to one another. Fucking classic.

In the background, she sweetly sang the first two lines, her sobering sentiments echoing through the speakers.

Truer words were never spoken.

46

My body moved without thought, compelled by the emotion of the song, starting off slow and gentle only to crescendo with the swell of the music. There were moments of frantic, angry motions into which I threw all my frustration, hatred, confusion, and betrayal. The intensity grew as my memories came forward; so much pain I'd never dealt with, both recent and past.

I launched my body across the room in true contemporary style. I ran, jumped, crashed into the floor, reached in futility for something that didn't exist. So many things that didn't exist.

My emotions were boiling over from the dance to my eyes. It took a brief reminder that my new policy was in full effect—no more crying. I struggled to maintain the balance between control and expression, and the scale was tipping away from the former.

Her words pushed through my defenses, settling into my mind, allowing my subconscious to take over. So much for balance, and my policy for that matter. My eyes stung as I fought the pooling tears that threatened to spill while her verses pounded in my head.

As the last line was sung, I crashed to the ground on my knees in a deliberate but painful move, and pressed my face tightly to the floor. The flood had broken the levy, and tears poured out everywhere.

Would something always bring him back to me?

In my sadness I felt, rather than heard, someone enter the room. I was in no mood for company.

"Coop, please. Please leave me alone," I whispered, unwilling to lift my head to face him. He said nothing in response, but didn't move away. He must have heard me carrying on from downstairs.

I'd never wanted to be alone more in my life. I didn't know why that was so hard to understand. I lifted my gaze to plead with him, to send him away. The face I expected to see was nowhere to be found. Instead, I found myself eye to eye with Sean, who'd knelt down to the ground to be nearer to me. Before I could say a word, he leaned forward, carefully cupped my face in his hands, and kissed my tears away.

He thought I needed his comfort, his strength. He thought I was weak.

I'll show you weak.

I slapped his hands away and shot to my feet.

"Why are you here?" I snarled. "Aren't you supposed to be long gone? Don't worry, Cooper is an excellent message boy." He looked genuinely wounded.

"I came because I had to see you before I left. I just couldn't do it without..."

"Taunting me beforehand? Wiping my face in it for good measure?" I spat, cutting him off.

"No, no, of course not," he said, deflecting my anger with his hands.

"Oh, of course not," I said in my most mocking tone. "That'd be *totally* beneath you, wouldn't it? You wouldn't do that, would you?"

He was starting to visibly breathe deeper, presumably trying to keep his shit together while I totally lost mine all over him. My anger was fully and completely irrational, and unfortunately, very unstoppable. I was hitting him in the chest with every word I spoke, beating emphasis physically into what I said.

"You're getting this all wrong, Ruby. I came over here because I wanted to tell you that I..."

"That you're going back to the PC homeland for good? Gonna spill the beans about my little bloodbath in Utah? And here for that matter?" I said accusingly.

"No!" he shouted in his defense. "Well, sort of. But it's not how you're making it out to be."

Jackpot...shaken the unshakable.

I was starting to get some emotion from him and it felt good. It further fueled my rage.

"That's me, the village idiot, barely capable of rudimentary function, Sean. I must be at fault here because your perfect ass would never do something unbecoming or incorrect."

He finally clasped my wrists to keep me from punching his chest. I doubted that I was hurting him, but I was certain it was difficult to think while your body was being used as a bass drum.

"ENOUGH! You *will* listen to me!" he commanded.

I stared him down, doing my best impression of *her,* my inner beast.

"I'll do whatever the fuck I please."

"I came because I need you to understand something," he said.

"Oh, I understand *many* things, Sean," I shouted. "I understand that you're leaving forever. I understand that you were going without so much as a 'nice knowing you.'" He took a moment to look the slightest bit stung by that.

"But what I understand most," I started, with a sudden eerie calm to my voice, "is that you're leaving to be with Sophie, that you are to be together and always have been, and that whatever trivial emotions you have for me pale in comparison. And they always will."

He looked floored. He didn't know that Cooper had overheard their conversation, though I'm sure he was not at all surprised that he'd share that little tidbit with me if he had. I paused for a brief moment before delivering the final blow.

"I. Hate. You."

I sprang up off the floor and brushed past him as I walked towards the door. I was done with him and the situation entirely.

The pain hit me as I neared the threshold and I clutched my chest in a fruitless effort to relieve it. My lungs tightened with every step, and I stopped just before exiting, leaning on the door casing for support. I furiously rubbed my ribs, trying to massage the breath in and out of me.

Calm.

I felt his energy calling to my own, soothing me. It was familiar and welcome, and it sparked something in my consciousness that had silently gnawed at me ever since he'd told me what I was. He said that RBs could not be influenced by others, making them dangerous and unpredictable. It never fully made sense to me because he could affect me. He always had. But my wolf and I were not one, but rather two separate entities comfortably sandwiched into one body, and though his being could not speak to her, it sang to me. Beautifully.

I heard him slowly step closer, and with his every advancement, my chest eased. His broad palm slid from the base of my neck down to the small of my back. I shivered under it, but my breathing normalized. For a moment we both remained still, just breathing together.

His hand slid back up slowly to its starting point, gaining strength in pressure. He repeated that soothing path over and over for minutes in silence until changing course suddenly. His fingers wove themselves up into my matted curls and rubbed circles in their roots until finally grabbing them lightly, turning my head to face him. My body followed.

My anger with him was a cover-up.

My tantrum had been a mass of emotion based on pride, hurt, embarrassment, and slight. I didn't hate him at all. I loved him, the recognition of which threatened to physically tear me apart. Staring into his eyes was painful because of everything I stood to lose. I wriggled to get away from him, running being my default response, but he was having none of it. He held me kindly but firmly in place.

He slowly brought his face to my ear, his breath tickling me.

"You shouldn't believe everything you hear, Ruby," he said softly. "I thought you of all people would understand that by now." He went back to doing the scalp-rubbing routine with his fingers, and I had no clue how I was supposed to think clearly with that nonsense going on. "I am leaving. I don't know when I'll return, or if I will be able to at all," he admitted, sounding mournful.

Is this supposed to be helping?

"Sophie is complicated, as is our situation," he said, fingers still working through my curls.

Soooo not making this better.

"I came back here for one reason, and one reason only. I needed you to be clear on something."

I stood perfectly silent, hanging on his every word.

"You. Are. Mine."

And with that, his lips pressed brutally to mine, kissing me with a frantic passion that I feared would consume us both. I was even more concerned that it wouldn't have bothered me if it had. He broke it off as suddenly as he started it, looking at me with complete satisfaction. His mission had been accomplished.

He took my face in his hands again, admiring it for a moment.

"You truly are the most exquisite thing I've ever seen."

I stumbled in my mind, trying to think of something, anything, to say in return. The man whose face was the pinnacle of perfection in my mind mirrored that sentiment about me. Interesting how life could go from one extreme to the next in a blink of an eye.

I couldn't believe the moment was occurring, not having admitted previously that I'd wanted it to. I struggled for what I wanted to say to return the sentiment. It took a minute while he waited patiently.

"Ditto," I sputtered.

I had such a way with words.

EPILOGUE

It had been a month since Sean left, and still I had received no word from him. My emotions bounced around from concern to anger to hurt and back to concern again like a bad pinball game. I later found out that he had gone back to the Elders to not only plead my case, again, but his own as well. It seemed that there was dissention in the ranks, and one of his beloved brothers had ratted him out to the powers that be. I was looking forward to making that individual's acquaintance. I think we both were.

Sophie had gone with him, and visions of her nearly naked body draped all over him plagued my imagination. Perhaps she could be dealt with at the same time as the big-mouthed brother; make it a combo meal of sorts. The only glitch with that plan was that it required them to come back, and there didn't seem to be any of that happening any time soon.

Thankfully for me, something else *did* return. A familiar cramping sensation showed up one day, accompanied by the bane of every young woman's existence. My period was back and I couldn't have been more relieved. At least it made for one less complication resulting from my stay in Utah.

Cooper turned out to be less and less of a hindrance as time went on. I found out that he had a BA in accounting, so I put him to work at the shop to clean up the books. Despite his first two weeks of constant bitching about 'fiscal negligence' and 'systemic irresponsibility,' he turned out to be a godsend. Prayers really were answered sometimes.

It wasn't only prayers he answered, but also lingering questions about my Change and why it seemed so unpredictable. I knew after the attack at my apartment that my ring had something to do with it, but not why. Cooper solved that mystery for me. Apparently Sean had ascertained from Marcus during their time together that platinum was a Rouge et Blanc's kryptonite, a revelation that Marcus had stumbled upon centuries earlier with the woman I reminded him of so much. It explained everything, especially why I wasn't able to Change in Utah. I remembered the strange silvery lining of the iron manacles and realized that the Alpha had had them specially made just for me on Marcus's instruction. They kept the wolf buried deep within me, unable to be accessed. But now that she had officially been let out with my knowledge, things seemed to be changing and I wasn't sure if it was for better or worse.

Cooper and I spent a lot of time together working at the shop during the week. He handled the books and customers and I worked in the back, designing new pieces to beef up our inventory. I couldn't pay him much, but he worked off his room and board and seemed more than happy with the perks—the perks being the twenty-somethings that seemed to frequent the shop for repeat purchases ever since his arrival. It didn't matter to me—money was money.

I was worried about Cooper, though. For all his joviality during the day, his nights seemed haunted somehow. About two weeks after Sean left, Cooper started waking me up at night with his screams. His cries were short-lived given the continued state of his voice, which appeared to have been damaged during his healing with Sophie. When I repeatedly asked about the dreams, he played them off as nothing, but his attempts at casualness were failing.

I knew something was wrong.

AMBER LYNN NATUSCH

*we all have
skeletons in
our closet*

HAUNTED

BOOK TWO
THE CAGED SERIES

HAUNTED EXCERPT

"I cowered away from him, unable to formulate a coherent sentence. Questions ran through my mind, though none made it past my lips. I wondered how this could be happening, what he wanted, and what major injustice I'd brought against the universe in this life or another to bring a fate such as this upon me.

Perhaps being born was reason enough."

After his near-death experience only months earlier, Cooper's behavior is rapidly deteriorating.

So what does Ruby do? She adds a new roommate into the mix. When her friend Ronnie is abruptly called away for a family emergency, Ruby takes in Peyta, Ronnie's highly intelligent and overly observant teenage daughter. With an increasingly unstable Cooper in the house, Ruby fears for Peyta's safety.

But when Peyta's behaviors become as perplexing as Cooper's, Ruby finds herself juggling a series of lies to ensure their safety as well as her own.

Then the balls, and the bodies, start dropping...

ABOUT THE AUTHOR

Amber Lynn Natusch is the author of the bestselling *Caged*. She was born and raised in Winnipeg, and speaks sarcasm fluently because of her Canadian roots. She loves to dance and sing in her kitchen—much to the detriment of those near her—but spends most of her time running a practice with her husband, raising two small children, and attempting to write when she can lock herself in the bathroom for ten minutes of peace and quiet. She has many hidden talents, most of which should not be mentioned but include putting her foot in her mouth, acting inappropriately when nervous, swearing like a sailor when provoked, and not listening when she should. She's obsessed with home renovation shows, should never be caffeinated, and loves snow. Amber has a deep-seated fear of clowns and deep water...especially clowns swimming in deep water.